THE THREAD OF THE UNICORN

BOOK 5 OF THE AGENCY OF THE ANCIENT LOST AND FOUND

JANE THORNLEY

PROLOGUE

*hâteau Saint Chappelles, France, 1432*

FATHER LOUIS PRAYED in the tiny chapel, prayed that he would be forgiven for what he was about to do. He was not a man for whom disloyalty came easily but neither was he one who could permit the murder of a young girl—a saint in peasant clothing—to go unchallenged.

It had been he who had heard his king's confession just hours before the royal hand dispatched the message to the English that agreed to the trial of Joan of Arc. King Charles knew that his actions would result in what transpired—the burning at the stake of that poor but blessed girl—he knew! This king, for whom Louis had striven to preserve his soul through all the decisions that governance had laid upon his feet, knew that the message he sent that day signed Joan's death warrant. Louis had tried to stay the king's hand, pleaded that allowing Joan to die was as good as consigning the king's own soul to hell. Joan was a saint sent by the angels to save France.

That had angered the king. Did the priest not realize that unless he allowed the English to take Joan's head, more troops would die, more citizens felled? How the king had roared, storming off through the castle calling to his advisers to assure him that he was right. Antoine Le Viste had been among those in the inner circle that day and his eyes had met Louis's across the long hall. Together they would give voice to their outrage, ensure that the truth was told, buried though it was deep within layers of art and artifice. Foolishly, they believed their secret was safe.

Many months would follow before they learned of their mistake,

They were fools. Too many spies lurked behind the seats of the mighty in the courts of kings. Somehow word reached Charles that a tapestry telling the true story of his treachery existed somewhere and that his challengers lay among his closest confidants. When the king threatened to grill every courier until he identified his censors, Louis had sent word that he was to blame. Let the secret die with him, for not even Le Viste knew where the tapestry lay hidden.

Slowly, Louis climbed to his feet. They would arrive soon. Now all he could do was reach deep within himself to find his courage and his God. Better that he take the secret with him to the grave than Le Viste. Antoine had a wife and children whereas he had nobody, except perhaps Joan.

Joan had become his only light, the maid of his soul. Her sacrifice burned bright within his heart as an example of true bravery and sacrifice. If not for her, King Charles would not sit upon his throne over a unified France. If not for her, both the country and its would-be king would have languished. And for this, she was burned alive? A horrible end for anyone, but for one such as she, it was nothing but a wicked travesty of justice and truth. He could not bear it.

Had he not heard her confessions many times, too? Had he not touched the head of that brave maid and known deep within that she was all that was right and true? He well believed that she had been touched by the archangel Saint Michael himself, making her death an insult to God. That's where he consigned his loyalty—to God and to justice, not to mere mortal kings and bishops.

Slowly, he picked up the canister and strapped it over one shoulder. They would never find it. There could be only one hiding place for him and their secret but he would not descend into the darkness alone. He stepped from the chapel in time to see the line of torchlights marching up the château from the village.

They were coming! Swinging around, he bolted for the old keep.

He could not believe that he, Father Louis Saint Chappelles, was running for his life through the bowels of his own château, chased by the very soldiers of the man for whom he had dedicated his life. There could be no more loyal man than he, no more obedient servant to God, but when the time came to choose, there was no choice to be made. To God he pledged his ultimate allegiance.

He could see the torches behind him as he pounded down the stairs of the old keep, the sound of their boots thundering in his ears. They would expect him to sneak out through a hidden tunnel, those passages well-known to the king's spies, but they would be wrong. Louis would not sneak away; Louis would go meet Joan at last in the one place he knew she waited for him. But first he must cross into the darkness.

At the base of the stairs, he tossed his own torch into the tunnel to draw the soldiers away while he scuttled across the stones in the opposite direction. He had the portal ready for his arrival but still he hesitated at the edge. Clutching the canister, he teetered on the brink of forever, cast one look over his shoulder and prayed with all his heart.

And then he jumped.

1

―――――――――

$\mathcal{I}$t began in Paris, which deserves an explanation.

One day in the spring of 2022, a potential client emailed me to arrange a Zoom meeting to discuss a possible case. Since I mostly lived my workday fixed to a computer, that sounded reasonable enough right up until the moment she mentioned her location. Paris. Suddenly technology lost its luster. If there ever was a city that warranted an in-person visit, it was Paris. I assured her I'd be in the area and that we'd arrange an appointment.

"Once I go, I can't help but worry about you," Evan said as we strolled down the Champs-Élysée.

"I appreciate your concern," I said while squeezing his arm, "but we have to stop fretting about each other when we're apart. We both have jobs to do." It sounded so reasonable, so adult. Meanwhile, I was attempting to savor every moment of our time together.

On our side of the boulevard, a little park blazed sweeps of red flowers while overhead a cloud of pink and white blossoms rained petals down over the sidewalk. Since it was drizzling, we huddled under a clear plastic umbrella. Does all this sound delicious? May I add that I had recently spent three days and nights with the man I adored. Yes, it was every bit delicious.

"I always worry about you," Evan told me, "always and forever."

"Nonsense," I murmured. "No sign of Noel here." I really didn't want to discuss the details of my sometimes fractious life right then.

"Unfortunately, I'm not your only admirer." He pulled me close and kissed me with that long languorous way of his that implied that he'd take all the time needed to do things properly. Let me just say that he applied that approach to every. little. thing.

"Yes," I whispered when I came up for air, "but I don't want to discuss that right now. We have about 15 minutes before you head for the airport. Let's not squander it."

But already he was steering us in the direction of our hotel where his luggage waited in the lobby, and I was the one about to do the squandering.

"Even though Peaches will be nearby, don't let your guard down for a moment," he reminded me. "Remember, Noel may still be in hiding but that doesn't mean he doesn't have you watched every second. He could be lurking behind this mysterious client of yours."

"Said client insisted that she needs to protect her privacy, which doesn't mean that she's part of Noel's cartel." That did it: my bliss cocoon collapsed. "That's where you're going, isn't it, to track down Noel?"

Since Evan worked for Interpol and many of his assignments fell into the Top Secret category, it was pointless asking for details. That never stopped me. As much as I tried to shove my nemesis ex into the back of my brain, he was always festering away back there.

"You know I can't disclose anything, Phoebe, but in ways other than my Interpol life, there's nothing I wouldn't share with you. Consider me an open book, an interesting open book, I hope, one with multiple chapters, a strong opening, a diverse and developed character, a satisfying style—note the leather jacket—a strong internal logic, a—"

I was laughing now. "And the oh-so-modest blurb on the cover, but you don't need to sell me—I've already bought the whole Evan series. Here's a short review: 'Evan is a great and satisfying read and I can't wait for more except that some parts remain unreadable such as those sections labeled with a nondisclosure clause and redacted footnotes.'"

The brows arched over those fine hazel eyes as if this was the first time he'd heard this.

We were crossing the boulevard, the Arc de Triomphe visible down the road, the honking horns and pedestrians racing by eroding the last of my romantic haze. A niggle was a niggle, after all. "There's something you're keeping from me, Evan Barrow, and as long as you hide it, I'll keep wondering what it is and why you're hiding it."

The need to know always drove me.

"And do you think you know what this mysterious something is?" he asked. "Because I don't have a clue what you're referring to."

"I suspect the truth and it seems so inconsequential, bafflingly insignificant in ways, but the fact that you refuse to tell me has made it grow to monumental proportions." The Arc de Triomphe brought that word to mind.

"Phoebe, I have no idea what you're talking about." He stopped mid-sidewalk. "Monumental? What in my personal life is so monumental that you would bring it up three times during our brief time together and at least once back in London? You know that I was previously married and you have even met my former wife and son, so what could possibly be more personal than that? At least give me a hint."

I was into it now. "Keeping with the book analogy, this involves your opening chapters, possibly the prologue or foreword, that's forward of the backstory variety. Is that hint enough?"

His gaze briefly veered skyward. "Absolutely not. Do you mind providing a translation, as in one that doesn't speak in riddles?"

Okay, so he was irritated now. The man was devastatingly handsome when those eyes flashed and the skin tensed over his high cheekbones. I fought the urge to stroke his cheek. Before I could soothe the savage beast, however, I spied Peaches striding toward us, her long legs encased in hyacinth-blue leather jeans.

"Ev! Hell, man, you look even more debonaire in Paris," she called before wrapping him up in one of her legendary hugs that put them nearly nose-to-nose. She squeezed him so tight it would have crippled a lesser man. "Is that even possible? I mean, God, he looks good," she said, winking at me. "And you spent three days with this one? That must have been sweeter than all the sugar in a French pastry shop."

Evan, not even mildly embarrassed, gently disentangled himself. "You are looking amazing yourself, Peaches. Sir Rupert would approve of the couture. Chanel?"

"A knockoff but don't tell on me. Anyway, I have been shopping," she admitted. My friend-cum-bodyguard had dropped her easy Caribbean spandex style for something closer to Parisian chic, at least that's how I interpreted the Hermès scarf knotted over the leather bolero-style jacket all in that astounding hue. I could never pull off chic no matter what the city or color. I wore my hand-knit shawls as a badge of honor, the artsy shag look.

"Peaches," Evan said with a smile. "Take care of my girl here, would you?" He checked his watch. "I must run."

"Woman," I corrected, "as in 'take care of my woman.'" I could be such a pain.

"My apologies. Of course, that's entirely what I meant," he said as he swept down for a parting kiss. The kiss was long and weak-knee-inducing to make a point. Let's just say that I couldn't speak for a couple of moments but had no doubt that he considered me fully adult. A few minutes later, he had jumped into a cab and was gone.

"If that kiss is any indication, I'd say you two had a dynamite couple of days, as in hot, hot, hot." Peaches fanned her face with her hand as we watched the cab disappear.

"It was pretty amazing," I agreed, still dazed.

"Care to divulge?" she asked.

"No way. Consider the Do Not Disturb sign on my virtual door. Come, we'd better get going." Trying to steer my brain back to business, I checked my phone. "Okay, so I'm to meet my client at a café a couple of blocks in this direction."

"I didn't mean that kind of detail," she scoffed as she strode along, me taking two strides to her every one. "I have my steamy romance books for that. I meant relationship stuff. You know, like how's it going? Is he officially your boyfriend now?"

"What does that even mean?" I sighed, almost tripping over a small powder-puff-size dog attached to an elderly gentleman by a rhinestone leash. "'Boyfriend' is not an appropriate term for an adult male."

"Partner, then?"

"Sounds like a business arrangement."

"Companion?"

"A lapdog."

"Main squeeze?"

I laughed. "Is that Jamaican? That suggests a giant plush toy to me. Evan may be many things—*is* many things—but teddy bear isn't one of them."

"Definitely not teddy bear, then. What about significant other?"

I snapped my fingers. "'Significant maybe.' That works. How about that?"

"You're joking. 'Significant maybe'—seriously?" She stared at me aghast. "Think I can't detect commitment issues when I hear them? Are they yours or his?"

"His. He's keeping something from me."

She gave me one of those sidelong glances I knew so well. "Shit, woman, unless it's either your car keys or your passport, drop it."

She had a point. In any case, we had arrived at Le Café de l'Époque, the location my client had just messaged me. "Here it is."

Totally old world as the name implied, the café gave every indication of being the epitome of a French brasserie right down to the "Maison Fondée en 1826" emblazoned on its green awning.

"Founded in 1826," I translated, as if Peaches couldn't do that for herself.

She pulled me back into the doorway of a building. "The place is under surveillance," she whispered. "See that guy behind the magazine across the street and the one gazing off into space at the outside table far right? One's wearing a wire and the other hasn't taken his eyes off the entrance even though he's hiding behind *Paris Match*. Are you kidding me? What amateurs! Anyway, they're staking someone out, maybe you, but they're mostly focused on the café. What did you say about this client of ours?"

"Nothing, as in she wouldn't disclose anything by email and only sent me the name of our rendezvous location two minutes ago. I'm to come alone. She said she wanted to interview me first, something she was only willing to do over Zoom or in person."

"Hell, you mean you're being interviewed?"

"I prefer to think of it as being vetted."

"Doesn't she know who you are? She'd be damned lucky to have Phoebe McCabe working on her case. Why did you even agree to meet her under such circumstances?"

"Because Madame Cointreau is a mystery and I love mysteries," I told her. "I also love Cointreau and Paris. Is that a sign or what? Do you think she's the subject of this stakeout?" But I didn't wait for an answer. "Anyway, I'm going in. I'll go first and then you follow."

I crossed the side street heading for the topiary-flanked café with its outdoor tables shielded from the sidewalk by potted trees. I was to meet Madame Cointreau at an inside table away from the window. So far the whole setup struck me as delightfully clandestine, like something out of a spy movie. All of the lost family artifacts and missing-art cases I'd been offered lately couldn't compare to this. I'd felt electricity along my spine from the moment I'd read her email.

The interior was flooded with natural light. Marble-topped tables and woven chairs offered a welcoming ambiance. It was late morning so the handful of customers were mostly sipping café au laits and devouring decadent-looking pastries. Most diners claimed the window seats. Only a chic-looking woman in a broad black hat and enormous sunglasses sat at the rearmost table against the inside wall studying her phone. That had to be Cointreau.

I strode right down to her, skirting the maître d', who zoomed in to intercept. "Madame Cointreau?"

Though she was virtually hidden behind the sunglasses and enormous hat, I took her to be in her early thirties. Gold hoop earrings, full coral-pink lips, minty-green chiffon scarf, matching Chanel jacket. Okay, then, either wealthy or trying to look wealthy. Not a strand of natural hair showed beneath the head gear.

"*Oui*. Madame McCabe?"

"*Oui*." I preferred madame to mademoiselle. It swapped gravitas in lieu of youth. I sat down, wondering if the entire conversation was going to take place in French. Most Parisians winced at my occasional bouts of conversational fumbling and I so hated to offend the locals.

"Thank you for meeting me," she said in English. "Mind if I call you Phoebe?" American. Not a touch of an accent.

"Please. And you are?"

"Call me Lilly."

Lilly Cointreau. So far, the only French thing about her was the surname and maybe her choice of couture. "All right, then, Lilly, tell me what you want me to do for you. I admit to being very curious by all the secrecy."

The waiter appeared bearing the menus and also indicated the chalkboard lunch offerings hanging on the wall midway down. Lilly ordered a latte and I did the same. I could see Peaches sitting at the other end of the café eyeing the desserts trolley with an intensity she usually reserved for muscle-bound guys.

After the waiter slipped away, Lilly held up one pale hand while gripping her phone in the other. No rings. One gold bangle. "Wait. Are you here with anyone? I told you to come alone. My man outside said that someone came in with you."

Good surveillance. "So those guys staked outside are yours?"

"They're my bodyguards. Don't mess with me, Phoebe. Part of the reason I needed to meet you first was to establish trust. Trust is like super-important to me."

"You brought your bodyguard and I brought mine. So what? By the way, she's the statuesque black woman pointing out the lemon meringue pie over there. She noticed your guys, too. If they catch anybody else staking out either one of us, they're free to do their worst."

The coral lips turned up into a brilliant smile and I realized for the first time that she was gorgeous as well as vaguely familiar. "Touché. One of the reasons I needed to meet you first was to see if you were some pain-in-the-ass know-it-all who would annoy the hell out of me and my uncle, especially my uncle. I've been following you in the news and it appears that you've got what it takes. Do you?"

"Mind being a bit more specific? You must have already checked me out so you know that the Agency of the Ancient Lost and Found retrieves lost or stolen artifacts and artworks. What else are you looking for?"

"Discretion, loyalty, tenacity, and guts."

Right, so she needed a German shepherd. I sat back to study her more carefully, not that she revealed much. "I don't take on just any old case these days, either, and if you need to assess my character, know that I need to do likewise with you. So who are you really? Not French, but American, is my guess, and definitely attempting some version of incognito. Let's begin there."

She leaned over the table, briefly pulling back when our cafés landed in front of us. "Lilly Lin," she whispered, lifting her glasses only long enough to reveal her startlingly beautiful face.

"Lilly Lin, the Chinese American movie star?" I was shocked, briefly starstruck, even, since I was a fan. She was a hot ticket just then, riding a wave of nominations for her first serious dramatic role.

"Not Chinese American but Franco Chinese American—figure that one out—though I've lived most of my adult life in the US. Confused? Try being born in China, adopted by a Chinese mother and a French diplomat father, who happened to be the eldest son of the historic Saint Chappelles family. My real name is Liliana Saint Chappelles. In France, that makes me a permanent outsider and something else again in China, but in the US, right now, Asian actors are almost having a moment. I say almost because, like everything else, there's a flip side and it's not pretty. Anyway, forget all that." She waved her hand again. "I'm not here to moan 'poor little me.' I'm successful, I'm blessed, and I know it. I'm here to help my uncle."

I sipped my coffee. Right, the uncle. "And he is...?"

"Monsieur Henri Saint Chappelles. Heard of him?"

"Never."

"Good. We've both worked very hard to keep it that way. He's a recluse who prefers to maintain a low profile, an interior decorator whose heyday was back in the '80s. Now he just hides."

"Hides where?" I stirred the mountain of foam into my coffee.

"In the little village where I grew up. We used to live in the Château Saint Chappelles, but after my father died, Uncle Henri tried to keep the château going but didn't have the money. The only way Dad managed while he was alive was by accepting transfusions from me. Châteaus are like bottomless pits, even when you're charging visitors entrance fees. Finally, my uncle had to sell. Broke his heart. Château Saint Chappelles has been in the family for eight centuries off and on and he holds himself accountable for its current loss. But he's not to blame. First there was Covid and then there was more Covid and my uncle is more of a dreamer than a businessman, anyway."

"Um—" there was no delicate way to ask this "—but I'm sure you've tried to help since…"

"Tried and tried," she acknowledged. "Uncle Henri is a proud man. There was no way he is going to accept what he considers to be handouts from his little niece. I mean, how humiliating is that for the son of a family that once produced multiple French dukes? I didn't even know that he'd sold the château until it was gone. Same thing with his Paris pied-à-terre. All gone. Now he lives holed up in a gatehouse."

"Okay." Poor Uncle Henri. "So, where do I come in?"

Her phone pinged and she held up one coral-nailed finger as she read the text. "Shit. They found us. We've got to go. Come on. It'll be safer back at my hotel."

"Safer from whom?" I hissed. "Who found us?"

She dispensed 20 euro tips both to the waiter and the maître d' on her way out the door as I scurried after. I could see Peaches scrambling to catch up, her mouth full of pie. In moments we were diving into the back seat of a black Mercedes parked at the curb while people swarmed around us pointing their phones. The paparazzi—got it.

Lilly landed in the back seat first, me behind her, with Peaches bringing up the rear. It was a big car, but even so, three burly guys and three women was a bit of a squeeze. The guys sat up front, us in the back.

"Lilly, meet Peaches. Peaches, meet Lilly," I said by way of introduction as we zoomed down the street.

"Uh-huh. Hi." Peaches was glued to the rearview window. "What's that thing those dudes in the car back there are pointing at us?"

"Probably a telephoto," Lilly suggested, sliding down in her seat. "They won't see much. The windows are smoked."

"Doesn't look like a telephoto to me," Peaches said, using her own agency-issue phone's telephoto lens. "Looks like a bloody pistol with a silencer."

2

Of course Peaches could have been mistaken.

"Pont de l'Alma?" shouted the driver.

"Whatever's faster," Lilly called back in French.

We were zooming through the Parisian streets being chased by the paparazzi heading for the Pont de l'Alma tunnel?

"For God's sake, fasten your seat belts!" Peaches cried. I secured mine in seconds but Lilly was slow to comply.

Peaches nudged her. "Buckle up, buttercup. Shades of Princess Di."

"Oh, shit, yes!" Lilly exclaimed before securing her belt and settling into a tense silence as we dashed through the tunnel.

"Um, where are we going again?" I asked as the tunnel walls whizzed by.

"I had planned on going directly to my hotel," Lilly replied, "but changed my mind. We'll lose these scumbags and head straight for my uncle's. I need you to meet him so he can decide whether to hire you or not. Without his help, we'll get nowhere."

"And your uncle lives…?" I asked.

"In the village of Saint Chappelles, about two and a half hours' drive outside of Paris in the Loire Valley. If your agency is going to take on this case on behalf of the Saint Chappelles family, we'll need his blessing. Don't worry: I'll have you back in the city by ten p.m. at the latest."

We burst into daylight on the other side of the tunnel and breathed a collective sigh of relief. The driver was trying to dodge our tail but hardly in the skilled manner I've come to expect. So I was spoiled. I judged everything by Evan's calm, measured, and utterly impeccable technique. He could take a hairpin turn like a maestro. This guy was sloppy by comparison. We almost sideswiped two cars as he cut in between the lanes.

After several quick turns, we slid into a side street and slowed down. We seemed to have lost our tail.

Lilly leaned back against the seat and sighed. "This is what drives me nuts —the constant scrutiny. It's even worse here than in LA. In LA, it's manageable, somehow. Here and in London, it's like open season." She switched to French and instructed the driver to head for Saint Chappelles.

"Is the driver your usual guy?" I asked.

"I don't have a usual guy," Lilly said. "This crew has been hired from the foremost security group in France. The driver's Jean Luc, the guy with the topknot is Pierre, and the guy on the right is René."

Peaches and I exchanged glances but said nothing. All three were of a type: big, muscle-packed, and probably hired at least as much for their brawn as their skills. I guessed they had all been bouncers in a previous life and spent their downtime pumping iron at a gym. At least René was black, which gained him a few brownie points from Peaches.

Once we hit the main arteries leading out of Paris, Lilly threw off her hat, releasing a long glossy black ponytail, and pulled down her face mask.

Peaches stared. "Holy shit!" she exclaimed. "Lilly Lin? I'm such a big fan! I just loved the hell out of *Sacred Medallion.*"

I'd never seen Peaches gush.

"I mean, like, I've seen your *Princess Bai and the Mongolian Dream* twice, at least. I just love the way you do those action scenes—the flying air chops, the somersault back kicks—the whole shebang."

And gush.

"And when you conquered the genie monster with a—"

"Peaches." I nudged her.

"Right," Peaches said, subsiding.

"It's okay," Lilly said, leaning back in her seat. "I'm used to it, but, Peaches —cool name, by the way—as an Asian actress, starring in all those films is more of a stepping stone than a destination. I want to be cast in roles like my recent *The Human Zone*, not because I'm Asian but because I'm a good actress who happens to be Asian." She turned and smiled at her. "As a visible minority, I bet you get that."

"I totally get that. I always want to be seen as a person first and a tall black Jamaican woman second. For a minority, I'm way too visible."

Lilly grinned. "You're, what, six foot something? Good luck with that, but yes, and then there's the whole gender thing. Anyway, you've both passed my initial trust test so I'm really hoping Uncle Henri will accept you for the case, too."

"Which is?" I prompted.

"There's no point giving you the details until my uncle gives the nod. He's a hard nut to crack, I warn you. So I'll tell you this much: we've had an item missing in our family since the early fifteenth century or thereabouts. Or we think it's missing. Actually, we don't really know that it even exists."

I was studying her while half listening to the three guys discussing routes up front and simultaneously watching the road signs fly by. It took me a second to catch on to what she'd just said. "Wait, you don't even know that it exists?"

"My dad thought it did and Uncle Henri, too. Dad was obsessed with it. He died about five years ago, Mom two years back. Anyway, if it exists, its estimated worth should be in the millions, maybe more. Enough I think to buy back the Château Saint Chappelles, which is currently up for sale again. I'm hoping that if we locate the family treasure, Uncle Henri will dig himself out of his depression, buy back the ancestral pile, and live happily ever after." She shrugged. "Something close, anyway."

"How come you can't just purchase the château yourself, Lilly?" Peaches asked.

She grimaced. "Because my uncle refuses to accept handouts from me. Besides, I'm now an American citizen, which prevents me from buying it outright unless I'm planning to reside here. French laws are complicated."

"But since you were raised here, you're French," I pointed out.

Lilly rolled her eyes. "Growing up in France doesn't make me French. To most countries, if you say 'Made in China,' nobody accepts you. A little village like Saint Chappelles is no different than any tiny village anywhere and probably worse than most. I don't belong, never did. They want you to look French to be French. Nobody looks at me and sees French. They used to call me a French translation of 'Chop Suey' in school. I applied for US citizenship and got it."

"But you grew up here." I couldn't help myself. It was the injustice of it all, though I grasped the reality well enough.

"And it was unbearable at times. As much as I loved the village, it didn't always love me back. My mother finally had to pull us out of the community and send us to a school in Paris, against my dad's wishes, by the way."

"Us?" Peaches was quick to ask.

Lilly sighed. "I had—*have*—a twin sister. Fraternal. We're not close. In fact, we couldn't be more different. So, when they adopted these two little Chinese girls all those years ago, they had no idea that growing up in a château with at least one French parent would never be enough to protect the kids against racism."

"Damn, there were actually two of you?" Peaches took the words right out of my mouth.

"Yeah. Look, let me make the long story short." She spread her hands. "My parents couldn't have kids of their own so decided to adopt. Adopting kids from Asia has always been a thing, you know? And since Mom was Chinese, it sort of made sense. But they underestimated the problems. Mom should have figured it out since she wasn't exactly welcomed with open arms in France, either. Still, being wealthy and living in a château kind of insulates you. But not for kids. Once you send them to school, they're exposed to everything. Mom finally packed her bags and took us to live in Paris where it was only slightly better but at least there was—*is*—a Chinese community. It tore Mom and Dad apart in the end. Though they stayed married in name, they lived separately. I took off for the US as soon as I was old enough and never looked back."

"And your sister?"

Lilly gazed out the window. "She headed in the opposite direction—to China to live with Mom's brother, Uncle Tengfeng. After we hit our teens, we drifted apart. She runs my uncle's export business in Beijing now. I hardly ever hear from her anymore."

"But you're sisters!" Peaches exclaimed. "I'd give my eyeteeth for a sister."

Lilly continued gazing off into the distance. She shrugged. "Yeah, so Uncle Henri and my friends are my family now. Who cares for me matters more than who shares my blood."

"Yeah, I get that, too," Peaches said. "I consider Phoebe here like a sister now, though she's very white and a little on the short side."

Lilly smiled. "Are you an only child or something?"

"No, I have a brother of the criminal persuasion," she replied.

"Me, too," I said. "Like Peaches, I have a brother but both my parents are also gone." An attempt to connect, albeit a bit clumsy. "My brother and I used to be close but things changed when he stepped into the dark side."

"The dark side?" Lilly asked.

"His activities turned criminal, too."

She glanced at me and flashed a wry smile. "Criminal as in...?"

"Serving time for international art theft."

"Both your brothers are in prison?" Lilly exclaimed, turning in her seat to get a good look at us.

"Don't worry," Peaches assured her. "It's not contagious. But that's how we met: both our brothers were in the same line of work, you could say. The Agency of the Ancient Lost and Found was born from family drama—got to love it."

"Are you single, Lilly?" I asked.

"No, I have a boyfriend in LA. We're planning on getting married sometime next year," Lilly continued. "He's a director." Thinking of him seemed to bring a light to her face.

Peaches caught my eye. "Note she said 'boyfriend,' not 'significant maybe.'"

"I heard," I said.

Lilly was watching us. "What about you two?"

"I'm single," Peaches told her. "And Phoebe is confused."

"I'm not confused," I said in my own defense. "I'm just hung up on the names we give the men—or women—in our lives."

"Okay." Lilly shrugged. "But what difference does it make if everybody understands the meaning?"

"My point exactly." Peaches shot me a grin.

Lilly returned to gazing out the window. "Anyway, forget all that. Forget about my parents, forget about my sister, my boyfriend, forget about me. This is about finding something lost. This is about my uncle Henri. I need to see him happy again. I love him to bits and he's all the family I have left."

"You two are that close?" Peaches asked.

"Totally. We both know what it's like to be different, to not fit the norm and to be marginalized."

"It can be worse in a small town," Peaches remarked.

"True. Things are better now, for sure, but in my uncle's case, it's like he hasn't noticed."

We fell silent after that, focusing on the scenery changing outside the window, at the turnoffs leading across farmland, the copses of trees, the stone-wall-edged rivers. In the distance, we'd glimpse clusters of tiled-roof cottages, the occasional barn perched in a field of crops, a few castles on hilltops, and finally a sign reading *Ville de Saint Chappelles*.

After cutting cross-country for a few minutes, the lane abruptly dove down into a little wooded valley where the river flowed closer to the road. We crossed an old stone bridge past a waterwheel into narrow streets where white stone cottages topped with tiled roofs huddled. Flowers spilled from window boxes everywhere.

Peaches pressed down the window. "Wow. Did they package this place for tourists or something?"

"Nope. It's totally real, as in quintessentially French," Lilly remarked, donning her sunglasses and reapplying her hat. "Not a Chinese takeout anywhere—bad joke. Put the window up, please."

Peaches did as requested. Meanwhile, the car slowed to a crawl, maneuvering the picture-postcard streets with care, slipping by the boulangerie, the patisserie, the boucherie. The butcher shop had a whole pig hanging in the window. "Just in case we don't know how that guy brings home the bacon," Peaches muttered.

"How that *woman* brings home the bacon," Lilly remarked. "The Boucherie Beaumont was taken over by the youngest daughter. She was the only one in my class I was sort of friends with, by the way. At least she got that the world was changing and treated me with respect. Mimi, on the other hand, clashed with everybody."

So, Mimi was the sister. I was so absorbed in thinking about the two siblings that when the car wound down a long lane, I wasn't quite ready for the turreted house that reared beyond the stone gateposts. Two conical towers plus one tall curved sharply slanted roof, a dovecote, mullioned windows, a tumble of vines crawling over everything, made it every inch the fairy tale, French translation.

"Where's this?" I asked as the driver pulled up to the wall and parked.

"Uncle Henri's place, the gatehouse," Lilly explained.

"This is the gatehouse?" I exclaimed, climbing out. "It's bigger than most homes in St. James's Park."

Lilly took me by the arm, drew me back to the other side of the lane, and pointed through a break in the trees. There, framed by the branches and perched on the crest of a hill about a quarter of a mile away, stood a white fortified château complete with pediments, multiple conical-peaked towers that matched the one before me, and something that could be a drawbridge. "All relative."

"Got it," I whispered. "If you used to live up there, then Uncle Henri's fallen on hard times."

Lilly smiled. "Can I leave you two out here while I go inside and prepare Uncle Henri for visitors?"

"Sure," I said. "Does he need priming?"

"Sort of. He's been depressed and in a funk since his partner died."

"Oh, I'm sorry. When did that happen?"

"Three years ago but Uncle Henri has never gotten over it. Hopefully this will give him a distraction. Stay out of sight, okay? The security team are going to check the perimeters to make sure we weren't followed or have photographers lurking in the bushes. If you and Peaches stay in the garden, I'll try to keep my uncle away from the windows."

"Right," I said.

Peaches and I stood watching Lilly march up the stone pathway under the flowering fruit trees and let herself in through the front door. A dog started frantically yapping from somewhere deep inside the house. The security dudes had already melted into the shrubbery.

"So what do you think?" Peaches asked as we wound our way through to the back garden.

"I think there's lots going on here besides a missing family treasure." But I was briefly enchanted by the garden, which was charmingly overgrown and delightfully tangled without looking messy or unloved. A weeping willow drifted branches into a lily pond flitting with golden koi and nearby sat a pair of waders with a scummy net propped against a marble bench. Birdbaths, a little fountain, and an arbor climbing with wisteria greeted the eye.

"It's sort of like a mangy Giverny," I remarked.

A flash of movement sent both Peaches and me scuttling behind a tree. Lilly could be heard calling for Uncle Henri through the open French doors. Suddenly, a tall lean man came into view carrying a screaming Lilly in his arms, twirling her around until she demanded that he put her down. I stared at the man with the gray-streaked ponytail and goatee, the denim dungarees over the red striped T-shirt, with a kerchief knotted around his neck. A diamond stud glinted in one ear.

A string of expletives mixed with endearments followed as Uncle Henri admonished his niece in French for not telling him she was coming, not calling often enough, not living in France, etc. What was he, anyway, yesterday's lunch? She was his little *"ma chérie," "mon poussin,"* the French equivalent of shit-face, and his little shrimp. She was a bad girl, a good girl, the world's best niece, as well as by far the worst.

By the time the fond expletives had trailed away, Lilly was standing before him, arms crossed, with a grin across her face. *"Fini?"*

No, he was not finished. In fact, he launched a new tirade, this one even more impassioned and more creative with the salty Anglo-French adjectives thrown in until finally Lilly held up her hand. "Enough," she told him. "I have something very important to discuss with you, uncle, so let's not waste any more time." In moments, she had tucked his arm in hers and led him deeper into the house.

I turned to comment to Peaches but she'd shifted several feet deeper into the wisteria arbor. "Wait here," she whispered. "I thought I saw movement in those hedges. I'm going to investigate."

"Maybe it's the security dudes," I suggested, but she had already disappeared. Right, so I turned back to stare through the two French doors. I spied color and pattern. Color and pattern call out to me like Circe to the sailors. I had to investigate.

I stepped inside what looked to be a breakfast room with a round table spread with blue and white toile fabric. Vases of lavender and garden flowers seemed to spill from every available receptacle, infusing the air with fragrance. The shelf closest to the door was amassed with a mix of unmatched crockery interspersed with neatly stacked books.

Wandering from one room to the next, I found books everywhere, not shelved so much as arranged. Big coffee-table books propped face outward on a ledge as if their covers were part of the decor, along with the oil paintings and watercolors, which hung everywhere. On every colored wall (no white walls existed), some interesting collection had been composed—a series of old tiles in one corner, a selection of Indonesian batik blocks in the other.

The fireplace in what must have been the main sitting room was completely tiled above the marble mantelpiece with corresponding vases on little pedestals about the room. The deep yellow walls seemed to hum with color like living sunbeams caught in the center of a buttercup. Chintz wing-back chairs, plump overstuffed sofas, and gilt-legged Louis XIV seats abounded. I was totally overwhelmed by color, pattern, and texture. The man was a collector, a lover of all the things I adored, and had to be as besotted by color as I was. I liked him already.

Suddenly a yapping white mop burst into the room and dashed for my ankles, stopping feet away to bare its little teeth.

"*Qui diable es-tu?*" a deep voice demanded.

I turned. There stood Henri Saint Chappelles, looking like a cavalier farm-hand in dungarees, grey goatee, and sweeping mustache. There had to be an ostrich-plumed hat stashed somewhere.

"Hi, I'm Phoebe McCabe, finder of lost things. What can I locate for you, Monsieur Saint Chappelles?" I thought that a suitably jaunty opening.

"Uncle Henri," Lilly said in French, moving between us as if she half expected either dog or uncle to lunge for my throat, "this is the woman I told you about."

"She who enters my house as if she had been invited? I do not like this person. She must leave immediately! I will not tolerate such an insult. Go at once, I say! Immediately!" All delivered in French while flapping his hand as if shooing away flies.

Truly, the man might have been a bit frightening had I remained looking at him but by now I was crouching beside the *petit chien* with my hand outstretched muttering doggy endearments. "Is he a Coton?" The Coton de Tulear breed hailed from the once French colony of Madagascar and looked very much like a white fluffy cotton ball. I'd never met one and I was charmed. This one gave my hand a tentative sniff followed by enthusiastic tail-wagging.

"She," I was told imperiously. "*She.* You insult Mademoiselle Le Chouchou now?" Henri said in French. "How many insults must we endure? If you do not leave on your own volition, I shall pick you up and toss you into the road on your ear, you tawdry little English upstart," Uncle Henri raged. The tawdry little English upstart bit was delivered with racy expletives and included a few professions I'd never explored. Still, I was more amused than offended.

Then Mademoiselle Le Chouchou jumped into my arms and covered me with kisses and I knew in a flash that the matter was settled: if I passed the doggy test, I could stay.

And then in strode Peaches.

"Hi, you must be Henri." She entered the room as if she owned the place. Naturally, she didn't waste any time waiting for greetings from monsieur. In seconds, she had taken his hand and pumped it energetically before exclaiming: "I love the decor! I love your look!"

Henri was staring at her, his mouth half-open. "Who is this magnificent creature?" he asked in English.

"The name is Penelope but you can call me Peaches. Okay to call you Henri?" Not that she waited for an answer. "So, you have a couple of oddball stalkers lurking on your property, Henri—oddball as in they can run like hell and disappear into the shrubbery like shadows. They don't look like paparazzi to me—too fast. More like professionals. What are we searching for here, anyway, the French crown jewels?"

"Okay to tell them?" Lilly asked, turning to her uncle.

"Tell them," he agreed, standing with his legs apart and his fists dug into his waist, smiling at Peaches.

"A missing panel of the Lady and the Unicorn tapestries," Lilly announced, her tone ta-da and her expression expectant.

"The Cluny Tapestries?" I pulled my face from the dog's fur.

Peaches looked to each one of us in turn. "The Clooney Tapestries, seriously? As in George Clooney?"

Lilly and Henri broke into gales of laughter. Only I knew that she wasn't joking.

3

$\mathcal{P}$eaches never was big into textiles, no matter how old or how historic. She was, however, big into George Clooney. Luckily, the Saint Chappelles thought she was just kidding around.

"She is very funny this Peaches, *non?*" Henri exclaimed, taking Chouchou from my arms, "but of course she knows that La Dame à la Licorn tapestries are one of the wonders of the Middle Ages, a priceless testament to the weaver's art, is that not so, Chouchou?" He was gazing at the dog, who licked his face in agreement.

Peaches wisely remained silent, leaving me to exclaim excitedly: "You're actually looking for, what, a seventh tapestry? The six tapestries in the Cluny Museum are masterpieces and to think there might be another, well, that's just incredible!" We all have our gush points. I could easily enthuse about this topic but suddenly the possibility of a missing panel struck me as unlikely. "Wait, why do you even think there is a seventh?"

"Do you know the history, mademoiselle?" Henri inquired coolly.

I was close to blurting out my credentials but kept my ego in check. "Could you please just call me Phoebe? And I know the basics. I know, for instance, that the tapestries were probably commissioned by a Jean Le Viste from Lyon sometime in the late 1400s and that they were designed in Paris but probably woven in Brussels. They are believed to be allegorical, representing the five senses with the biggest, the sixth, *À Mon Seul Désir*, possibly referring to the lady's love or possibly her virginity but there are other interpretations. Right so far?"

"*C'est exact.*" Henri nodded, putting the dog down.

"Okay, then. Here's where things get a bit fuzzy. Historians assume that the tapestries were commissioned for Le Viste's marriage to Genevieve de Nanterre in 1475. He hailed from a wealthy family, she from a noble but broke one, making the union particularly beneficial to both families despite the age difference. But, if I remember correctly, the tapestries were actually completed about the time of Le Viste's death. They could have been commemorating his marriage to Genevieve since the Viste crest is prevalent throughout and it could easily have taken many decades to weave six panels of that detail, but it's puzzling."

Henri now stood with his arms crossed but otherwise did not appear ready to throttle me or erupt into a tirade.

"So why do you believe there's a missing seventh panel?" I asked.

"Because, Mademoiselle McCabe, my family is in possession of a secret letter written by a relative of mine, a Louis Saint Chappelles, to a member of the Le Viste family referencing a seventh," Henri continued in English. "He is writing to a Monsieur Le Viste but we do not know which one. He promises to keep the seventh panel safe, that he hopes someday it will hang with the others. Louis Saint Chappelles was a priest and spiritual adviser to the King of France at the time."

"How extraordinary," I remarked. "What else does it say?"

He shrugged. "*Rien.*"

"But where does the missing tapestry come in?" I pressed.

"The letter, it references *À Mon Seul Désir,*" Henri said with a flourish. "That is most important. My late brother and I, we thought the letter was to Jean Le Viste, who may have commissioned a seventh panel in secret and requested help from my ancestor, the priest."

"Seriously?" I asked. I could have shaken the information out of him if I could.

"Seriously?" Henri repeated, drawing back. "Do I not appear serious enough for you, mademoiselle?"

"Sorry, what I mean to say is that as exciting as that all sounds, does it really indicate a missing seventh tapestry?"

That was a mistake. Henri's long face had turned so thunderous I swear his mustache twitched.

"Anyway," Lilly intercepted, "this letter has haunted our family for centuries and sent my dad and uncle off on quests that have unearthed nothing."

"And yet, we believe a seventh tapestry exists, *n'est-ce pas?*" said Uncle Henri, turning to his niece.

"We sure hope so," Lilly agreed, "but for that to be proven, we need an expert in locating lost things, don't we, uncle?"

Uncle shrugged.

"May I see the letter?" I asked.

"Non." That was Uncle Henri. "Why should I hire you for such an important case when some of the most well-regarded detectives in France have had no success?"

"Because my skills are unique," I suggested.

"Phaw!" That was a Gallic snort. You had to experience it to grasp its full gravitas.

Peaches stepped forward. "What, Henri, you haven't heard of the famous Phoebe McCabe?" She held out her phone on an article about me finding the lost Botticelli. She loved that one. "Phoebe finds things others can't—paintings, lost temples, family jewels—you name it. What's a missing tapestry?"

Yes, embarrassing, but I was trying to own my worth. "I believe I can help you," I insisted.

Now Henri was temporarily transfixed by Peaches again. One long stride and he was before her, taking her free hand and kissing it. "So magnificent," he murmured over her knuckle. "Will you help me find the lost tapestry, mademoiselle?"

"If you hire the agency, I'm part of the package." She caught my eye over Henri's bowed head. "I'm her bodyguard, by the way."

"Bodyguard? Why does one such as she require a bodyguard?" Henri lifted his head and peered at me skeptically.

There was the crux. If told him my full sorry tale, both Lilly and Henri might assume that I'd attract unsavory types from the underside of the art world—justifiably, I might add. Though I seriously doubted that any of my usual admirers would be that interested in a tapestry, I didn't want to alarm my employers unnecessarily. Lilly drew enough attention on her own.

But Peaches had it all figured out. "Bad ex," she explained. "My friend here has an abusive ex-boyfriend who won't leave her alone."

Henri straightened. "Abusive?"

"Oh, completely. Just a few months ago, he locked her in a cave and tried to kill her. Controlling bastard."

Funny, I had never thought of Noel Halloren as an abusive boyfriend or even an abusive significant maybe. Then again, I had never considered myself a victimized girlfriend, either.

Henri swore in French. "I have such contempt for men who abuse the ladies! What is it about these tiny men—" he brought his thumb and his forefinger together to measure these minuscule beings "—these tiny, tiny men, these *putains*, who must abuse the much weaker sex?"

Lilly, Peaches, and I exchanged glances.

"Anyway," Peaches assured him, "I'm around to keep her safe. I'm particularly good at bonking bad guys but I could assess any structural difficulties you may have on the side. I have a degree in architectural engineering, too." She was distracting him. Clever. "How's your foundation and your roof? I've already seen two areas of concern regarding the structural integrity of this cottage. Take that beam directly overhead…"

All eyes turned ceiling-ward. A thick whitewashed beam, no doubt hailing from the days when trees were allowed to grow into ripe old age undisturbed, ran the full length of the pitched roof and seemed to brace the supports on either side.

"See that crack running down the center?" Peaches asked. "Ordinary age as in wear and tear, I'd say. What is it, about five hundred years old? So it's allowed to have a few wrinkles. It might hold up for a while longer but already I can see fissures in the plaster there and there—" she pointed "—which means it's starting to buckle. If you don't get that attended to soon, this whole thing could come tumbling down on your head." Peaches stared at him.

"Would you do the work yourself?" Henri asked softly.

She shrugged. "Could be tricky working with a French crew but I could stay on hand to consult, certainly."

Then it was as if he snapped to. "What do I say? I cannot afford such renovations!" Henri proclaimed, throwing up his hands. "I am but a poor man."

"Okay, then," Peaches said with a shrug. "Let's get your house in order and make you a rich one. Let's find this missing tapestry of yours and turn the Saint Chappelles fortunes around. Show us the letter so we can get started."

And just like that it was done. We were hired, or so I thought.

Minutes later, I was trailing behind with Lilly as Henri led Peaches on a tour through the house, supposedly en route to view this letter from Father Louis Saint Chappelles. But it seemed that nothing would be done quickly around Henri. He insisted on stopping every few feet to explain his collections, the decor, the colors. "This hue is called," he noted at one point, "'pipi de vache,' named after that wonderful shade that flows from the pipi of cows fed on mangos."

"Cow pee, seriously?" Peaches stopped to gape at a sunflower-yellow wall, the predominant hue in the house.

"There really was such a color in the eighteenth century," I told her as we followed Henri up the stairs. "Colors have fascinating stories."

"If you say so," she whispered. "Never putting cow piss on my walls, just sayin'."

The upstairs opened up onto a series of small chambers, several of them bedrooms furnished with oversized grand furniture but also cozy libraries and studies, every room crammed to the rafters with furniture and collections.

We were led into a room where a wall of mullioned glass faced onto the garden; it seemed at first glance to be a cabinet of curiosities crossed with an art gallery with a dash of a storeroom thrown in. Among the oak cabinets and wall-to-ceiling books, watercolors hung along with several Dutch oils that would have fetched a few thousand euros had Henri been inclined to sell. It looked as though a few had already gone since two vacant rectangles remained empty as if in memoriam.

Lilly went directly to a chest sitting in the center of a desk, me in tow, while Henri continued pointing out his treasures to Peaches.

"It's in here," she said as she pulled a fob of keys from her pocket. Inserting a tiny brass key, she flipped open an ivory inlaid Chinese chest and pulled out a piece of paper. My first thought was *They keep an old letter in a box?* but soon realized it was only a photocopy.

"What happened to the original?" I asked as I took the page between my fingers. Standard quality photocopy in stark black and white. Surprisingly brief.

"Stolen way back when we still lived in the château."

I looked at her. "How long ago?"

She shrugged. "Maybe twenty years ago, before I left for the States. Dad was still alive then. Lots of guests staying at the château back in those days since Mom and Dad always entertained. Glad we kept copies just in case."

"Do you have any idea who took it?" I asked.

"None. It could have been any one of about twenty-five people. Dad didn't even know how long it had been gone when he discovered it missing."

I peered down at the page. It was barely legible and the date above the salutation was completely indecipherable.

Lilly read it off by heart: "'Dearest Monsieur Le Viste, to my sole desire. I

shall guard the seventh panel with my life, as promised, and will prevent—'
there was a big hole in this line so we never knew what was to be prevented
'—ever learning of its existence. I hope to someday see it complete with my
own eyes and dream of the day when it may hang with the others—' the rest
of this line was ruined, too '—yours faithfully, Father Louis Saint Chappelles.'"

Not much to go on but intriguing nonetheless. "And you believe the
seventh panel refers to the Lady and the Unicorn tapestries?" I asked.

"That has always been the family's belief," Lilly said, "and the Saint Chappelles family was related to the Le Vistes, which is yet another connection.
The family rumor was that the Le Vistes used to come to our château because
of this connection—cousins or something. Father Louis Saint Chappelles was
supposedly a priest in the court of Charles VII when Le Viste was the
barrister."

I pondered that for a moment. The timeline didn't quite add up. "Is any of
that substantiated?" I asked.

Lilly shook her head. "We're kind of light on the ground in tracking down
any real historical information here, which has always been part of our problem. My dad hired a few detective types. There was a Louis Saint Chappelles
in the court of Charles VII and he was a priest. That's all we know. Most of
the findings are historical texts you can find in the national archive."

"Primary?"

"Pardon?"

"Firsthand accounts?"

"Oh, yes, I think so. The Saint Chappelles were all supporters of Charles
VII."

I turned. Henri was standing directly behind us. "The same king of France
that Joan of Arc helped crown against the English-backed army?" I asked.

He nodded. *"Exactement."*

A tremor of excitement hit. *Joan of Arc.* "We've got to get back to Paris to
see the other tapestries and begin research—the sooner, the better."

"Agreed," Henri said, "but then you must return here, *non?*" He was
pointing out the window. "The tapestry is hidden there in the château. This I
feel in my soul." He tapped his chest. "My brother and I, we searched and
searched but never found it, but I know it must be there. You must look."

I gazed out the paned windows toward the hill where the imposing
château stood glorious, magnificent, and at first glance rendered all mere
mortals to mere serfs.

"You must start there," Henri insisted. "The owners, they have turned it
into a *lit et petit déjeuné. Travestir!* Why not a Rocco Forte? Why only room and

breakfast? That was the plan but they say they have not the money so they scrimp." "Scrimp" was spoken as if synonymous with defecating in a corner. More French curses followed. "It is no wonder that they fall on their heads, *non*? They close half of the château off for the spiders and open up but a few rooms for guests but the guests do not come. Now that the Covid wanes, maybe they do, but it is too late, *oui*? *Les DuBois*, they lose money. Phiff!" He shrugged. The Gallic shrug spoke volumes and involved a combination of expression and gesture implying that the poor buyers deserved their fate.

I was at a loss on how to respond. "That's sad. So many businesses failed during Covid. Of course we'll book ourselves in there."

Henri snapped his fingers. "You must roam the house. The owners, they ask for my help to prepare the château for sale. I will say that you will help me, designers from London, *non*?"

No, because I couldn't imagine anyone French requesting anyone English as a design consultant but what did I know?

"They want to stage it," Lilly explained.

"But they only have to do a little research to discover that design is not our business," I pointed out.

"If I recommend you, they will look no further. Of course, it is me they want and I will make myself available. They want *l'original*," Henri added. "*C'est moi*, Monsieur Saint Chappelles, last remaining son of the *famille de Saint Chappelles*, I am an original. When I appear, they fall all over themselves. This they have done since purchasing the château from me in 2020. I will say that, with your assistance, I will make the château more, um, buyable to the Anglais or Americans."

"Salable, marketable?" I offered in English.

"*Oui*."

"But didn't you tell them that you wouldn't help them anymore, Uncle Henri?" Lilly asked.

He lifted his chin. "I said that I would not help if they would not permit me to choose the next buyers and they refused this, so I refuse them." He was gazing toward the château, so much pain grooved into his long face that I thought he would cry.

"And now?" Lilly prompted after a few seconds.

"And now I change my mind so Peaches can find the tapestry."

Lilly visibly sagged with relief. "Good. We'll get started, then, but I thought you liked the DuBoises?"

Henri shrugged. "For them, the château is but a business. For me, it is blood. The DuBoises let me visit any time I want, that is a good thing."

"They've been...very gracious," Lilly said.

Henri gazed down at her. "But what if new owners will not let me come whenever I choose, close the doors to the Saint Chappelles forever? How could we bear this?"

Lilly sidled up to him and gave him a hug. "Don't worry, dear uncle. Phoebe and her agency will find the tapestry and then you can buy back the château yourself."

Daylight had leached from the room by then and Peaches was staring out the window. "Where did you say your security dudes were posted, Lilly?" she asked.

"I didn't. Actually, I don't know where they are." She pulled out her phone and tapped in a text. "Um...Jean Luc and Pierre are at the end of the driveway. No word from René."

"Why aren't they surrounding the house?" Peaches demanded. "Do they seriously think bad guys only enter through the front door? There should be one guy out front, one out back, *and* one watching the driveway! If we're going to work for you, Lilly, I need to be put in charge of security."

"Magnificent creature!" whispered Henri.

"Why are you so agitated?" Lilly asked as we scrambled down the stairs behind Peaches moments later.

"Because I saw movement in the garden just now and if it's not the security dudes, then who the hell is it?" Peaches didn't wait for a response but ran straight out the door into the garden, little Chouchou at her heels. Henri called the dog back.

"Peaches, wait!" I hissed but she had disappeared.

"It's just a pap. He'll get the photos he wants and then be gone," Lilly said as the three of us stood together peering into the shadowy woods.

"These photographers, they have no respect," Henri muttered.

"What bugs me is that this means they've tracked me here, uncle. Shit!" Lilly turned away and tapped her phone. When Jean Luc and Pierre strode up the drive, she demanded in French, "Where is René?"

The two men glanced at each other. "I thought he was watching the door here," Pierre, the topknot guy, replied. "He's not answering his mobile."

"Then find him! Peaches saw somebody in the bushes. Maybe it was him," Lilly said. As the men strode off, she turned to me. "I promised to get you back to Paris by ten."

"But you have only just arrived," Henri complained.

"We'll return tomorrow, I promise. Phoebe and Peaches have a hotel they have to check out of tomorrow morning, uncle."

"Come, I give you something to eat before you drive back, something light —soup and baguette?" Henri offered.

"Perfect." Lilly turned to walk with her uncle into the house when Peaches called out behind us. Turning, we watched as she dashed up to us, Jean Luc and Pierre carrying someone between them.

"Found René," she panted. "He's been shot."

4

*A*ctually, shot wasn't correct, more like *chopped*.

By the time the doctor had arrived followed by the police, it appeared that René had received a blow to the head, not fatally but definitely incapacitating. The poor man lay in one of Henri's upstairs bedrooms while the doctor tended him, and the police waited below until he could be questioned. There was still some debate over whether he should be taken to a hospital for further tests but René himself wanted to wait until his return to Paris for that.

Meanwhile, the area surrounding the property was thoroughly searched with no signs of an interloper detected, not even a footprint that didn't belong to either Peaches or the security team. The rest of us remained in Henri's cow-pee-colored salon while two police officers grilled us until we were crispy.

"Mademoiselle Williams, you say you went to look for Monsieur Bouchard?" asked Monsieur Cappat, a member of the regional police force, a pleasant-faced man with closely cropped hair and a ready smile packed into a dark uniform so close-fitting it molded his body like a second skin—impeccable French tailoring. He spent an undue amount of time interrogating Peaches, who, he pointed out, was the only one in the vicinity when René was accosted.

"I said I had," Peaches told him again. "After I saw movement in the bushes, I ran out to check and found René several yards back in the orchard flat on his face. The other two joined me seconds later." The fact that Peaches refused to call Jean Luc and Pierre by name indicated how disgusted she was with their overall security skills. "That wasn't the first time I'd caught movement, as I've said. I saw a shadow back there earlier."

"Let me just clarify, if you please," Monsieur Cappat continued with excruciating courtesy. He was, it appeared, the senior officer. "You are here protecting Mademoiselle McCabe, and the three men from Forces de Sécurité à Paris are protecting Mademoiselle Lin, yes?"

"That's right," Peaches told him.

"Correct," Lilly agreed.

"That appears to be a great deal of security for two women. Mademoiselle Lin I understand, she being a famous person, but what is the nature of your protection of Mademoiselle McCabe?"

Peaches gazed at the officer as if he had spent his days perched on an inflatable water toy. "Haven't you heard of Phoebe McCabe? She's famous, too." I tried to catch her eye but she was fixed on Cappat. "She's notorious for finding lost treasure, missing art, countering art thieves, and putting criminals behind bars. I watch her back. Check out the Agency of the Ancient Lost and Found's website if you don't believe me. It's not fake news, either. Everything you read there is verifiable."

The second officer, Monsieur Boucher, tapped something into his tablet and passed it over to Cappat, who was not the only one who understood English between the two as I first assumed. Whispering ensued. I caught the French translation for *Interpol stooges* where I sat with Chouchou on my lap. That rankled but I said nothing.

"I invited Phoebe here to meet my uncle," Lilly explained, "in hopes that she could help us find a missing family heirloom."

"Which I intend to do," I added.

"Family jewels, a rare painting, a stash of ancient treasure, perhaps?" Cappat asked while skimming the tablet.

"Just something lost, monsieur," Henri was quick to assure him, "and we are quite certain that whatever happened to the security man that lies incapacitated in my room above is not connected to what we seek here. Another photographer—such a nuisance! Lilly is always being harassed by these types."

"We were chased by the paparazzi in Paris but believed that our driver shook his tail," Lilly said, "but who knows if someone managed to follow us here in order to catch a few photos?"

"*Oui,*" Jean Luc interjected in French. "We were contracted by Mademoiselle Lin to assure her safety after she arrived in Paris three days ago. The paparazzi were harassing her." None of this was new information but repeating the same questions in different ways was a familiar police technique.

Cappat was still reading about the agency, his expression hard to decipher. Meanwhile, Jean Luc perched forward in his chair looking ready to spring while Pierre kept glancing upward as if concerned for his wounded comrade upstairs.

"So," Cappat said, lifting his gaze at last. "It would seem that Mademoiselle McCabe may attract attention of her own. Perhaps not the best choice for your seeker of lost heirlooms considering you fear for your privacy, Mademoiselle Lin?"

Though he was addressing Lilly, Peaches jumped in. *"Au contraire, monsieur d'agent*, we were contacted because we are the *best* finder of lost things. Lilly chose her agency well." She probably hoped to detract from the true point of the officer's statement. By then I feared that Lilly may have been regretting her choice.

Luckily, further commentary was aborted when the doctor arrived to say that it was all right to question René. That sent the two gendarmes upstairs and left us staring at one another in the salon. Henri leapt up to fix us a light snack, leaving Lilly twisting her hands.

"I didn't realize that you might attract that kind of unwanted attention," she said to me. "Is this from your abusive boyfriend?"

"He was—*is*—an international art thief," I admitted, feeling guilty for not filling her in on the sordid details. "But he's not involved here. I can feel that in my gut."

"Phoebe has the kind of gut that knows these things. Call it a sixth sense," Peaches explained. "If her gut tells her that her ex isn't involved, then he isn't involved."

Lilly looked unconvinced.

"Lilly, attacking a security man isn't my ex's style. He's more into dramatic staging on an impressive scale and prefers big-ticket items that can be quickly turned into profit. A possible seventh Lady and the Unicorn tapestry, should one exist, will probably need years of conservation once found. Noel prefers quick turnarounds like gold and jewels."

Since Henri returned with plates of bread and cheese, we dropped the subject to eat. I was temporarily entranced by melt-in-the-mouth cheeses which reminded me how incredible the fresh varieties could be. The store-bought varieties held only a thin resemblance to the original.

By the time we'd brushed away the last crumb, the police announced that we could go. René could provide no information about his attacker. He claimed that he felt a sharp crack of pain in the head and then went unconscious. With no footprints and no clear sighting of anything conclusive, the police resolved to blame the attack on a rabid photographer. They would make inquiries in the village about strangers hanging around and move on to other things.

It was already 10:30 by the time we left for Paris, René leaning against Peaches's shoulder and Lilly up front with Jean Luc and Pierre.

"You okay?" Peaches asked René.

The wounded man only mumbled and stayed put. By now Peaches was taking a personal interest in his well-being, due, she assured me via a whispered exchange, to the fact that he was the only one of the security team worth his salt. At least he had been prowling the property like a proper guard when he was wounded, she said. The fact that he was tall, well-built, black, and good-looking probably didn't hurt, either.

After dropping René off at the hospital in the care of Pierre, Jean Luc drove on to Lilly's Hotel Crillion.

"We'll rent a car and meet you back at Saint Chappelles the day after tomorrow," I said to Lilly as the car slowed to a stop outside the lobby. "First I want to research here in Paris."

"Hold on to the research part until I get back to you," she said as a bellman opened the door. "I'm not sure hiring you was the best idea, like I said. I didn't realize that you attracted such notoriety."

I leaned forward in the seat. "We're absolutely the best ones for the job, Lilly, and you know it. Whatever happened to René had nothing to do with us."

"You don't know that," she said without looking at me. "I have never had a paparazzi attack a security guy ever. That just doesn't happen around me. Anyway, I've got to think about this. Mind getting a cab to your hotel? I'd feel safer if Jean Luc escorts me to my suite."

"Of course."

That left Peaches and me standing by the hotel entrance while a bellman hailed us a cab.

"I feel like I've just been dumped after a bad first date," Peaches muttered.

"We're not being dumped," I told her. "Technically we haven't begun dating. I still have time to convince Lilly."

"How?"

"I don't know yet but I'll find a way. If there's a missing panel to the Lady and the Unicorn tapestries, I'm going to find it, no matter what."

"Are you getting any tremors in your gut, any sense that we're on to something big?"

"Not a thing," I admitted as we climbed into the cab's back seat, "but I rarely feel anything this early."

I had no intention of waiting for Lilly to give us the nod before launching my research. In fact, I intended to begin a preliminary web expedition as soon as I reached my room. But first things first. I had promised to keep all members of the team informed of any case I was on, as in step-by-step, a fallout from my recent Grecian experience. Rupert, in particular, had grown irate when he had learned how quickly events had accelerated during my presumed vacation. Now I did due diligence accordingly. Sort of.

"Heading straight for bed," Peaches said with a yawn. "Can't believe how tired shopping and bodyguarding makes you. See you tomorrow morning."

"Night."

Peaches and I parted ways at the doors of our adjoining rooms and I stepped into my suite with my phone in hand, trying not to imagine Evan standing there the way he had been only a few hours before. I wondered if he'd messaged me and, if not, maybe I should contact him. Before I did anything, however, I crafted a brief group message to all team members bringing them more or less up to date.

I had no sooner hit Send when a text from Rupert popped up on my screen: *More detail required.*

I knew what this meant; in fact, I could have added a postscript: *I expect a detailed description of every case ASAP as per our agreement. Any attempt to brush me off will not be tolerated.* I imagined his plumby vowels rolling between my ears.

Taking a deep breath, I called him immediately. "Hi, Rupert. Hope you're enjoying working in our new lab. Anyway, to keep it short, the client hasn't signed us up yet so there's really not that much to report." The term "short" and "Rupert" rarely coexisted but I was ever hopeful. "In fact, she may not hire us in the end."

"Whyever not? If she has something of value worth retrieving and is herself a discerning individual, she would be foolhardy not to hire us for the task. After all, we are foremost in the field. Who is this woman and what does she seek?"

Crud. My answer would pique his interest above all else. "A family heirloom," I said quickly.

"Who is the family to whom the heirloom allegedly belongs?"

I sighed inwardly. Why did I think I could keep this off his radar? "The Saint Chappelles."

"*The* Saint Chappelles?"

"Yes, the same. You've heard of them?" Of course he had. He was more up on French history than I, having spent many seasons in France. "Anyway, the potential client is Lilly Lin, the movie star. Yes, I didn't make the connection, either. Long story. She and her uncle, Henri Saint Chappelles, are hoping to find a seventh panel to the Lady and the Unicorn tapestries." There, I said it. Done and dusted. In my case, more like done and dynamited.

"Henri Saint Chappelles, the celebrated interior designer?"

"The same."

I counted the seconds before he spoke again. His tone was as frosty as the North Sea. "You disappoint me. You have been withholding pertinent information, Phoebe, something which I find unbearably difficult to accept given our history. After all these years, do you truly believe that I am unable to tell when you are dissembling?"

I sighed. "Sorry, Rupert. It's just that this case is in such early stages that I'd hoped to be on a firmer footing before engaging you or the others. The Saint Chappelles family believe that there may be a seventh panel to the Lady and the Unicorn tapestries that went missing from their family sometime in the fifteenth century. While I'm at it, I may as well tell you that there was an incident earlier today where Lilly Lin's driver suffered a blow to the head. She's constantly plagued by paparazzi being who she is but she believes that our notoriety may be responsible. There, that truly is everything."

I counted ten beats of silence. "How extraordinary," he said. "I will be on the next flight to Paris and will book at the Étoile, too," he said finally. "That is where you and Peaches are staying, I presume?"

"The Splendid Étoile, yes, but, Rupert—"

"Pray do not check out until I arrive."

And then he hung up. I stood for a moment, phone in hand, silently swearing. Of course a possible missing Cluny tapestry would send him flying over, not to mention any hint of a historic French family coupled with the dual bonus of meeting a famous film star and an apparently noted French designer. Like it or not, Sir Rupert Fox was on this case.

Looking for a distraction, I gazed down at my phone again, hoping for a message from Evan. Nothing. Next, I checked the agency's tracking map, which showed his dot flying across the Mediterranean. That pitched me into muttering my latest mantra: *I will not be needy, I will not be needy.*

Wherever this relationship went with Evan, if it progressed anywhere at all, the last thing I wanted was to become a woman who needed a man so badly that she had to know where he was every moment of the day. Even worse was the thought of waiting on tenterhooks for a message or a phone call. No. Phoebe McCabe was never going to be that woman. She had work to do, fulfilling, engaging, and important work. Men were secondary.

With that, I dug out my laptop, activated my phone's intruder alert, and launched the first of many online research excursions beginning with the history of King Charles VII of France circa 1422-61, the Saint Chappelles, and the Le Vistes.

5

$\mathcal{T}$he first thing the next morning, I called to arrange an appointment with a Madame LaForte, one of the curators at the Cluny Museum, and received an appointment that same day. Finally, I thought, the Agency of the Ancient Lost and Found had begun to open a few doors. Such appointments were rarely organized so quickly and I was feeling incredibly lucky. The fact that I had not yet heard from Lilly was something I chose to ignore for now.

"You got an appointment just like that?" Peaches asked as we headed for the museum on foot under a cloudy Parisian sky. It was so tempting to linger over coffee and croissants on our balcony that morning but my lingering-in-Paris days were over. However, I did glimpse the Eiffel Tower punctuating the sky in the distance, which almost made it better.

"I expected to have to wheedle and throw a few names around to arrange a meeting so quickly but it turns out I didn't need to. Good thing. Now we can interview Madame LaForte before Rupert arrives."

Peaches cast me one of her sidelong glances. "Think so?"

"Why do you say that?" I shot back.

"I checked the agency map this morning and it looks like he's already here."

I stopped dead in the middle of the sidewalk, nearly banging into the woman behind me, which prompted me to say *excuse me* in three languages before remembering where I was. "No!" I said to Peaches. "I was only talking to him last night."

"So, he works fast and flights from London to Paris are frequent. Why the problem? He's your friend and a member of the team."

"He is both," I acknowledged, resuming my pace, "but this particular case—an ancient tapestry, a historical French family—is the sort of thing that will make him jump in with both well-heeled feet and possibly hijack the case. He loves this sort of thing and he's bound to confangle everything."

"'Confangle'?"

"I just made that word up but, trust me, it works when applied to Rupert."

"Sometimes I think you'd rather operate alone without other agents kicking up dust in your sandbox, at least until you need them," she remarked.

Ouch. There was truth to that. Sometimes I wondered when my colleagues would clue in to that reality but it seemed that Rupert already had.

My appointment wasn't until 2:30 so Peaches and I had a few hours to explore the museum on our own. My friend was naturally fascinated by the architecture so was keen to study the building itself, it being the best-preserved medieval mansion in Paris, while I wandered from room to room, soaking in the stained glass, the kingly effigies, the exhibit of golden objects.

Any time thoughts of Evan interfered with my historical pondering, I quickly shoved them away. I refused to be enslaved by my emotions unless those emotions were incited by ancient art, of course. In my effort to remain focused, I only permitted myself to check my phone a few times per hour, which, by the way, was how I knew that he had landed in Sardinia.

The stained-glass exhibit was mesmerizing. Staged in a darkened room so that the light could illuminate the medieval glass, I spent considerable time bathing in the colors. That was the first time I sensed that I was being followed. A tug on my senses, a prickle at the nape of my neck, was all it took to alert me that someone in that gallery—shadowy figures all—might be more interested in me than the glass.

Turning quickly, I glimpsed a figure scurrying away at the back of the gallery. I didn't chase him, partly because I was used to such scrutiny and partly because I had better things to do. I was in a museum, after all.

I saved the tapestry room for last. Though it wasn't my first visit to pay homage to the Lady and the Unicorn, every encounter was as fresh and vivid as the first. The six tapestries hung in splendor in a curved room where the lighting was designed to illuminate the jewel-like colors of the wool and silk against a darkened background, and even to this day they represented the height of a weaver's art.

The colors sang out in rich red and woad blue with the millefleurs—millions of flowers—background enlivened with white, green, orange, and yellow, a design which the weavers of the Netherlands, where the tapestries of this kind were created, had perfected. Every blossom was identifiable, every creature romping in the foliage clearly defined. Even after all these centuries, the artistry was incredibly detailed, as much akin to painting with fiber as any existent woven art then or since.

They were presumably commissioned around the mid-1400s by either Jean Le Viste or Antoine Le Viste, both of whom had been involved in the French court. Exactly which one was behind the work, no one seemed to know for certain. According to the scholarship, the subject of the tapestries remained an enigma, too, thought by general agreement to be dedicated to the senses with multiple symbols of courtly love hinted at throughout. Each panel featured a beautifully adorned lady often with her handmaiden standing in a millefleurs background flanked by a unicorn on one side and a lion on the other. In most cases, the animals held a banner emblazoned with the Le Viste emblem and both the expressions of the central ladies, who changed from panel to panel, and the animals themselves, were unique. Sometimes the lion frowned, sometimes he grinned. Sometimes the lady looked happy, at other times sad, even resigned.

The first panel shows a lady holding the Le Viste pennant flanked as always by the lion and the unicorn. In this panel she is holding the unicorn's horn, which is believed to represent the sense of touch. In the next, the lady and a maid stand together playing a kind of table organ resting on an intricate carpet. This piece reportedly represents sound. Another tapestry supposedly representing smell has a lady removing carnation blooms from a basket her maid carries while a monkey sniffs a flower in the background. For sight, the lady holds a mirror up to the unicorn, who is resting its forelegs in her lap while looking at its own reflection. For taste, the lady appears to be reaching for a sweet in a basket while a parrot flaps over her hand as if eager to get at the treats. In the sixth and most enigmatic panel, the lady stands before a tent held open by the lion and the unicorn while her maid holds a chest from which the lady is either removing or returning a jeweled necklace. Written on top of the tent are the words *À Mon Seul Désir*. Was "to my only desire" referring to love, as is often interpreted, or something more mysterious?

I stood staring at the tapestries as other viewers circled around me, struck by the multiple interpretations the medieval artistry presented. Even the rabbit was symbolic, suggesting lustful urges, while the monkey represented whimsy and mischief. The little lapdog in different versions appeared near the lady in all the panels and could represent loyalty or devotion but the fact that they were always collared might also imply captivity. Was the unicorn itself referring to the tale of the unicorn that could only be tamed by a virgin, a powerful myth dominating the Middle Ages?

These were only a smidgen of potential interpretations that frolicked in this rich and storied hodgepodge of medieval symbolism. The tapestries were probably designed to thrill, entertain, physically enhance a space, as well as to baffle the viewer all at once. They must have been displayed in some magnificent hall similar to the building in which I stood where the rich and mighty wined and dined.

If Jean Le Viste had commissioned them, I couldn't believe that his sole purpose was to decorate his drafty manor house or simply impress everyone with his wealth and taste, though no doubt those reasons factored, too. If a seventh tapestry did exist, that could be the piece of the puzzle that unlocked the entire mystery once and for all.

I stared at the faces of the women in the tapestries, each lady's expression exquisitely rendered. Weaving faces in tapestries was no small feat. The weavers followed a cartoon or drawing while actually working the images in reverse, never able to see the work as a whole until the piece was removed from the loom and unrolled months or even years later. These weavers were technically and artistically brilliant, something more evident in these magnificent tapestries than any of the others I had seen or studied.

My phone pinged. It was Peaches reminding me that our appointment was drawing nigh and that she was waiting for me in the main hall. I thought I caught a shadow flicking past as I retraced my steps back to the entrance, someone short, dressed in total black, but the moment I caught sight of Peaches, I put it out of my mind.

She stood brimming with enthusiasm beneath the effigy of an ancient king. "Fantastic place! You wouldn't believe the foundations here and I just read the most incredible thing on flying buttresses. So where do we meet this Madame LeForte?"

"This way." I indicated a sign discreetly hidden beside a brass plaque saying *Ne Pas Enter. Personnel Seulement.* "But first, I'm to let the information desk know that we're coming."

I strode up to the desk and told the clerk that we had arrived for our appointment. Moments later, a slim woman estimated to be in her early forties and dressed in a maroon cardigan over a black pencil skirt and low heels approached me with a welcoming smile.

"Mademoiselle McCabe. I am Ella LeForte. A pleasure to meet you," she said in faintly accented English. She extended her hand and quickly pulled it back. The days of handshaking had apparently died during the pandemic but she appeared to regret the lack of physical congeniality. "Come with me, if you please."

We followed her, me studying her clothing as we went, a habit gleaned from a conviction that what we wear says much about who we are. Or want to be. Her apparel was well-tailored of excellent quality and yet plain enough to imply that the wearer wished to stay very much in the background. Her short curly hairstyle spoke of wash-and-go ease and her glasses leaned on the practical rather than stylish side. She also walked a lot, judging from her muscled calves.

We climbed up a curved wooden staircase and through a side door, down a long hall, and finally to a spacious room at the end. The door was open and the figure of a man stood backlit against a tall arched window.

Rupert. *Well, damn.*

"Phoebe, you have arrived at last but I must say that I do feel as though I have been waiting forever—a bit of an overstatement, I confess, but you do get my drift. Nevertheless, Ella and I have been happily reconnecting in the interim. Did you know that I have worked with the esteemed tapestry curator in the past? Yes, indeed. She has kindly assessed several of my French pieces over the years. I—"

"Rupe!" Peaches exclaimed. "What a surprise!"

"Greetings, Peaches, and may I say you look divine. Is that Chanel?"

But Peaches dove in for a hug despite his efforts to avoid her enthusiasm. "Sure, if you want it to be." She squeezed him repeatedly until he was gasping for breath and managed to shove her away long enough to fetch his fallen glasses.

"Bulletproof, I hope?" Peaches asked as she swept the glasses from the floor and attempted to replace them on his nose while he swatted her hand away.

Ella was regarding the display with amusement. I sensed that she grasped exactly what was going on. Turning to me, she smiled. "Please sit and explain how I may be of help."

While Rupert readjusted his spectacles and straightened his tie, I took the seat opposite Ella and got right to the point. "Thank you for seeing me so quickly, Madame—"

"Ella, please."

"Ella," I continued. "I realize now that Rupert probably played a part but I'm just grateful to connect with you so quickly." I cast a quick glance at Rupert, who was now seated and mustering his composure. I flashed him a smile, which he didn't return. "Anyway," I said, turning to the curator, "I have a prospective client who believes that her family may be in possession of a seventh Lady and the Unicorn tapestry, which they are convinced may be hidden somewhere in the former family château."

"Ah, yes, of course—the Saint Chappelles." Ella's hands lifted and fell. "Members of the family have approached many curators here over the years, me included. I was speaking on the phone to one member of the family only last week."

That had to be Lilly since Henri appeared to have stopped the hunt. "And may I ask what that conversation involved?"

"Mademoiselle Saint Chappelles wished only to know whether I thought the letter that had once been in possession of her family was authentic. We hold a copy here in our archives. I explained that since I have only seen a facsimile, it is impossible to say. A carbon dating and thorough assessment by an expert would at least place the letter in the correct time period but the original has been lost."

"Apparently it went missing decades ago."

"Yes, so I understand."

Rupert cleared his throat. "So, there is a letter?"

"Presumably from a Louis Saint Chappelles, which may reference a seventh panel." I passed him my phone, open on my photo of the letter. "It doesn't really say much but Louis Saint Chappelles was a priest in the king's court, though not of the same generation as Jean le Viste."

"Either way, that would place it in the Valois dynasty. Which king, Charles VI, known as Charles the Mad?" Rupert inquired.

"*Mais non*, King Charles VII, his son," Ella said.

"'Charles the Victorious?'"

"*Oui.*"

"This Louis was a court priest?" Peaches inquired. "You mean there were more than one in the same court?"

"Many, indeed, nuns, too," Rupert remarked. "The court would have many spiritual advisers on hand."

"And this letter is supposed to refer to a seventh panel? Unlikely but not impossible." Ella lifted her hands again. Bare of rings, close-cut nails, perfect for handling delicate textiles. "The interesting thing about the letter that causes me to doubt its authenticity is that it does not follow any of the social constructs of the day—no courtly language, nothing that indicates the importance of either the sender or the recipient, *non*?"

"It almost appears to have been written in haste," I suggested.

"Yes, I agree." She smiled. "Or by one who does not comprehend how a letter of the day would be scripted, a forger, perhaps."

Fair enough.

"And there is no way we can authenticate the handwriting?" Rupert asked.

"Mais non," Ella assured us, "little has been traced to either the Saint Chappelles or the Le Vistes except dates of marriage and deaths, all through church records. Though important members of the courts of two kings, there is no paper trail for these men. I attribute that to their turbulent times."

"Indeed, due to the Hundred Years' War and the ensuing chaos that it wreaked on France." Rupert realigned the knife crease on his gray flannel trousers and crossed his ankles, flashing his brilliant knit socks. "Indeed. Pardon me, but from your remarks earlier, Ella, I was led to believe that it is your opinion that it is doubtful a seventh tapestry ever existed."

"Most of my colleagues, and indeed the scholarly world, do not believe that such a tapestry has ever existed," Ella acknowledged.

"But do you?" Peaches asked.

"I prefer to withhold judgment but I think not. If you regard the tapestries in the series as they are now—" she indicated six poster-sized images of the tapestries framed on the wall over her desk "—you will see that the story appears complete with *À Mon Seul Désir*. Not only does this panel differ in height but it is the only one that depicts a tent and, with that tent, a label that appears to both define and complete the story."

I gazed up at *À Mon Seul Désir*. "What do you believe it means?"

"It most likely refers to the constraints of courtly love that guided the social behavior of the nobility at the time. Wealthy couples married for family betterment, as you know, for political, financial, and status reasons, but rarely for love. Love was as a game that couples played within the safety of the courtly rules. Such rules allowed couples to flirt, to pine, to write songs and poetry to one another, to *court* romantic love, without actually engaging in the physical act and often while remaining married to another."

"Amazing," I mused, gazing up at the images.

Rupert cleared his throat again. "So, in keeping with that concept, the lovers may be permitted to engage the senses depicted in the tapestries up to a point, for example to sniff the flowers, see the object of their desire, to sere-nade them, and whatnot, but that *À Mon Seul Désire*, if it could be said that consummation of physical love may be the sole desire, must be safely packed away in a chest, so to speak."

"That's brilliant, Rupert," I enthused. "That's one interpretation of the tapestries and I suspect there are others." A jeweled necklace representative of physical love? Maybe.

"Many others," Ella agreed.

Before we left, we exchanged contact information and I promised to keep her informed as I proceeded with the case. She also offered that I could run things by her as they came up on my search. She'd make herself available to help in any way possible, too. I thanked her warmly.

"She's great," Peaches remarked as we stood outside the museum considering next steps. "Nice, easy to talk to. So what's next—check out someplace else or what?"

"I'm sending an update to Lilly and asking for us to meet her later today," I said.

Rupert was staring at me. I finally turned to him. "Okay, Rupert, I'm sorry. I kept the details from you because I wanted to get a sense of this case without distraction. Am I forgiven?"

"You are not. The assurances you gave following the Delos case indicated that you would provide a fulsome description of each case as it unfolds. Instead, you attempted to smokescreen your activities as if you did not wish my involvement."

"Sorry is all I can say. Of course I adore you, Rupert, but I think I felt a bit possessive about this case because it involves textiles, and not just any textiles. I will try to do better, promise."

A response from Lilly popped up onto my phone screen: *Still not sure you're the right person for the job. Am returning to my uncle's. Will inform you of my decision tomorrow.*

"Wow," Peaches remarked while gazing over my shoulder. "Cold or what? It's not like we attacked René ourselves or anything."

"Who is René?" Rupert inquired while fluffing out his pocket jonquil-colored silk, which naturally matched his tie, which naturally coordinated with his socks.

"One of the security dudes that Lilly hired to protect her against the paparazzi," Peaches explained. "Really cool guy. He was whacked on the head yesterday by persons unknown. Kind of shook Lilly up. Look, maybe we should just hang around Paris until she makes up her mind?"

I feigned shock. "Peaches, that doesn't sound like you at all: waiting around for someone else to make up their mind. Did I hear that right?"

"You neglected to add the Paris part. That's important."

I grinned. "Right, but I have another idea. We'll rent a car and drive down to Saint Chappelles and restate our case to Lilly and Henri. Henri really likes you, and with the Sir Rupert Fox on board, our argument will be that much stronger."

"The *Sir* Rupert Fox?" Rupert inquired. "Are you attempting to placate me?"

"Yes. Is it working?" Linking my arm in his, I beamed my brightest smile. "Monsieur Henri Saint Chappelles is a bit of a character, a former Parisian interior designer, as you know. He had the notion that we should book ourselves in to the Château Saint Chappelles B and B as interior designers arrived to assist the owners to find a new buyer. He sold the family pile during Covid to cover expenses but now the owners are putting it back on the market. He believes that we could claim that we're 'staging' the property to give us more run of the château."

Rupert's brows shot upward.

"I know: How does one stage a château?" I said. "I have no idea, either, but let's find out. I'm all for telling the DuBoises the truth but I'm taking my client's lead in this."

"If we get in there as designers or something we'll have the roam of the place. The Saint Chappelles believe the tapestry may be hidden somewhere there," Peaches pointed out.

"Extraordinary," Rupert remarked. "I do rather like the idea of being a designer."

"I thought you might but there's a huge flaw in Henri's logic: he believes if he finds the tapestry in the Château Saint Chappelles, the tapestry will be his to claim."

"Which is not the case." He nodded.

"Definitely not but I haven't broken that to him yet. If we find it, it could be claimed by the current owners or possibly France itself."

"Indeed, but I suggest we worry about ownership when and if we find the tapestry. It is, after all, a long shot as they say. Meanwhile, if we are to arrive as designers, it behooves us to dress the part, which I must say, you do not, Phoebe." He was studying me over the top of his spectacles in a manner that always made me edgy. "One of your art sweaters or wraps will only work if paired with interesting separates that can be mixed and matched without looking too done or too, well, *boho*. Your total look at the moment does not say stylish, Phoebe, it says shaggy. However, I know just the shop and the person who can assist. Come along."

Which is how we came to arrive back at our hotel at 5:35 laden with packages and, frankly, exhausted. After retrieving our keys from the desk, the three of us were just crossing the lobby when a tall man stepped out in front of us.

I stood looking up at him, trying to figure out where I'd seen him before. "René?" I finally registered.

"René!" Peaches exclaimed. "Why are you out of the hospital?"

"I was dismissed," he said in broken English peppered with French. I'm sure he meant *discharged*. "But you I had to see. I remember something."

6

He remembered very little, as it turned out, but still enough to make things interesting. Just before René was chopped on the head—and he swore that's what it had felt like—he recalled seeing a small dark figure diving through the air toward him. For a brief moment, he thought it was a bird—a big bird.

"Like a bat?" Peaches asked.

"Non, trop grande. C'est très petite. Très quick. There were *deux*, ah, two, one in front, one behind."

Must have been two if somebody cracked the rear of his head while the bat thing was diving toward him. On the other hand, had the concussion muddled his thinking? Large bats don't tend to dive at people at dusk, contrary to popular opinion, unless they were Transylvanian and of the Dracula persuasion. Besides, did they even have cat-sized bats in France?

"Why did you not tell the police, dear chap?" Rupert asked as we sat in the lobby.

René gazed across at Rupert as if he were a hallucination, maybe as a result of Rupert's blazing yellow accessories. Shaking himself from his apparent confusion, the wounded security guy replied, "I only remember now and I do not like the gendarmes." He made it sound like a point of honor, *no talking to the police.*

I studied him, detecting what I thought might be a faint African overlay to his French and English accents. He was an immigrant, too, I guessed. "Where do you hail from, René?"

"Hail?"

"Come from. Where were you born?"

"Sudan," he admitted. "I come to France many years ago with mother. My true name Abdul. I change. French now."

I smiled at him. Being a black Muslim immigrant wasn't easy anywhere. "So, are you still working for Lilly Lin's security detail?"

His gaze sank to the floor. "She fired company; they fire me."

"But you were hurt on the job!" Peaches protested. "What about work-men's compensation, sick leave?"

He stared at her, baffled, maybe a little in awe. She was undeniably magnif-icent. "I do not know these things."

"That's all right. You'll come with us. We can use extra help on our case," Peaches said, reaching over and grasping his hand. "We're going back to Saint Chappelles this afternoon."

You have to love Peaches's take-charge attitude. Forget about the legal shenanigans of hiring a French national. In fact, forget the tricky details like offering employment to a man with a head injury unable to actually work. Still, René happily agreed and it was settled.

I caught Rupert's eye: *we'll pay him under the table.*

René offered to drive us down in his little Citroën. Rupert refused in the name of legroom and hired an Alpine A110 sports car, which probably had less capacity than the Citroën but better suited his style. It was bright yellow to match his socks but he swore that was only a coincidence. Peaches and the luggage drove with René and I kept Rupert company.

It was the first time I'd actually seen him behind the wheel. When he had been undercover, Evan had catered to his every need as the chauffeur extraor-dinaire. Rupert, however, managed the wheel like a pro and had even decked himself out in driving gloves, a peaked cap, and a white silk scarf reminiscent of some World War Two fighter pilot, minus the goggles.

At least now I had apparently been forgiven enough to enjoy a congenial drive into the countryside. I brought him up to speed on all the details I had been withholding as well as a few I hadn't had the chance yet to disclose. He listened intently, which in itself was a rarity.

"I'm still disgruntled with you," he said after a few minutes of blissful silence.

"I've apologized. There's nothing more I can do for now but consider this, Rupert: for all the years I've known you, you have hidden the truth from me, lied, dissembled, and far worse. It's only been in the last few years that you've begun playing it straight."

"Ah, but I was working to catch an art thief who I originally believed to be your then paramour and possibly you for a time," he pointed out. "My under-cover sleight of hand was completely necessary given the circumstances. Now I am compelled by the honor and integrity of our agency to be completely honest with you as a member—dare I say leader?—of the team, an approach, I am sad to say, that you failed to uphold with me."

"Okay, so I initially kept back the details of this case but—" and I took a deep breath "—you are still withholding things from me, too, personal things, I admit, but as friends, I can't understand why."

"I am holding back nothing from you, Phoebe. What an astounding thing to say."

"Forget it. We're almost here. Take this exit," I said just as the computer-ized navigator voice told us the same thing in French.

We fell into silence as the car wound its way down into the valley, me trying to focus on the beautiful French countryside, the hum of exquisite engineering, the plush leather seats, and not the niggle that chewed away at the back of my mind.

Pulling out my phone, I checked my screen: no word from Lilly, just a message from Max , my godfather and co-owner of the gallery end of the business, complaining that Rupert had left without saying where he was going, one from Serena, our gallery manager, sending a photo of a carpet they were eyeing at an online auction, and…nothing from Evan. Damn. Didn't we just share a wonderful few days? Does such romantic bliss simply end without a postscript? I was an adult, I reminded myself, not some insecure teenager. I pocketed my phone.

As we drove through the village, I pointed the way to the gatehouse while the little Citroën followed behind. "We need to convince Lilly that we are the team for the job before we book into the château B and B," I remarked.

"Yes, indeed," Rupert acknowledged, "but I have taken the liberty of regis-tering at the château in advance under our assumed names."

We had assumed names now. "What about our passports?" I protested.

Rupert sighed gustily. "I will dispense both you and Peaches with false passports for the purpose of our stay in order to support our little ruse." He shot me a quick glance. "Phoebe, do not look so shocked. Surely you realize by now that the agency always has a selection of false passports on hand in the event that a mission may require undercover personas? Each of us have three or four that will do in a pinch. I doubt they will be too deeply scrutinized."

I kept forgetting. A part of me hadn't yet quite adjusted to this new life. "And I am…?"

"You are Phoebe Wentworth, a fledgling designer from London and the newest member of my firm, Carpe Diem Design Inc. I haven't had business cards made up—one can only do so much overnight—but I do have a virtual one on hand. Peaches is Penelope Guy Françoise from Haiti and a senior member of my firm."

"And you are the chief designer, of course."

"Of course, and you are our newest, least experienced member."

The fledgling. Got it.

"And yet, if I understand correctly, staging isn't redecorating so much as it is rearranging. It's about plumping up the curb appeal of real estate and making an interior more appealing for prospective buyers."

"Exactly."

"Which surely works better for houses than for castles," I reasoned. "So, what makes a castle more salable—a new turret, the latest in baronial hall chic, perhaps? Even a fledgling designer should know that much."

He smiled as we pulled into the lane beyond Henri's gates. "I believe you are overthinking this, Phoebe."

Two uniformed guards stood outside talking into their phones. Lilly must have hired a new security team. "Shit," I muttered.

While Rupert addressed the guards, I shot off a text to Lilly: *We're here just outside the gatehouse. Can we talk?*

She was marching up to me minutes later, Chouchou bolting out ahead of her, greeting me with excited yaps. "What's the meaning of this? I've un-hired you, I said." Today, casually dressed in gray joggers with a baseball cap, she was the picture of California chic.

I launched into my spiel immediately while gathering the dog up into my arms. "Lilly, we're the only ones who can locate this missing tapestry. You need us. We'll begin with combing the château since my agency has high-tech tools uniquely able to X-ray walls without moving a stone." I pulled back my head to avoid doggy kisses, then gave up and offered my chin. "However, in order to locate a missing ancient artifact of this importance, we need to better understand the period in which it was created. Once we understand the context, we're that much closer. I've already begun."

Lilly was gazing at me, clearly pondering the possibilities, while Rupert was addressing Henri, who had just ambled out in a pair of jeans and tall boots with a striped T-shirt over all, his look complete with a matching kerchief knotted at his neck.

Henri was busy inspecting Rupert and Rupert inspected him back. "Sir Rupert Fox? A member of the aristocracy?" he asked in French.

Rupert explained that he had married into a wealthy family but that his parents were actually working class and Jewish. I have no idea why he disclosed so much personal information—that was a first, to my knowledge— but Henri suddenly embraced him as if such candor was an expression of friendship.

Lilly and I turned in amazement to gaze at the two men. Rupert was now pointing toward the château; Henri, apparently excited and engaged, nodded enthusiastically. There was much hand flapping and exclamations going on. I released Chouchou to go have a yap at Rupert.

Lilly shook her head. "Looks like it's out of my hands."

"Does that mean that we're rehired again? It's like a meeting of the eccentrics, British and French versions, by the way. That's Sir Rupert Fox. He'll be booking into the château as designer extraordinaire, advising the owners on the best way to stage the property as per Henri's suggestion. Standing with Peaches you might recognize René, who was the security guy hit on the head yesterday."

"Why is he even here?" Lilly asked. "I fired them all."

"Peaches thinks he can be helpful. Have there been any further incidents?"

"No." Before she had an opportunity to continue, Henri approached with Rupert, and in the stream of French that followed, I gathered that the agency had been hired, as I suspected.

"Brilliant ruse!" Henri exclaimed. "We will surely find the tapestry now. Rupert—" pronounced *Rupair* "—has state-of-the-art tools and wall-penetrating radar in his phone, Lilly, imagine that!"

Rupert kissed Lilly's hand. "I am a great fan, madam, and my deepest congratulations on your recent nomination. The judges would be blind not to award you the highest honor for your flawless depiction of a serial killer. Masterful, truly masterful, and I eagerly await your next astounding performance." And so Rupert won over Lilly's resistance and the deal appeared further secured. Chouchou yapped her approval.

The enthusiastic discussion between Rupert and Henri continued all the way into the house where coffee, tea, and pastries were served while Rupert laid out the plan for finding the tapestry. After that, *Rupair* was given the grand tour of the cottage by Henri, leaving the rest of us sitting in the yellow salon trying to squeeze one more pastry under our proverbial belts. René remained in the garden at his own insistence, keeping watch while appearing to devour more pastries than the rest of us combined.

"Looks like Rupert and your uncle are of like mind," I remarked, brushing crumbs from my knitwear onto my plate. It's a little known fact that hand-knit anything gloms onto crumbs like a mass of fuzzy little incisors.

Newly decked out in a black 1999 Yves Saint Laurent *Le Smoking* jacket over leggings, compliments of Madame DesCartes from Au Revoir, Bon Jour, Paris's foremost vintage and consignment shop, I needed to wear my "artistic flair" minus the snack residue. My beloved Melancholy wrap added multiple shades of burgundy and teal to enliven my monochromatic vintage couture but presumably a dusting of sugar and crumbs might spoil the effect.

"Yeah," Lilly sighed. "Uncle Henri rarely makes friends but it sounds like he's found one in your boss."

I looked up. "Actually, Rupert's not my boss but I don't blame you for assuming that. He likes to play a few roles himself."

She grinned. "I figured as much. Where did you get that wrap, anyway? Oh, I just love it." Lilly reached over to feel my stitchery. "Wow, so soft. Silk and cashmere?"

"Yes," I said. "I'm working on one in berry shades interlaced with streaming tones of butterscotch and caramel with dollops of creamy silk, my tribute to French patisserie."

"Hey, Lilly," Peaches interrupted. "While the guys are up there discussing paint, maybe you could show me a few of the moves you did in *Princess Bai and the Mongolian Dream?*"

Lilly turned. "You know I had a stunt double who did most of those moves, don't you? And part of it was animated."

"Yes, but you must have learned something. Don't actors go into training for that kind of movie?"

"Well, yes, I was trained by a martial arts expert for months."

"Then show me something! I always longed to do some of those ninja moves."

Lilly assessed Peaches's long body for a moment. "Your point of gravity may be too long for some of these maneuvers. True martial arts maestros are much shorter."

Peaches shrugged. "If Keanu Reeves can do it, so can I. We're about the same height."

That provoked another grin. "Yeah, why not? Ninja is Japanese, by the way, but who cares? Come on, I'll show you a few tricks."

The moment the two of them stepped into the garden, I pulled out my phone and settled back into research. I was stuck on Charles VII for the moment, the king for whom one Le Viste had worked as a court lawyer. There were multiple Le Vistes, it turned out.

King Charles seemed to be an odd duck. Called "The Victorious" or alternatively "The Well Served," he came to the French throne under difficult circumstances. Not only did English forces backed by the Duke of Burgundy occupy Paris and other important parts of France at the time, but his father, Charles VI, had disinherited him back in 1420, naming the English monarch Henry V as his successor. I mean, seriously? Ouch.

So Papa Charles had thrown over his own son in favor of the English king? I knew that Europe was a muddle of cross-political monarchial successions but since when did a French king throw over his bloodline for an English monarch? For politics, as it turns out. French daughters married off to English kings to secure peace, which, in this case, failed miserably. An unstable king who was often forced to leave his rule up to regents, Charles VII's father only further stirred up a fractious Hundred Years' War. It appears that his queen may have been partially behind the disinheritance of Charles Junior.

I glanced up from my phone long enough to see a pair of long legs flying in the air somersault-style beyond the garden windows. My gaze returned to my phone to stare at a painting of Charles VII, where the monarch sat enrobed in red velvet with a sulky expression that made him appear ready to cry. For a man who had regained the throne against impossible odds, he certainly looked miserable. If it weren't for Joan of Arc, he wouldn't have stood a chance. Maybe his expression was partially guilt.

Moments later, Rupert and Henri entered the room chatting away in French.

"I do appreciate a finely turned furniture leg in mahogany with just a hint of inlay but my oak spindle-post tester bed is still among my favorite pieces," Rupert enthused.

And here I always thought his collection of Roman gold laurel-leaf crowns ranked as his favorite.

"And mine is, above all, my Louis XIV gilded canopy bed, a gift to one of the Saint Chappelles from the king himself," Henri countered.

"Which king?" I asked.

"*Pardonnez-moi?*"

"Which king did your ancestor receive the bed from?"

"Louis XIV. Why do you ask?"

I stood up from where I was perching on the settee. "I'm trying to find out more about one of your ancestors, the priest who may have been in the court of Charles VII, the relative to the Le Viste. King Louis was the wrong timeline. Did you have other Saint Chappelles working with other French courts?"

Henri blinked at me as if I had wrenched his thoughts away from the delights of antiques and decor to plunge him into the difficult mechanisms of French history. "But of course," he said, straightening. "Just as Jean Le Viste had worked for both the court of Charles VI as well as Charles VII, so did my ancestor, Father Louis. He was a religious adviser to both kings, a priest of some note."

"Why do you believe Jean Le Viste was the one who worked with Charles VII? His dates place him much earlier. Why not Antoine Le Viste?" I asked.

Henri shrugged. "But no one knows for certain, *n'est ce pas?* The dates are not clear."

"True, but if it was Antoine Le Viste, that puts your ancestor right in the thick of Joan of Arc's first meeting with Charles at Chinon where she convinced him that she had been visited by the archangel Michael and would help make him king of France. Your family could have been a key player."

7

$\mathcal{I}$f there ever was a woman betrayed by the mechanizations of male political power, it was Joan d'Arc. Named "the Maid of Orléans," she rose from being a peasant girl besieged by visions to the spiritual leader of a nation, one who had commanded armies into battle against the English-backed Burgundians to reclaim the throne for France. She was at Charles's side in Reims when he was crowned King Charles VII and went on to lead multiple campaigns that eventually ended the Hundred Years' War.

After leading armies to further advance on English strongholds in France, she was captured by Burgundian troops and traded to the English. Charles VII's efforts to release his champion is murky, but from the time she was put on trial by the pro-English Bishop Pierre Cauchon and charged with heresy, there appeared to be little intervention on the part of the king. In 1430, she was burned at the stake at age nineteen.

For decades, her name was besmirched as a heretic until Pope Callixtus III declared the original trial politically motivated and reversed the findings. She was eventually beatified and canonized.

I stared across at Henri. "France had a girl warrior supposedly backed by angels and saints whose leadership helped regain France's identity and release the nation against English-backed intrigue and invasion. For that she was burned at the stake. Sort of redefines one's definition of traitor, right? How do you think the Saint Chappelles felt about that, or any French family who lived during this time, noble or peasant alike? They would have heard about this incredible girl, perhaps even seen her riding through the villages—an amazing sight at any age, a girl and a peasant in charge of an army and she delivered on her promises. For that she was tortured, *burned!*"

Henri slapped his hand across his heart, his eyes wet. "A travesty! The pain the French still feel in our hearts here." He thumped his chest. "Jeanne d'Arc is our martyr, France's own patron saint, well-loved forever."

I stood. "What I'm getting at, Henri, is that Joan of Arc was betrayed by the very king she helped crown. He did little to save her. Meanwhile, your family was somewhere in the thick of it. Your priest Louis must have seen it unfold in court, possibly even begged his king to rescue the holy maiden, yet ended up forced to watch her die for political expediency. Maybe he was even his king's confessor."

"Left alive, Joan was too much of a threat," Rupert agreed. "She could rally supporters around her at the drop of a gauntlet and would continue to rage against the pockets of English supporters at every opportunity. After his coronation, Charles had to don the mantle of diplomacy and negotiate with the straggle of still powerful Burgundians in order to unify his country. In all probability, Charles VII had bargained behind the scenes to let her trial go forward. He sacrificed her, in truth."

"And thirty years after Joan's death, the tapestries were presumably commissioned, though no one really knows for certain when," I said. "The drawings may have been done much earlier and hidden before the Le Vistes believed it safe to formally launch the commission. Possibly they were commissioned by Antoine Le Viste, another prominent lawyer but in Charles VII's court, or they were a family secret through two generations. Along with the Le Vistes, the Saint Chappelles were also at the same court only as spiritual advisers rather than legal ones."

"Phoebe, what the devil are you getting at?" Rupert demanded.

I stared at each of the two men in turn. "I don't know," I said, "but I'm getting that itch in my spine again. I'm on to something."

In strode Lilly, busy plucking leaves from her joggers, while Peaches trailed behind practicing air chops. "Okay," Lilly puffed. "It's almost 4:30. Are you going to take the design team up to the château and introduce them to the DeBoises, Uncle Henri? I thought I'd book us all in for dinner at 8:30. The DeBoises have a very good chef they bring in from the village. All I need do is call to say we're coming."

After we had tidied up a bit, we climbed into two cars, Chouchou included, wearing a natty little embossed leather collar with a pink bow catching her topknot, and drove about a mile up a hill toward the château, arriving shortly after six p.m. To say that the structure was impressive under-stated the effects of a looming white stone multiturreted building constructed as much as a fortress as a home. The French knew how to make a castle, leaving the English versions no more than austere bastions in comparison.

"It has been many times renovated over the centuries," Henri explained as we piled out onto the gravel drive surrounded by shaggy topiary and crum-bling cement flowerpots. Once I imagined those yew trees ahead must have been shaped into fantastical creations but now looked more like clusters of badly behaved puppies lounging by the foundations.

Henri muttered his disgust under his breath.

"Indeed," huffed Rupert, gazing up at the spires and turrets sprouting from the multilevel roofs like some kind exuberant *Game of Thrones* birthday cake. "I recognize traditional French, Renaissance, and baroque influences here."

"Oh, yeah. It was once a castle and then a château, right?" Peaches was studying every inch of the structure, too.

"What's the difference?" I asked.

"A castle is defensive, a château is not. See the squarish central structure with the surrounding thick stone walls branching out? That would have been initially built to withstand attacks. It's a kind of keep and those sections must date as far back as maybe the 1300s. Then successive renovations after that are when the sharply pointed turrets in the architectural promenade style came in." She was pointing overhead. "And then that part rising up there is pure Renaissance with the arched windows. Cool."

"This was once a moat, *n'est ce pas?*" Henri indicated the deep depression that surrounded the foundations. Sometimes it was difficult to tell whether he was asking or telling when he mixed French with English. "The Duke Saint Chappelles drained it in1602 because les mosquitos buzz-buzz." He flapped his hand and Chouchou barked.

Moments later we were crossing the drawbridge into a courtyard where a man and a much taller woman strode across the pavers toward us.

Eduard DuBois, greeting us with a ready smile, was a lean man of about thirty with short-cropped blond hair dressed in a white shirt and blue linen pants with bare feet tucked into woven leather loafers. Dark-haired Natalie DuBois was equally svelte in her red silk palazzo pants and high heels, the gold bracelets gleaming on finely toned tanned arms.

My first impression was of two people who very much wanted to be to the château born. I had learned on our way up the hill that Eduard had made his first fortune in advertising, Natalie in PR, both originally hailing from Paris. It seemed they had now resigned themselves to returning to the city to regain their careers and possibly in order to refresh their capital after maintaining a château during the pandemic.

Much enthusiastic greetings between the DuBoises and Saint Chappelles followed after which we were introduced as the British design team arrived to help put the Château Saint Chappelles on the international castle market/grand estate map. The whole thing struck me as bizarre but Rupert had risen as star performer and managed to infuse an air of credibility while Henri enthused away about Carpe Diem's fame. Peaches stood by with a regal tilt to her head while I smiled and tried to shake off a knob of crusted sugar I saw clinging to my wrap. Chouchou had bolted across the courtyard for the open door and Lilly took off after him.

"This is the grand hall," Eduard explained in French as he took us through to the baronial space, a huge long room the size of an auditorium with a black-and-white zigzag pattern decorating the stone walls. A high timber-peaked roof rose overhead while wooden balconies encircled the entire space. I gazed up at the circular wagon-wheel-sized wrought-iron candelabras dangling at regular intervals along the room and suppressed a wave of vertigo.

Eyes back down, I focused on the comfortable furniture that had been gathered around several round tables with additional seating areas near the two monstrous fireplaces at each end. Over the thick stone walls several eighteenth-century-style pastoral French tapestries hung in an attempt to warm the room, replicas all, with a few Persian-style rugs thrown over the flagstones here and there.

"In this room we serve breakfast," Natalie was saying, "and the couches against the wall are for the guests' pleasure. The television room is through that side door and next to that we have a library stocked with a range of English and French titles. At first we had hoped to welcome many American and British visitors but our timing was very bad with the pandemic. Do you see how this area might be improved, Sir Fox?"

"*Mais oui,*" Rupert assured her, lifting his hands as if about to conjure up accents. "More pillows of velvet and needlepoint would enhance the sense of regal comfort immediately. Small touches such as huge bouquets of flowers are always appropriate as are other small items that give the appearance of grandeur without compromising comfort. In my own estate, I have employed these things." He was definitely in his element.

"The bedrooms are up there," Eduard was telling Peaches while indicating the rooms along the balcony. "We try to restrict the guests to this part of the château and keep doors into the other wings locked as we have been unable to afford full renovations."

I had finally shaken the sugar bit onto the slate-tiled floor and watched Chouchou lap it up in seconds when I remembered that I had a role to play in this little pantomime. "But of course. However, we will need to investigate every inch of the building, you understand."

"Every corner," Peaches added, standing arms crossed, staring straight ahead at a set of armor that appeared to be staring right back.

Eduard shot us a tense smile. "That is inadvisable unless either I or Natalie accompany you. These old châteaus are filled with dangers—crumbling stone, unstable planking. My wife suffered an accident just this winter when a chunk of plaster hit her on the head in the west wing. You cannot investigate the château alone, *non?*"

"*Oui*, we can." Peaches fixed him with a brilliant smile. "We have arrived to assess the building for resale and complete honesty is necessary, meaning that I and my colleagues will study every inch for structural integrity." Her French was a bit spotty but her message was clear.

A cloud crossed Eduard's pleasant visage. The poor man seemed alarmed to the point of panic. "But no, you are not real estate agents but staging agents so the structural integrity is not your concern."

Peaches appeared startled. She had forgotten that point.

"Ah, Eduard, *mon ami*, do not be so stern," said Henri, throwing one long arm over the younger man's shoulders. "I know that you worry over this great responsibility that burdens you. Worry, worry, that is the price of owning a château, *non?* The insurance costs alone are so extreme, the things that need to be repaired endless. But my friends, they have come to help you prepare this château for sale and maybe I buy it back so we must permit them free rein, *oui?*"

I looked up and smiled. "Besides, we're bonded. Would you mind showing us to our rooms?"

Natalie seemed eager to comply. René, who stood beside me, looked ready to topple over and I needed to get him horizontal pronto.

"This way." She smiled as she moved to help me with my luggage. I had only a roller and a carpet backpack so I shook my head.

"Tell me, Natalie," I asked as we climbed the wooden stairway to the balcony level passing by mounted swords and shields, many of which were no doubt replicas, "I heard Eduard say that you had been injured over the winter. Hit on the head by flying plaster?"

Natalie turned back to me as she paused by a thick arched door. The skin over her high cheekbones seemed to tauten and her blue eyes fixed on mine widened. One hand flicked a length of long brown hair from her face. "Plaster does not fly but—" she shrugged "—this one flew. It was strange. I was inspecting a leaking roof—we have had many—but this one needed immediate attention. It seemed to grow by the day. Eduard was in Paris arranging roofers and I was here alone with only a handful of helpers hired from the village to clean, cook. It was a horrible winter, one I never wish to repeat. Suddenly, I see something big and black flying from one of the windows. Before I could cry out, I was hit on the head and shoved to the ground. Eduard found me hours later in a pile of crumbled stone. It was horrible!"

"I'm so sorry." Now I understood how the DuBoises were not only financially eager to be rid of the château but terrified to remain.

"I will help protect you," René said.

She smiled and touched his arm. I could tell instantly that she had assessed his state of health and possibly his nature, too. "What a sweet man you are! So gallant. Perhaps you would like to rest now in this room. It has a big tester bed perfect for a large man. Dinner is at eight o'clock." She gave him a warm grateful smile and opened the door to urge him to enter, which he did.

"Have you experienced any other unusual events here?" I asked as we continued down the hall.

"*Mais oui.* It is so strange. We enter abandoned rooms and find piles of stone, not like they have fallen down but as if they have been removed piece by piece. It makes no sense."

Ah, but it did. It meant that we were not the only ones looking for something valuable in the Château Saint Chappelles.

8

*J*ust before supper I texted Peaches and Rupert to meet in my room.

"After everyone goes to bed, we'll go through the castle room by room using our X-ray apps," I told them, holding up my phone. "If we divide up, we can take it in sections. The app may not reveal much since it only picks up metal but Evan added a new feature that maps depressions or cavities through stone. That will help."

"Just be careful of the security system," Peaches said. "Believe it or not, they actually have one here, even if it does only secure the main living quarters. No problem, though. We can deactivate that pretty quickly." She leaned forward. "Hey, a text from Evan just popped up onto your screen."

I pulled back my phone and replaced it in my pocket to read later. "So, look, Natalie tells me that there's been strange occurrences going on around here. She was hit on the head while investigating one of the deteriorating wings this winter. She thought she saw something flying toward her. Sound familiar?"

"The same sort of flying thing that hit René? Have they determined whether they have killer bats in France?" Peaches asked.

"Not likely. I'm thinking that there is definitely another interested party searching this château, maybe the same group watching the Saint Chappelles, but they're not of the nocturnal beastie kind," I said. "We need to be careful."

"In that case, we'd best perform our searches in pairs," Rupert pointed out before doing the math. "Well, that will not work unless we include René, will it? I do not think the lad is up to it tonight. Perhaps we three must remain together."

"But that will take too long," said I. "This place is huge."

"Lilly and Henri will help and they know the château," Peaches said.

"Good idea. I shall ask them at the next opportunity," Rupert said. "Shall we convene in the hall outside at 1:30 a.m.?"

"Great. What about the guard team Lilly hired?" I asked.

"I suggest that we leave them to watch the grounds," Rupert said.

Just then, the gong rang for dinner, a deep sound reverberating with an almost teeth-rattling intensity.

"What the hell was that?" Peaches asked, gazing upward.

"It does sound like one of those Chinese Bao gongs, a mite incongruous for a French château, *n'est ce pas?*" Rupert stood to straighten his dinner jacket and readjust my blouse collar while he was at it. This was the very same silk couture top that my Italian friend Nicolina had bought me years ago and the most expensive thing in my wardrobe. "So last year," he muttered once satisfied that I looked reasonably pulled together.

"What's the difference between 'vintage' and 'so last year'?" I asked, not bothering to hide my irritation.

"It's all in the eye of the beholder, my friend." Turning away, he added: "Let us descend to discover the source of that metallic ding-dong."

René was waiting in the hall wearing the same gray joggers and hoodie he'd worn all day.

"Dear boy, do you not have anything more formal?" Rupert inquired, looking up at him.

"*Non.* A pair of jeans and a shirt."

"Well, do go get changed and I will lend you a tie. Will lime-green silk suit?"

Clearly René didn't care. He emerged from his room moments later and stood obediently while Rupert tied a Windsor knot on his plaid shirt. After that, we met up with Lilly on the stairs. She had donned a black silk tuxedo suit over jeans with a pink boa tossed over all.

"Natalie prefers her guests to dress in gowns for dinner but this is as dressed up as I'm going to get."

"Lilly, about the gong—" I began.

"A gift to my mother from Uncle Tengfeng. When Uncle Henri sold the château, he didn't want the thing so we left it for the new owners. Follow me, guys. We'll dine in what I consider along with the library to be the best room in the château."

Down the stairs through room after room, passing pseudo suits of armor with a few genuine antiques thrown in until finally we ended up in a wood paneled room that to me spoke pure château.

"Ah, *magnifique!*" exclaimed Rupert as he gazed about the long space hung as it was with two genuine Flemish tapestries that I inspected closely before I could do another thing. I had glimpsed Henri seated at the far end of a banquet table in a tête-à-tête with Eduard but was too enchanted by the sixteenth-century hunting tapestries to pay much attention.

"These are genuine!" I gasped.

"Those were sold with the château, too," Lilly said. "So sad. I would have hung them in my LA condo in a minute."

"What a stunning room!" Rupert enthused.

"*Merci.* This is where we poured most of our renovation euros. The paneling has been restored and we installed new windows into the garden at, oh, so much expense. Ah, well. We had capital in those days."

I turned. Natalie had just stepped in carrying two wine bottles with a maid following with a tray of hors d'oeuvres. For the first time I noticed the graceful arched wall of paned glass at the room's far end that looked out onto a fairy-lit back courtyard. "It is similar in design to the library, which is next door," she added.

"You can see the Loire River from out there. Had it been warmer, we would have invited you to taste the valley's finest vintages while seated in the garden but, as it is, we will remain here, *non?*" our host said, standing and offering a seat with a wave of his hand while his wife poured the wine, two glasses each, white and red.

"The Saint Chappelles once owned a vineyard," Henri sighed. "Now it, too, is gone. All gone." In his lap sat Chouchou as if one of the dinner party. By the looks that Natalie cast the little dog, she was not pleased by the arrangement.

Rather than spreading out along the sizable table, we had all joined Eduard and Natalie on one end where the table had been set for ten.

"Do you have other guests coming?" I asked, picking up a glass of white along with a slice of brie. I reminded myself to take it easy with the wine but to enjoy it, anyway.

"*Mais oui*, two more just booked earlier this afternoon. We are so excited to have our château filled with guests at last!" Natalie smiled and took a seat, unfurling her napkin in the process. Garbed in a sapphire-toned silk flowered gown, she seemed so much more at ease, almost happy. "Know that Eduard and I are thrilled that you have come to help us to sell but by coincidence this new guest arriving says that she may be interested in purchasing a château. Imagine that? All these good things happening at once after a winter of trauma."

Over the table I caught Rupert's eye. Was he thinking what I was thinking, that the last thing we needed was more guests underfoot while we combed the grounds for possible textile treasure?

If it weren't for the fact that our goal might eventually result in a happy outcome for both the DuBoises and the Saint Chappelles, I might have felt guilty about our ruse. Now I was more afraid that the new guests might actually buy the place from right under Henri's nose. The poor man had blanched the shade of boiled haddock.

"Seriously?" I asked. "You may have a buyer already?"

Leaning forward, she added: "She did not say that she was necessarily interested in purchasing the Château Saint Chappelles, just that she always wanted to own a château, so I think why not this château? It is the first possible buyer we've had. Others phone and ask questions but never follow through with a visit."

"Except that couple who only came for a good meal last summer," Eduard added. "They said they were serious buyers but piffff!" He shrugged. "They were more interested in eating and drinking our wine."

"What price are you asking?" Rupert inquired while Henri still sat in stricken silence.

"Approximately two million euros," Eduard said. "Cheap by British standards, *non?*"

Henri snapped one hand over his face. "*Sacré bleu!* But I sold it to you for one point five!"

Another shrug from Eduard. "That is the way, *mon ami*. You sold it to us during the first pandemic wave. The market improves as things open up, *non?*"

"Right now condos in Toronto are going for over a million dollars so a couple of million for a château sounds like a bargain," I exclaimed, sipping my wine while wondering what Henri had done with all that loot.

"The real estate market has hyperventilated in many North American cities and towns, it is true, with prices far exceeding expectations, partly as a result of Covid," Rupert remarked while holding up his glass to study the color and "legs" of the wine. "But it is sad to say that this same rise in prices is not translated into the French estate market, as I understand. However, in your case, my dear hosts, the key will be to convince your prospective buyers that owning this château is a business opportunity. Allow me to raise a toast: to a successful staging venture. My colleagues and I will look forward to assisting you in this undertaking! Cheers!"

Throughout the evening the wine flowed; the coq au vin was magnificent, the confit de canard interesting, the salade Niçoise delish, and don't even get me started on the chocolate soufflé. The conversation was relaxed with both Eduard and Natalie seeming to enjoy being hosts. I could see why they had longed for this particular enterprise, though I guessed that their current joviality had something to do with the prospects of achieving liberation from the glorious albatross overhead.

The prospective buyers did not arrive in time for dinner or even dessert. Apparently they had been delayed in Paris but were on their way. While my companions continued to enjoy the wine, I excused myself in order to get a few hours' sleep before the long night ahead.

Rupert was deeply engrossed in a conversation with Henri while Chouchou nibbled at delicacies Henri plucked from the table for her enjoyment and Natalie looked on with dismay. Eduard was deep in conversation with Peaches over his problems with shoring up the east wing's roof system. Lilly, however, looked as weary as I. We escaped together.

"That's what the DuBoises and my uncle talk about all the time—dissecting the château's restoration needs. Uncle dreams of the day when he'll hang the missing tapestry in the great hall and people will come from all over the world to see it."

That was a long shot but I didn't have the heart to say anything just then. "What happened to the money that your uncle received when he sold the château?"

"It went to his creditors. He had gone so deep into the hole trying to keep on top of the renovations that he thought he'd never dig himself out. All he's left with is enough money to keep himself in relative comfort in his cottage until whenever."

On the way back to the central staircase we took a different way, passing by an enormous brass gong framed on its carved cherrywood stand.

"Wow. That must have cost something to ship from China. Did your uncle Tengfeng visit often?"

"Twice, I think. When he did he always seemed to get in an argument with Mom. He didn't like her marrying Dad and even less about her raising two Chinese kids in France. Mimi and I were sent to stay with him for a month in Beijing when we were in our early teens. He was very big on trying to teach us what it meant to be Chinese. It was interesting, but for a kid like me, I just wanted to watch American television and eat potato chips all day. As far as I was concerned at the time, Chinese was a race not a disposition."

I laughed. "And Mimi?"

"She was his A student, always trying to please her uncle Tengfeng." We had arrived at our floor. "Do you think who we are is in our genes or in our upbringing?"

"Both," I said. "It has to be, doesn't it? But I think mostly in our upbringing, which is when we humans study what's on the proverbial table and decide who and what we want to be. You decided not to be Chinese but your sister chose differently."

She smiled sadly. "But I am Chinese and proud of it but why must I be either or? Just because I'm proud to be of Chinese descent, doesn't mean I have to hate everybody who isn't. Still, maybe Mimi is less conflicted than I am because of her choice is so black and white, not that I really know her anymore."

"So you've chosen from two tables and not just one. That's the choice of a global human."

"I guess, but sometimes that leaves me feeling like nothing is truly mine and that somehow I need to start from scratch and define myself my own way." She shrugged, a pure French gesture that echoed her uncle's. "Anyway, see you at 1:30. I thought we'd start at the oldest part of the château first. It's in the worse shape but may be the most logical place to begin."

"Lilly."

She paused, hand on the doorknob.

"I don't think the tapestry is here. I'm going through the motions because your uncle is so convinced. I just need to tell you that."

"I know but Uncle Henri is desperate to believe it's here because that's the only hope he has of laying claim to it."

"If it exists, he probably can't lay claim to it, anyway. Still, I'll find it one way or the other and we can worry about legalities later. If the provenance leads clearly back to the Saint Chappelles, there may still be a case for the family's ownership," I told her. "We'll worry about that when the time comes. See you later."

I entered my room, a grand yet cozy space with high ceilings and a cheerful toile-blue-and-white wallpaper to ward away the mental chill. Switching on the Tiffany-style lamps, I bolted the door, and sat down to savor Evan's message. It filled my screen with a picture of a Sardinian sunset, all liquid gold and flaming orange. Below the picture, I read:

You are constantly in my mind, as illuminating as any sunrise or sunset, filling me with warmth, hope, and joy. I cannot wait to hold you in my arms again and I spend far too many moments imaging the two of us together.

And then he added a few lines of poetry by the French poet Paul Éluard:

AU BOUT de tous mes voyages
    Au fond de tous mes tourments,
    Au tournant de tous les rires
    Sortant de l'eau et feu

AT THE END of my travels
    At the bottom of all my torments,
    At the turn of all laughter
    Coming out of water and fire

ENTRE MES BRAS je t'ai vue
    Dans mes rêves je t'ai vue
    Je ne te quitterai plus

IN MY ARMS I saw you
    In my dreams I saw you
    I will not leave you anymore

I WILL NOT LEAVE you anymore. But of course he would leave me as I would leave him. The two of us had our work, our passions. Then we would return to one another. Therein lay the power, the excitement, of love.

Did I just think that word? Yes. Closing my eyes, I fell back on the bed with a smile on my face. I didn't even read the other messages that had crowded onto my phone screen.

Apparently, I fell asleep in that position because it seemed like only moments later that my phone pinged and that someone was knocking on my door. I checked the time: 1:45 a.m. already.

Lurching up off the bed, I slid back the bolt to find Peaches standing outside dressed in her skintight black stealth gear, Lilly standing behind her.

"You'd better change, woman. Hear that?"

A dog was yapping somewhere deep in the château. "Chouchou? But why isn't he with Henri?" I asked.

"That's the problem," Lilly said, poking her head around the corner. "My uncle's door is wide open and he and Chouchou are gone. He didn't even take his phone!"

9

*L*illy followed the sound of frantic yapping and we followed Lilly. So far, the rest of the house appeared to remain undisturbed, including the DuBoises, whose rooms were at the end of the hall. The two other closed doors I spotted must be the late arrivals.

We downed several flights of stairs, entered multiple doors to cross gloomy chambers where we briefly sliced the darkness with our phone lights. Peaches deactivated all the security features right up until we reached the part of the château that had been cordoned off. The huge oak door hung wide open on its hinges, the scent of mildew emanating like a foul presence from the darkness beyond.

Once we had entered the first unused corridor, Lilly began calling for her uncle and Chouchou. The dog had stopped barking, which was worrying. We navigated empty spaces while flashing our phone lights over moldering curtains, splotched wallpaper, and the occasional piece of broken furniture shoved against the wall. One room seemed to be tiled completely in mirrors.

"The ballroom," Lilly remarked.

"Venetian glass," Rupert muttered. He was having trouble keeping up and occasionally spent too long investigating a patch of wallpaper or textile or something else until either Peaches or I pried him away. Otherwise, we trailed along, Lilly, me, Peaches, and Rupert, in that order. René always brought up the rear as if watching our backs.

The rooms seemed to go on and on, deteriorating by degrees the deeper we went. "Lilly," Rupert puffed, "do you really know the lay of the land?"

"Of course," she said without pausing. "I grew up here. My sister and I made the château our playground. Nothing Mom and Dad could do could kept us out. The fact that it was dangerous made it all the more enticing."

"Look," I said, flashing my light on a tumble of stones that appeared to have fallen from a wall. "Those didn't just crumble by themselves. Somebody pried them out."

"With a crowbar, by the looks of things." Peaches pointed to the gouge marks in the plaster.

"Come on, guys!" Lilly urged us. "I think I hear Chouchou whimpering ahead!"

We quickened our pace, navigating around various impediments that appeared to have fallen from the roof or a wall.

"This is one of the oldest parts," Lilly said as we entered a round flagstone space open to the sky. "Used to be a tower. Dad always wanted to restore it but it's so far away from the main living areas he couldn't get around the logistics. Chouchou! Uncle Henri!" she called. "I thought I heard the sound in this direction."

The five of us suddenly stilled. A chill breeze was howling in around the crumbling battlements overhead creating an eerie cry like ghosts caught in the mortar. I shivered.

"Is that what you heard?" I whispered.

"I don't think so. This was always one of the creepiest parts." Lilly was aiming her flashlight overhead to where tuffs of grass and shrubbery grew out of cracks in the wall. "But it sounded…different. See that hole covered up over there?" She beamed the light down on a cement square in the center of the space. "The oubliette is underneath that. Nothing down there but bones. Dad long ago covered it up."

And then a human cry shattered the air.

"This way!" Peaches pushed past Lilly and bolted through an arched opening. Soon we were all racing into a little courtyard, or at least that's what it looked like.

Henri was splayed facedown on the stone attempting to push himself up. Overhead a black figure was scaling up what looked to be an outer wall. Peaches attempted to climb up after him while I aimed my laser app in his direction. The first blast missed the figure by a foot and by the time I'd taken aim again he had disappeared.

Lilly and Rupert were beside Henri; Henri was crying for Chouchou but the dog was nowhere to be seen. Peaches was balancing on top of the wall cursing as she tried to pick her way across the broken surface looking for a way down while René rushed to help, calling out in French for her to fall into his arms.

"You've got to be bloody kidding me!" Peaches shouted down in English.

I left them and climbed out through a jagged break in the wall onto what looked to be a broad hilly meadow where I could see the village lights far below. I didn't know exactly where I was going but knew that the dark shadow thing couldn't have gone far. There was only one direction for it to escape: straight down the wall and away.

The château was perched on a knoll overlooking the Loire Valley with nothing nearby but copses of trees and piles of ruins. Using the phone and starlight to guide me, I ran blindly, looking for movement in the shadows ahead, but saw nothing significant. Everything seemed to move—tall grass, trees. It was only by chance that I caught the shape of something small and white crouching in the grass. If it hadn't twitched, I would have missed it.

In seconds I was crouching down, shocked to find Chouchou hunched and shivering. Some bastard had wrapped the dog's snout in duct tape! I picked up the shivering bundle to comfort the little thing, so angry I wanted to scream. Who would do this to an animal? I knew I couldn't easily get that stuff off her by hand without causing her pain. Then I caught movement and the flick of a light far to my right.

"You stay here, sweetie," I cooed, stroking the little dog. "I'll come back and get you as soon as I break a face."

With that, I bolted for the light, readying my body for every possible trick of hand-to-hand combat. I was no expert but mad enough to do some damage. Or so I thought. Something jumped me from behind and set me flying while at the same time that another something appeared to flash before my eyes only to be intercepted by a second figure.

Pushing myself back onto my feet, I struggled to make sense out of what I was seeing. Two figures fighting? Three figures? Someone crying out in French, another swearing in Italian while firing a gun overhead? One figure kicked away the other and leapt to its feet. That one disappeared into the shadows with the other one chasing after. "What the hell?"

"Phoebe, are you all right?" said the figure with the gun.

I knew that voice. "Nicolina?"

"Of course it's Nicolina," she said, running up to me. "You knew I was coming. Did you not read my text?"

_A_EN

* * *

WE SAT TOGETHER in the library, Natalie, Lilly, Rupert, Henri, Chouchou, and Nicolina, a fire crackling in the hearth, various mugs and cups scattered around the tables as we helped ourselves to tea and coffee.

Eduard, René, and Peaches were still off combing the grounds looking for the perpetrators but, of course, the attempted burglars would be long gone. A quick peek at my agency map assured me that Seraphina was still on their trail, her spot placing her somewhere near the village.

Was I surprised that the agency's Rome division had joined us? Actually, I should have expected it. As soon as I posted that internal all-points bulletin, my European colleagues were bound to rush to the scene.

And it would have helped had I read my texts.

Henri was unhurt but obviously in shock after being knocked to the ground by an unseen assailant. He sat cradling a whimpering Chouchou. We had sliced the tape off her snout but not without leaving little patches of bare skin here and there and now the two of them seemed to huddle together for comfort.

"Chouchou began barking and would not stop," Henri said for at least the third time, "and when I open the door to see what upsets her, she runs out very fast. Then I follow deep into the keep and...someone takes my petite Chouchou and tapes her jaws together. Why would they do such a hideous thing? I should have protected her."

"It's all right, dear man," said Rupert, leaning over to pat his knee. "No one blames you or the *petit chien* for this monstrous evening."

Lilly had yet to utter a word.

"They are back again, that is it," Natalie said, sitting wrapped in a silk kimono trembling almost as much as the dog, "these monsters that plague us. What could they possibly want? Why do they do this? I apologize so much for these terrible events, countess. I promise you it is not always this way."

Nicolina sat regally, not behaving the least like a disgruntled guest. The fact that she was also dressed in black leather and that her companion, Seraphina, was still off somewhere tracking down the infiltrators didn't seem to strike Natalie as odd—yet. She was clearly in shock.

We agreed not to call the police. "The police, they have come many times and find nothing, do nothing, do not assist us in any way," Natalie explained. She would not report another break-in, endure another round of questioning, only to be left with the implied sense that the victims were somehow to blame.

We were happy to oblige.

Meanwhile, we awaited the others' return and for our hostess to leave us alone long enough to talk freely. Finally, Natalie received a call from Eduard and dashed from the room, phone pressed to her ear.

We all spoke at once.

"Nicolina, did you get a good look at the perps, and how come you told the DuBoises that you were looking to buy a château?" I asked. Leave me to thread a major concern together with something minor.

"Dear man! Did you see who jumped you? And, Nicolina, do you think it wise to discharge a firearm on the property?" That was Rupert. "It will tip off the DuBoises, surely, and ruin our cover."

"Would you really buy the château?" Henri wailed at Nicolina. "It is a terrible place! Not good at all. I could recommend others much better."

Nicolina, that would be Countess Nicolina Vanvitelli, head of the Rome office, held up her hand and spoke in English. "Please, one at a time. First, I thought that arriving as a prospective buyer would also allow me full range off the property, and no, I will not consider purchasing it—too many villas to renovate as it is. Why add another ruin? I pretend only, yes? And I did not get a good look at the perps, as you call them, because they were all wearing black masks and I do not mean the Covid kind but full-face ones with holes for the eyes."

"All?" Henri inquired, staring at the tall lethal-eyed leather-clad beauty in wonder and possibly a dose of fear.

"I counted at least three but they were very fast and, by the way they fought, trained in martial arts. They used no guns but relied totally on their body parts." Nicolina paused for a moment, considering her words. In English they came out a bit risqué. "Not all body parts, just two, well, four. Yes, four," she amended. "The firearm was discharged into the air to alert the band that we were serious. They are an organized group but my assistant, Seraphina, will tell us more when she returns. She is also skilled in martial arts."

Henri began to weep quietly into Chouchou's fur. "They must be after the tapestry, non?" He sniffed. "But why?"

That was an odd thing to say. If the tapestry was the assailant's real target, then the why part was pretty obvious. The who part could do with a bit of explanation. Furthermore, I reasoned, though taping a dog's snout was cruel, they could have easily knifed the little creature, which would have been crueler still.

I fixed on Lilly, who sat staring down at her hands. Why didn't she say something? Her uncle kept trying to meet her eye but she kept her gaze fixed on her hands.

The sound of slamming doors alerted us to someone's arrival and soon in strode Peaches and René. "The bastards got away. Hell, they're fast! No wonder René thought they were bats. They leap and dart and chop and kick—I got hold of one but he backflipped me onto my stomach so fast I didn't know what was happening. Couldn't even get my knife out of my belt."

René sat down with a thud. "I caught one with bare hands but he slipped away. Very fast, like catching fish."

"We found the two security dudes tied up by a back wall—useless twits," Peaches continued. "I told them to get their butts back to Paris."

"The enemy is truly worthy combatants," Nicolina said, flexing her fingers appearing pleased at the prospects of throttling somebody. "I should have shot one in the leg to get answers. Next time."

I glanced at Henri, now clutching Rupert's hand while staring stricken-faced toward his niece. Lilly still avoided his gaze.

Getting to my feet, I slipped up beside her. "Lilly, can we talk in private for a sec?"

She looked up. "Sure."

Moments later, we were alone in the hall. "You know who's behind all this, don't you?"

Nodding, she opened her palm to reveal the black and silver thing she'd been grasping all evening.

Picking it up, I studied the inch-wide silver embossed disc, one half of the curved image formed of an inlay of onyx, the other inset mother-of-pearl, all set in thick silver. A hole at the top indicated that it was designed to be worn around the neck. "Yin and yang?"

"It's my sister's. I'm wearing one just like it, a gift from our mother for our thirteenth birthdays. We made a pact to wear them always, and when I can, I do. Mom always called us the yin to the other's yang, so different yet insepa-rable in ways. I found it in the hall outside my door, deliberately placed there like she wanted me to find it. Yes, I know who's behind this. It's Mimi Saint Chappelles and I'm betting Uncle Tengfeng is with her."

10

"Your sister?" I gaped. "But why steal from her own family, from you?"

She turned away, tugging her ponytail over one shoulder. "Because it's a game she thinks she can win. When we were kids, it was always a race to find the tapestry, the two of us taking off every day during our vacations to find the famous family treasure. We'd make bets over who would find it first, but in the end, neither of us did. Life and other interests took over, but for Mimi, it was always about winning. That's how she measures success. Now she wants me to know she's winning."

"But why would she try to steal from her own uncle?"

Lilly turned to face me. "Because she doesn't consider Uncle Henri to be her family, you see? She's chosen a different allegiance and it's not to us or France. China is her home now, Uncle Tengfeng her family. He must want this tapestry for the money, yes, but equally for the prestige. It would fetch a fortune in China going to some wealthy collector or be a point of honor to hang in a Chinese museum. Imagine the status, a French treasure on Chinese soil? And it would trump the country he knows did not welcome his sister and her children with the respect he believes they deserved. Uncle Tengfeng is in the export business so he might even have a key buyer lined up. Mimi just wants to beat me at the game."

"Hell, it sounds like Mimi is your evil twin," I remarked.

"I wish it were that simple." Lilly began pacing up and down before the suits of armor standing guard in the hall. "We are always in a struggle with two sides of our beings, dark and light, and that is the way of both nature and humanity. None of us are totally evil, none of us are totally good."

"That's true enough," I remarked.

"Absolutely. The great philosophies of ancient China like I Ching and Confucius will always be relevant. Mimi's studied the Chinese Thirty-six Stratagems of war, which Uncle Tengfeng applies to business. Mimi just continued with her studies while I chose another path. Don't get me wrong: the Chinese culture is rich, complex, and founded on ancient philosophies. Much of it is deeply spiritual and purports the principles of good and not doing harm to either man or nature. But, like every culture, there's a dark side. My sister fully embraces success as measured by material goods. She looks at it like a war game. Mimi intends to find that tapestry."

Just then Peaches flung open the library door and sped down the hall. "Got to get some salve for little Chouie."

I stood there listening to her footsteps fade. "Does your uncle Henri know?"

"I'm pretty sure he's figured it out. I'm guessing Mimi bound Chouie's jaws to keep her quiet but she's too much of an animal lover to silence her permanently, at least not until it's absolutely necessary. She can be ruthless. He also knows that Mimi has studied kung fu and that Uncle Tengfeng is a grand master."

"So he's in on it, too?"

"Definitely. Once Mom died, he stopped trying to connect east with west. Now it seems he sees them as adversaries."

"But isn't kung fu as much of a spiritual practice as a martial arts one?"

"It is, but like I said, nothing is simple. The original practice began with monks and has been tied to both Taoism and Buddhism, but like everything else, it can be corrupted. Now Mimi and Uncle Tengfeng are using that practice to win this game. They want the tapestry. I just hope they don't want it so badly that they'll employ any tactic to get it."

Peaches reappeared and dashed toward us holding a jar of one of her creams. "I'll have the little girl feeling better in no time." She opened the library door and was gone.

I gazed at Lilly. "They know that the tapestry exists. Now we need to find it first. They've been poking holes in the walls—not very strategic so far, or at least not to my eyes. We'll use something stronger."

"Like what?"

"I don't know yet but it's coming to me." But something else hit me first.

We had to be under surveillance by something our bug detectors didn't pick up. I felt it as sure as anything but what had we missed? Then it struck me.

I put a finger to my lips and pointed to Lilly's neck. Catching on in an instant, she fished out her pendent and dropped it into my hand. I sped into the library, finger still on my lips holding the discs toward Rupert, who silenced everyone in the room with his hand before snatching the discs and dashing from the room. I followed him out and placed a hand on Lilly's arm as he passed us down the hall.

"I think I just discovered how they've been listening in on us. We'll find out soon enough when Rupert returns. While we wait, tell me more about these stratagems and how Mimi and your uncle might be using them."

"For instance, they could be punching holes in the walls as a ruse," Lilly pointed out. *"Deceive the enemy with an obvious move that will keep them occupied while taking a direct approach in the real direction.'* Loosely translated, that means they could be just fooling us by making like they believe the tapestry is hidden in the château. We could be wasting our time looking for it here when it really lies elsewhere. *'Loot a burning house'* also works. The DuBoises clearly can't cope with this ruin of a place."

My eyes widened. "Are those stratagems?"

"Míng xiū zhàn dào, àn dù Chéncāng."

"I thought you weren't paying attention when your uncle gave you Chinese culture lessons?"

She grinned. *"Wú zhōng shēng yǒu.* In other words, I pretend not to pay attention to hear better. Actually, I've studied my heritage just as Mimi has only with a different teacher."

I laughed. "Damn it, Lilly! You, too, make a worthy opponent."

She bowed.

We were back in the library to continue strategizing our next moves when Seraphina dragged herself into the library, cut and bleeding from multiple scratches on the face and arms yet appearing remarkably jubilant.

Nicolina leapt to her feet. "What did you discover?" she asked in Italian.

Seraphina said in English. "I follow them into village to campsite. There are six: five men, one woman. They drive in a black camper hauled by truck. I hide and watch."

"And?" Nicolina prompted.

"They stay inside but one comes out to use toilet and I jump. We engage in combat. His pants were down or I maybe lose sooner—his fighting skills very good. With pants down, not so good. Before I taser him with phone, I insert tracking device."

"Insert where?" Peaches asked.

I almost didn't want to hear the answer.

"In pants."

"Which will only work as long as he wears the same pants," Peaches said.

Seraphina glared at her. "I also place one under camper and under truck."

"And then what?" Nicolina prompted.

"Then I run very fast."

It took a few moments to digest all that. Lilly was watching Seraphina in amazement; the DuBoises and Henri had gone off to rest and make breakfast, respectively. Good thing. Trying to explain Nicolina's fierce little assistant to anybody else would have been a challenge.

"Seraphina works for Nicolina," I explained to Lilly.

"Doing what?" she asked.

"Whatever I request," Nicolina replied with a smile.

Seraphina held up her phone. "Battery going but I monitor their activities when charged."

Nicolina nodded and Seraphina was released from active duty to have a shower and recharge her batteries while the rest of us continued our plotting.

"When Rupert returns, we'll see if my hunch was correct," I said.

Moments later, he entered wearing a self-satisfied smile. "I inserted a penknife into the crease between the two halves of each disc and, as Phoebe suspected, they contain surveillance devices. I have sent a picture to Evan for further instructions but in the interim took the liberty of battering the innards of one onto the patio pavers. The other I have left inside your room, Lilly, while we ponder ways we may use it for sending the enemy false information."

"Very wise." Lilly nodded. "I suspect that my sister hoped I would not guess about the eavesdropping, which I did not. I'm glad you did."

"Excellent," I said, "now we can get back to work, hopefully free of eaves-droppers. We have checked and double-checked this room but should we go someplace else to discuss next steps?"

"Why not the grand hall?" Peaches suggested. "If we stand in the middle of the space, there's nothing nearby in which they can hide a device."

In moments, we were standing in the center of the grand baronial hall as far away from anything as we could get. I carefully placed my printouts and assorted historical abstracts on the rug along with everything I could find on the Saint Chappelles family, the Le Vistes, Charles VII, and Joan of Arc. All of it simmered in my brain like a cassoulet and yet I could still not pick up the scent. The DuBoises had given us the run of the library and the printer so we had all the tools we needed, just not the lead I craved.

"Why do you think Joan of Arc is involved?" Nicolina inquired, gazing down at my little packet of Joan information.

"Because she was at the center of a political bomb in the war between France and England," I told her. "Everyone in France must have known the Maid of Orléans story and, on top of everything else, she was a religious icon. What if the missing seventh tapestry references Joan of Arc in a way that was not flattering to the kings of either France or England? What if the unicorn represents Joan and France while the lion represents England?" I opened my phone on images of the six tapestries and slipped through them, one by one, while the others looked over my shoulder.

"But the unicorn is always depicted as male. There's that little matter of the horn supposedly with its phallic references," Rupert pointed out.

"But Joan was a warrior who dressed in men's clothes and wielded a sword," I countered, "plus she was a virgin and infused with what many believed were magical properties. A white unicorn is a perfect image for Joan of Arc."

"And the lion has been traditionally an emblem for England, notably English royalty dating back to William the Conquerer. If ever anyone in the Middle Ages would wish to choose a symbol for British might, it would surely indeed be the lion." Rupert appeared convinced.

"And in every tapestry panel, the English lion is on one side and the unicorn on the other," Nicolina said.

"So what does the woman in the middle represent?" Peaches asked.

"I think she's France herself caught between the two powers, one noble and magical, the other mighty with claws and teeth," I suggested. "She's in a tug-of-war masquerading as a noble lady."

"Following with your line of reasoning, why would a member of the Le Viste family commission such a thing and why involve a member of the Saint Chappelles to assist him?" Rupert asked.

"Because both men had watched Joan's rise and downfall from vastly different perspectives in the French court and were equally appalled? Because they conspired together to change the Maid of Orléans' fortunes but ultimately failed? Because they were forced to stand by mute and helpless as the heroine was imprisoned, charged through trickery and deceit by members of the church itself, and ultimately sentenced to death without rescue from the man she'd help crown?" I was on a roll.

"Yes, the Maid of Orléans was betrayed multiple times in the name of political expediency," Rupert acknowledged.

"And if people were standing by watching all that, wouldn't they want to express the truth?" Peaches suggested.

"Yes," Nicolina said, touching Peaches's arm. "I like that thinking very much. I would feel such a thing."

"I just read the transcription of her trial—unbelievable," I said. "They grilled her on the nature of her apparitions so they could trick her into saying something that would nail her for witchcraft. Every time they tried to trap her, she was too quick for them. She refused to tell them what Saint Michael wore, for instance, or whether he appeared before her clothed. They wanted to prove her visions were satanic. She may have been a poor, uneducated peasant girl but she was brilliant and brave. In the end, they had to lie to declare her guilty of heresy."

"And so Antoine le Viste commissioned a tapestry that told the story hidden in multiple layers of meaning," Lilly marveled.

"And perhaps Louis Saint Chappelles was friends with Antoine Le Viste. Maybe the seventh panel was an afterthought and, once completed, too risky to put on display, forcing the two men to hide it?" I suggested. "I'm betting that the actual drawing for the tapestries was complete many years before the tapestries were officially commissioned."

"So the Lady and the Unicorn tapestries were about courtly love only on the surface?" Peaches asked.

"On the surface, yes, but like anything else in the Middle Ages, multiple meanings exist simultaneously," Rupert explained.

"Scholars have long suspected a hidden meaning to the series," added Nicolina. "This could be the one."

"I'm guessing that the first six were safe enough to display while the seventh was far too dangerous." I rubbed my eyes, suddenly exhausted.

"This is giving me a headache, too. Let us have breakfast." Rupert sat down heavily on the nearest chair while the rest of us gathered up the research to return to the library. We all agreed that after food rest was in order.

After breakfast, I trudged back up to my room suddenly exhausted. Understanding a possible secret meaning to the tapestries was only part of the quest. Usually, I'd have a stronger inkling of where to go next but this case seemed to elude me.

I lay in the tub up to my neck in lavender-scented bubbles allowing the elements of the case to steep in my brain. I seemed to be tied up in knots both muscularly and in terms of my thought processes.

Where would these two co-conspirators hide a seventh panel? There was a tapestry, the Le Viste family, a French heroine, betrayal, and incredible bravery. There were angels, court priests and lawyers, kings, warriors, and politics. And there was a disparate Chinese element that sounded like a gong disrupting everything.

After dozing in the tub, I dried myself off and wandered into my room where the drawn curtains cast a deep blue glow. We needed to find that tapestry before Uncle Tengfeng and Mimi. Did they know where it was hidden? Maybe not if they were still hiding out in a nearby campground. But would they try to trick us by using ancient battle strategies? Maybe they'd wait until we led them right to it. Surely that, too, was an ancient war tactic: when seeking something, let the enemy find it first.

I was almost asleep on my bed when my phone pinged.

Evan: *I hear you are on the trail of a seventh Lady and the Unicorn tapestry while being chased by Chinese nationals. Interesting conundrum. Has the oracle spoken yet?*

Rupert had obviously filled him in. Evan and Peaches were the only ones who knew about the golden key I wore around my neck, the only souvenir from my Greek vacation. Referring to it as the "oracle" was only half in jest. We all wondered that, given its provenance, whether it might actually drop hints into my subconscious mind when needed. However, in this case, no such luck.

I sat up and typed. *So far, nothing. I'm baffled by all the seemingly disparate elements in this case. History claims that the tapestries were commissioned by Jean Le Viste but I'm thinking that it was more likely Antoine Le Viste, which places their commission sometime after the Joan of Arc debacle. Nobody knows for sure.*

Evan: *Joan of Arc? Phoebe, you always pull out the strongest threads in any circumstance and tug at them until the truth comes into the light. Keep pulling, my love.*

So that gave me butterflies. That he called me his "love" and glommed on to a tapestry/weaving/fiber analogy, too. There was a reason why we were so drawn to one another. *I worry that this one may be beyond me. Everything is so tangled that I just can't find the strongest thread.*

Evan: *You'll find it as long as you keep seeking. You never give up, that's one of your many strengths. "It does not matter how slowly you go as long as you do not stop."*

Me: *Okay, so that's a quote. Name your source.*

Evan: *Confucius.*

I laughed. *I should have known that you'd have the words of a great Chinese philosopher at your fingertips.*

Evan*: Must pull myself away. I am picking up a lead that we thought had grown cold back in Delos last fall. I'll be in touch soon.*

After he signed off, I sat gazing down at the empty screen. He'd told me more about what he was working on than he'd ever disclosed before. He *was* following Noel. Shit.

I fell back on the pillows thinking I'd never be able to relax because I'd be fretting about Evan chasing that cutthroat bastard. And yet, I fell into a deep sleep almost immediately.

The next thing I knew, I was sitting straight up in bed saying aloud: "Saint Chappelles! There must be a chapel around here somewhere!"

Minutes later, I was dressed and downstairs, tracking Henri onto the patio where he sat in a patch of sun stroking Chouchou with her bare little snout and gazing off across the Loire Valley.

"Henri," I said, "The château, the village, and your very last name indicates that there must have been a chapel around here once."

"But of course," he said, turning toward me. "Not the famous one in Paris but a smaller one, a family chapel, yes? It is nothing but ruins now, just old stone."

"We must go there today."

Gently placing the dog on the pavers, he got to his feet. "What are you thinking?"

I took a deep breath. "Imagine for a moment that you are a priest in the court of King Charles. A warrior maiden has just liberated your country, a maiden who now stands on trial. You have been asked to hide something by a friend, one who believes as you do that the maiden has been falsely accused. This object, if seen by the king, would surely anger him and perhaps see the beautiful but politically sensitive item destroyed and you with it. Where would you hide it?"

Henri stared at me. *"Mon Dieu!* In a chapel or a church!"

"Exactement!"

"Let us go!"

"Let's confer with the others first."

"And while you do that, I will drop petite Chouchou at my housekeeper's where she will be safe."

"Good. I'll meet up with you later."

The idea was to do everything in daylight when Mimi and Tengfeng least expected us to engage in nefarious acts. Somehow they must know that the

DuBoises had no idea what we were up to while also being aware of our every move.

"But how? They are privy to inside information somehow." I was standing outside the library with Peaches, Nicolina, and Seraphina. The DuBoises were content to leave us to use the room as our office while regularly supplying refreshments. Rupert was at the desk inside busily drawing up staging plans with Henri, and Lilly was in her room resting. Henri had agreed to say nothing of my idea until we knew it was safe to speak aloud. "I was followed in the Cluny Museum, remember, and we were also tailed down to Henri's cottage. They were on to us even then. We found one source but there may be others."

"Did you scan for bugs?" Seraphina demanded from Peaches. Seraphina was the bug expert. I imagined that she had a collection like a tray of electronic insects with pins stuck through their innards.

"Of course: agency protocol," Peaches answered. "I searched every inch with the debugging app, naturally."

"Every inch?" said Seraphina with a snort. "Of this big château? I do not believe this. I search. If there are bugs, I find!"

Peaches rolled her eyes. "There are no bugs here," Peaches insisted. "The app beeps if it detects anything within 15 feet."

"Not all kinds," Seraphina argued. "Newer types only beep when inches away. I am expert. I know these things." She was stabbing her chest with her thumb, daring Peaches to deny her expertise. I figured Peach would rather engage with a combine harvester.

"Go, then." Nicolina dismissed her assistant with a flip of her hand.

"If the DuBoises want to know what you're up to, say that you're studying the walls. Or something," I called after her.

"Let's wait until about three o'clock and then check out the chapel ruin. Maybe we can do that much undetected. Just Henri, Peaches, and I will go. We'll make it look like we're taking a walk."

Fifteen minutes later, when we were all in the library waiting for the lunch gong, I had an idea. "Henri, did you ever receive a gift from Uncle Tengfeng?"

Henri bobbed his head back and forth like a water bird. It was an odd sight. "A porcelain good luck cat with a spring head. I think why would he give me a good luck cat? Do such things appear like my taste?"

Exactly. Why would he? I seem to recall seeing those in San Francisco's Chinatown and they were mass-marketed for tourists. "Where is it now?"

"In my basement. Somehow I accidentally broke it." He grinned.

"Any other presents?"

"*Non.* He gave Puilan the gong and I leave it here."

Puilan must have been Lilly's mother. I sent a quick text to Seraphina suggesting she double-check the gong, not that I believed that a reverberating sound mechanism would make the best place to hide a sensitive listening device.

When Lilly entered the room, I spoke pointedly toward the disc she now wore around her neck. We had decided to use it as a deflecting device of our own.

"Tonight we go through the château again," I said to the disc.

She smiled. "I suggest we concentrate on the east wing this time. It's a continuation of the oldest parts of the structure dating from the thirteenth century. We'll need ladders to really get up into those walls to scout around." She ended with a sly grin.

"Good idea," I said.

Rupert opened the door and remarked: "We must rest up. It will be a long night."

11

$\mathcal{W}$e began using the second disc to send decoy information to our infiltrators. According to Seraphina's bug monitor, neither the camper nor the truck had budged since the night before, leaving us to hope that they were buying into our ruse.

After lunch, Henri, Lilly, and I set out to investigate the chapel, leaving Nicolina, Rupert, Peaches holding Chouchou, and Seraphina to watch our backs and keep the DuBoises busy. René kept an eye on the front entrance and prowled the grounds looking for lurkers. Lilly had claimed that she would be taking an afternoon nap and placed the yin yang disc in her bedroom with the occasional sounds of running water and a flushing toilet to strengthen the effect, compliments of Seraphina.

"I'm trying not to think what Mimi's been listening in on for all these years," Lilly exclaimed as we slipped out the back door and wound our way through the keep toward the crumbling outer walls. We figured that the oldest parts of the château offered us the best protection from prying eyes.

"When was the last time you saw her?" I asked as I maneuvered a pile of tumbled stones.

"Years ago."

"But you do not always wear that thing, *non?*" asked Henri, his arm around his niece's shoulders.

"No. In fact, I often take it off and leave it lying around when I'm on set or doing a red carpet stint," she said.

"Then, you see, she had much opportunity to work her wickedness," Henri said. "Much opportunity."

"It's not really wickedness," Lilly tried to explain. "It's a game."

"A wicked, wicked game," Henri insisted. "She tries to steal from her own uncle, from *me*. What have I done to deserve such treatment?"

"It's not about you, uncle, it's about me—well, Mimi and me. It's hard to explain. She needs to prove something."

"Prove what, that she is just as good and talented as her beautiful, famous twin? It is an old story, *non*? She was always jealous of you."

"It's not that simple, believe me, though I'm not saying that jealously isn't a part of it. She always called herself the ugly one even though she's far from ugly. She always thought she wasn't good enough but she was, she *is*. Now she has to prove she's better."

Henri was right: it was an old story but this one came with new twists.

"She's the math whiz, remember?" Lilly continued. "She was always the brilliant one academically, but even for that she was teased at school and nobody championed her the way they did me. They said that doing well academically was in her genes because she was Asian, as if she didn't work hard to earn everything she got. Think about it, Uncle Henri: it's true. I was the performer, I got all the accolades. I was more conventionally attractive and got all the acclaim, too. It's not fair."

Henri kept his gaze fixed on the ground as we stepped through the crumbled wall into the meadow. "Perhaps, but that is no excuse. Life is not fair," he mumbled. "Somehow, we as individuals must rise above, is that not true? You and I were always closer than I was with Mimi. I did not think I treated you differently when the three of us were together, but perhaps I did. Your parents, though, they loved you equally."

"It wasn't our family so much as the world that treated her worse than they did me."

"Ah, just so," whispered her uncle. "Beauty is its own currency, yes? This makes me very sad. Perhaps I should have made more effort but it's still no excuse for doing bad things to people."

"True," she admitted.

We crossed the meadow, slipping among the trees where possible to remain shielded until we reached a pile of stones over which rose a single arch, all that remained of the family chapel. Backed against the Loire River winding away in the valley below, it was a postcard-worthy sight.

"Do you know how long ago it was destroyed?" I asked.

"But no," said Henri, still appearing deep in a reflective mood. "For as long as I can remember and much longer than that. I believe it was ruined by fire sometime in the fifteenth century."

"Fire," Lilly mused. "But it looks like the chapel was mostly made of stone."

"But the pews, the altar—all wood." Henri shrugged.

I began running my phone's X-ray app over the foundations. That and the arch were all that was left standing of the little building. I guessed that over the centuries much of the stone had been scavenged by other builders in the village.

"What do we seek?" Henri inquired.

That wasn't clear even to me but a chapel for the Saint Chappelles family, who had once counted a priest for the king of France among their members, warranted investigation. "I'm not sure," I told him, "but I'll know it when I see it."

As expected, all that showed on my app screen were irregular pockets of air, none of which were the right size and shape for what I was seeking.

"Come."

I turned to find Henri beckoning me through the rubble toward a narrow passage. Lilly and I followed him into a grassy opening that must have once been the nave. I gazed around, prodding my inner senses to feel something, anything, but no revelations came.

Lilly was tracing the rectangular shape of the building in the air with her fingers. "If I were trying to hide something in a chapel, where would I put it?"

"In a crypt?" I asked, turning to Henri.

"A crypt..." He pondered for a moment, one finger tapping his goatee. "I do not remember a crypt on the property. The Saint Chappelles are buried in a crypt in the main cemetery outside of the village. There is a fine church there."

"Maybe now but what about five centuries ago? Wasn't it common for wealthy estates to have their own crypts?" I pressed.

"Oui." Henri gazed downward. "But there are no plaques, no signs, anywhere here. Usually such burials have the names of the departed embedded in the floor, and the Saint Chappelles would know that our ancestors lay there."

"Where was your priest Louis buried?" I asked.

"No one knows," he said with a shrug. "All mention of him disappeared from the records. There is no record of his burial."

"Don't you find that odd?" I asked.

"Not so odd for the times. People who lived during the Hundred Years' War did not leave peaceful lives. Many disappeared without a trace."

"That makes sense." I followed his gaze to the ground and ran the phone app over the grass looking for depressions. There were none. Underfloor graves such as seen in many medieval chapels and churches would be clearly revealed as rectangular depressions on my screen. "I guess the Saint Chappelles chose to bury their dead elsewhere."

"What if we check the village cemetery?" Lilly suggested.

"Cemeteries are like an invitation to looters. If the tapestry is hidden somewhere in the area, I can't imagine it would be there." How could I explain that I felt no tugging at the back of my mind, no tingling along my spine? "Besides, I'm thinking that the tapestry was probably hidden in a hurry. We need someplace accessible. Now that I think about it, anything that involved digging and pulling up the floor of an active church wouldn't do. And a grave would be the worst place to hide a tapestry."

The chapel having borne no fruit was abandoned on the spot and we trudged back the way we had come.

"We need to think the way a long-ago Father Louis Saint Chappelles and his allies might have thought. Attack from one faction or another was afoot and if a member of the Saint Chappelles family did hold an item that criticized the kings of two countries as well as the church in some way…"

"Then he would hide it in a hurry. A sorry matter." Henri waited while Lilly and I climbed through the opening in the wall into the roofless tower.

"Mimi was the history-lover of our family, though not usually of the French history variety," Lilly mused.

"How seriously did you two hunt for the missing tapestry?" I asked.

"It was a game to us, a chance to run around the château at night," she replied.

"Okay, so did you ask yourselves where somebody would never think to look?"

"Georges and Puilan were so furious at the girls when they found out what they were up to," Henri exclaimed. "I was working in Paris at the time and I am certain I could hear them roar."

We were passing by the cemented opening for the oubliette. All three of us stopped and stared at once. A six-inch-thick slab of cement sat directly on the ground topped off by a layer of grass.

Mais non! exclaimed Henri, staring at it in horror.

"How long ago was it sealed like that?" I asked.

"For decades," Lilly replied. "Ever since Dad caught Mimi daring me to go down there. Before then there had been this rusty iron grille over the hole with a padlock attached. That very same day, Dad had this cement covering built."

I was walking around the slab looking for signs of tampering but the layer of grass and soil that covered it clearly had remained undisturbed for years. "Has anyone ever gone down there that you know of?"

"Never!" Henri exclaimed. "No one would dare."

"Even in the past?"

"The family stories say that it has remained undisturbed for centuries. No one would descend to such a horrible place. It would be like climbing into an open grave! The bones of the unfortunate dead must still lay there even now," Henri insisted.

"No forensic archaeologist wanting to get down there in the name of research?" I pressed.

Henri's look of horror said it all.

"It was designed so that once someone was dropped into the pit, they would never be seen again," Lilly said. "They called it 'the forgotten room.' There's no way to access it from the bottom, either. Dad found an old sketch for it in the château archives once. It's a horrible thing."

I looked at each of them. "And a perfect hiding place. Someone could throw something down the hole in a hurry and almost guarantee that no one would descend to the bottom to find it." But I could tell from their alarm that I needed to let the subject go for the time being.

An hour later we had all gathered back in the center of the hall, the diagram of the château spread across the table with a separate one of its oubliette beside it, the corners weighed down with paperweights. Where the château diagrams appeared to have been drawn in stages over the centuries, the oubliette's seemed to have been hastily sketched. I guesstimated the date of its execution to be in the early 1400s.

"It is rather an unusual design for an oubliette, is it not?" Rupert asked Henri. "It appears to be sectioned like…an intestine."

I had thought the same thing. First came the long esophagus-like drop that opened into a small stomach-shaped chamber, which squeezed into an even narrower tunnel leading down from that. There was no way out except back the way that you came and, except for the first drop, it looked natural rather than man-made.

"My brother and I, we believed the oubliette was constructed in a natural cavity in the earth. Many caves are found in these parts."

"So no poor sod was forced to dig the wretched thing out except for the opening hole, at least." Rupert was claustrophobic. Even gazing at the sketch seemed to be making him queasy.

"It is true. It was not designed to be a place to keep people like a prison—there were those in the original castle, also—but a place to forget them," mused Henri.

"Indeed," said Rupert. "'Oubliette' does mean *forgotten room* in French, after all." He turned away to stare into the garden as if he needed to glimpse the flowers to erase his imaginings.

Nicolina and Peaches were both watching me in an uneasy silence. I knew what they were thinking but had vowed to say nothing until the time was right.

"Henri, perhaps we must soon own up to what we're really doing here to the DuBoises. What do you say, my good man?" That was Rupert desperate to change the subject. "The DuBoises deserve an explanation, do they not? They appear to be decent people and keeping the true nature of our presence here has become desperately difficult." He turned to his new friend.

Henri nodded. "*Mais, oui.* I have thought the same thing. Perhaps we should explain that these scoundrels harassing them at the château are searching for something of value and that we only thought to find it before they did without disclosing the details. True enough, *n'est-ce pas?*"

"True enough, indeed. We shall say that we did not wish to heighten their anxiety but believed that the problem arose over, er, family problems," Rupert suggested.

"Why not just tell them the truth?" I said.

"The truth?" Henri turned to me, a storm brewing in his eyes. "That we have been duping them so that I can locate a priceless object that might save the château for the Saint Chappelles family? Would they not want the tapestry for themselves, which will only deepen our difficulties?"

"It's not that clear-cut," said I, taking a deep breath. "Legally, and providing that we can prove a relationship between the Saint Chappelles and the tapestry, there's a case for the ownership going to your family," I began, "but the French government will definitely have a say in something of such national importance. They could confiscate the tapestry and keep it for years while the matter is battled out in court and maybe then give you some portion of its worth—maybe—but only years later. Finding it will not be an easy fix."

Henri fixed me with a baleful look. "Why did you not say sooner?"

"Because until I believed there was a tapestry, it seemed better to wait. Also, now that I see better what we—I mean, *who*—we are dealing with, the more important it is to alert the French branch of Interpol ASAP to help us find this treasure before Mimi and Tengfeng get hold of it." I turned to Rupert. "Don't you agree?"

Rupert touched Henri's arm. "Sadly, yes, my good fellow. I will send the necessary information forward when we believe we have enough to justify such a position. At the moment, that is not the case."

"I will find what we need." After I moment, I added, "Soon, I hope."

Henri still looked angry enough to shake my teeth out and, in truth, I didn't blame him. I should have told him sooner.

Seconds later, Seraphina burst into the room and flung her phone onto the table. "The enemy moves," she said. "First I think they go nowhere, do nothing, but look." Picking up the phone, she pinched open the screen image to show a red dot crossing the countryside.

"Where do they head?" Nicolina demanded.

"I do not know yet," said Seraphina. "Possibly toward Paris. Only the truck moves. The camper does not."

"Is there anyone inside the camper?" Rupert asked.

"I do not know," she replied.

"Well, have you picked up any conversations with your devices?" Peaches pressed.

Seraphina kept her gaze fixed on Nicolina. "I hear nothing. No one speaks."

"Well, how bloody useless is that? That means they're on to us," said Peaches. "The moving truck could be a decoy."

"I agree that looks to be the case," Rupert said.

"I follow," said Seraphina, making for the door.

"Not yet," I said. "First we need to finish up our business here in the castle. Like Peaches said, the truck is probably a decoy."

"Why do we wait to chase it?" Seraphina demanded.

"Because we have work to do here first."

"Shit, I knew it," Peaches muttered, turning to me. "You expect me to descend that oubliette thing, don't you?"

"No, I don't," said I. "I have to do it myself and it has to be tonight."

12

$\mathcal{I}$ was not one of those Gothic heroines who penetrated spooky castles at night where no one in their right mind would be caught dead—no pun intended. Wait, let the pun stand. I needed to go because I was the only one who knew exactly what I was looking for, who could recognize the receptacle typically used to transport tapestries of that importance from place to place, and because I was the one with the itchy spine. Yes, I was being that kind of a control junkie.

The tapestry panel would have been carefully rolled together with layers of cloth and placed into a canister probably at least five or six feet long or the width of the weaving. Perhaps the receptacle itself would be made of oiled leather and covered in heavy cloth to further protect the fibers during transport. It might even be encased in lead. Travel between France and the Netherlands would have taken weeks, depending on whether it was initially shipped by land or sea. Considering that the countries along the way were in various states of war, probably by sea made the best sense, but then they had the damp to contend with.

"Couldn't you just tell us what to look for?" griped Peaches. "Besides, with today's technology, there's no need for any human being to descend into that hellhole."

"I agree, Phoebe. My word, we can send a special camera down there to do the proverbial dirty work while the rest of us remain safely above ground where members of our pitiful species belong," said Rupert, pressing his palms together as if praying for me to agree.

"And how long would that take?" I demanded. "You couldn't get one of those special units here much before tomorrow afternoon and certainly not without multiple people knowing about it. Besides, even a camera like that doesn't have the mobility and flexibility of a person. There will be uneven surfaces down there and a little height will be needed at times. No, it has to be me and it has to be tonight."

Peaches swore.

"What I need can be purchased in any hardware store—a rope, a sling, something that roofers might use, and maybe a pulley to hoist up something heavy, if I find anything. Peaches..." I turned to my friend and bodyguard, now so angry at me I thought she might blow a gasket. "You can use your engineering mojo to rig something up while all the strong arms we have on hand will move that cement lid aside."

"Don't try to placate me," she said with a snarl. "I know what I have to do."

"I bet René could help," I plowed on. "We can't waste time. I'm guessing that the Tengfeng-Mimi contingent have either dismissed the oubliette out of hand or they don't know what they should be looking for in the first place."

"Or they are on another track entirely, working on information we lack," Nicolina pointed out.

The debate went on for several more minutes but I won in the name of reason. The last volley thrown against my idea was that Seraphina should go in my stead because she was lighter. Seraphina didn't appear too keen on the idea so didn't put up much of a fight and I argued that I needed her to remain up top watching out for bad guys. "Given that you'll fix me in a secure sling to lower me down, the more important issue is for trustworthy people to be up top watching my back." I stared at each of them pointedly.

"Aren't you afraid of ghosts?" Henri asked in a small voice.

"Yes and no. My definition of ghosts differs from the traditional one," I said. "I believe the real specters live inside us all and answer to energetic opportunists that lurk in the dark. There are exceptions, of course. I've encountered them before." Unconsciously, I touched my Pythia key under my shirt. "But those aren't the kind that usually hide out in dark pits. Unless they're stuck," I added.

At last, it was settled: as soon as Seraphina and Peaches returned with the necessary equipment, we would begin. That left Henri and Lilly to explain the truth to the DuBoises while René, Nicolina, Rupert, and I figured out how to move the slab off the oubliette. The latter took several trips back and forth until we'd worked out the logistics.

An hour later, Natalie and Eduard DuBois entered the library accompanied by Lilly and Henri.

"We knew you were not designers," Natalie addressed Rupert and me at once. "And you, countess, though you are apparently the real deal, it seems you also work for the agency."

Eduard added, "We knew immediately after Sir Rupert booked that you were not being truthful."

"Seriously?" I said, turning to face him.

"You thought us so foolish that we would not research the big-name designers from London? I found the web page that Sir Rupert posted but our previous experience in advertising told us that it was fake," Eduard said, his usual friendly face crossed with anger.

"Hastily made," his wife clarified.

"Yes, hastily made. Then we find all the real details of your occupations— finders of lost treasures, art repatriation, association with Interpol," Eduard continued. "All over the news."

"But we know Henri and Lilly so we think, what are they up to? We will wait and see," said Natalie.

"And we knew you would not harm us, at least, because you work with Interpol and we think it must be safe to have you stay here and fill our bedrooms with company, which you have done." Eduard was focused on Henri now. "We knew we would learn the truth in time."

"That much pleased us—the company—but now we hear the truth and even we are surprised," added Natalie, today donned in casual jeans and over-sized shirt. "An ancient tapestry?"

"I explained my hopes to buy back the château with funds from the sale of the missing tapestry," Henri said with a shrug. His eyes were wet. "I am deeply sorry."

"But why do you want to take back the château?" Natalie swung on him. "This is madness! You always say how difficult it was for you with the constant upkeep and the bottomless hole it creates in your bank account. You were almost destitute when we bought the château, you said, and now you want it back?"

"It is my home!" Henri said with a sob. "This is the only home I have ever known, where I dreamed to retire, where all the memories live. I miss it terribly, poverty and all."

Lilly sidled over and slipped an arm around her uncle's waist. "We're sorry for the ruse, Eduard and Natalie. You deserved better than that and we clumsily tried to play you. Now we know that my sister is behind the attacks in the château and that she's after the seventh Lady and the Unicorn tapestry, too. Even if Phoebe and her agency find it first, we understand that it will not solve my uncle's problems and maybe it shouldn't. We'll have to work that through on our own. Can you forgive us?"

"You are forgiven." Natalie dismissed the notion with a flick of her hand. "But we are disappointed in you both, of course. Still we will rise above it, yes?"

Lilly smiled. "I certainly hope so."

"And I believe I may be of help to you regarding the château," Nicolina assured them, "though now is perhaps not the right time to discuss my proposal."

Rupert stepped toward the couple to take one of their hands in each of his. "In any case, I extend my deepest apologies, madame, monsieur, along with profound regret. Our actions were callow and unworthy of the generous hospitality upon which you've rained on our ignoble heads, yet we behaved so only to better study the premises without raising unnecessary alarm while continuing to locate the significant object in question. Meanwhile, we ask for your forbearance for a while longer as—"

"In other words, we're truly sorry, all of us," I interjected, stepping forward. "But matters are growing more desperate and we're running out of time. Would you mind if we continue looking on the premises? We promise to keep you posted of every aspect of the case as it unfolds, as we should have from the beginning, which brings me to the next request: would you permit me to descend the oubliette this evening? It will mean removing the covering but I promise we will return it to its original condition one way or the other."

Eduard gaped. "You are serious? Lilly said that you wanted to go down there but I could not believe my ears. Do you really expect to find a priceless tapestry in that death pit?"

"Not really," I admitted, "but it's too perfect a hiding place not to at least give it a try. Tonight, as a matter of fact." I checked my phone. "Sometime before it's completely dark. My colleagues just texted to say that they're on their way back with equipment. As soon as they arrive, I'd like to get started. We have plenty of preparations to make."

In the end, it only took a crowbar as a lever and a bit of René's and Eduard's might to topple the slab off the trapdoor to reveal the black opening. At first glance, it looked like a well, covered by a badly rusted grille, which broke into pieces in our hands.

When Peaches and Seraphina returned, they were put in charge of constructing the tripod-like mechanism over the hole where a sling would lower me down by a pulley. They had also purchased two big spotlights to illuminate the outside up top and a smaller version to wear around my neck. When they weren't arguing over who knew more, they managed to get the job done fairly quickly.

Eduard had leant me a pair of waders that though too big were a welcome addition to my non-designer wardrobe and offered some protection against whatever I might find underfoot.

While we watched them work, Evan texted me: *Phoebe, are you certain about this?*

Me: *Please don't try to talk me out of it. I need to do it. I have to do my own dirty work this time.*

Evan: *I'm not going to try to talk you out of anything. If it's what you need to do, then it's the right thing and I'll be behind you all the way. I just wish I was physically there to take you into my arms the moment it's over.*

Me: *I'd love that, too, only you'd probably insist on going down yourself.*

Evan: *Probably.*

Me: *Who told you the details?*

Evan: *Both Peaches and Rupert texted me. I've alerted my French colleagues. A possible seventh Lady and the Unicorn tapestry sends shivers of anticipation through my network.*

Me: *I bet.*

Evan: *I also launched an inquiry about Tengfeng Yu Ho and Mimi Saint Chappelles, who now goes by her adopted mother's maiden name of Yu Ho. They've been running a network of stolen art under the guise of the Lucky Ho Export Company out of Beijing. My informants tell me that they may have been responsible for the theft of the Blue Globe diamond from the museum in Chennai, India. The diamond was probably sold to a private buyer since it hasn't appeared on the market. They are professionals, Phoebe. I don't need to warn you to be careful, but just in case you believed this was just a family matter, it is not.*

Me: *Got it. Thanks. Better go. It looks like the pulley is almost done.*

Evan: *Use the geocontour map app. Click the button on your phone that looks like the sketch of a mountain peak. Once activated, this will allow you to detect an object's shape as far away as 20 feet by sending radio waves out to transcribe outlines onto the screen. This should help you find whatever you seek.*

Me: *Thank you!* And I sent him a couple of hearts just because I could. He sent ten back but his were animated.

That left me staring at the contraption suspended over the opening of the oubliette. It reminded me of one of those old-fashioned tripod cook fires where a caldron is hung over open flames, only in this case I would be the pot and nothing that lay below me even remotely warm. A sudden shiver ripped through my being. What the hell was I doing? If I fell, I could break a lot more than a leg or two.

"Phoebe, are you sure you wish to go through with this? It would only take another eight hours at the most for a camera to arrive." Rupert was gazing at me with concern while Nicolina stood by backing him up.

"I could call our Rome office and have it couriered overnight. There is a man I know who specializes in these things," she suggested.

"Why is everybody so worked up about this?" I asked. "Haven't we all done worse things—haven't I?"

"Of course you have," Nicolina agreed. "But you are our friend and we worry."

"It's just a pit," I pointed out.

"A pit that nothing has been down for a very long time—" Rupert began. "A deep pit, a—"

I held up my hand. "Don't make this worse than it has to be. I'll be down and back up within 20 minutes, at the most."

"We check oxygen levels down there," Seraphina said, stepping up to me. "Meter shows ample air to breath now that cover is removed but you must remain close to opening."

"Well, that's a relief. I'll be able to breathe, at least." I stepped up to the oubliette and studied the pulley system Peaches had rigged. Though I knew nothing about these things, it looked secure enough. She had fashioned a sling seat for my comfort on descent.

"Either call up or tug the rope when you want to return," she said. "The first sign of trouble, we're hauling you up. I figure you'll be too busy using your phone to text. Sounds should echo down there so we should hear you if you just yell."

I studied the hole now illuminated by a spotlight that beamed straight down into the darkness. The only thing visible on the bottom was a jumble of grayish brown things, maybe bones. I took a deep breath. "Let's get this over with."

Peaches grabbed my arm. "Let me go with you. I'll go first, then you come down after."

"No," I told her with a smile. "I appreciate the offer but I really do need you up here."

"Are you kidding me? There's like three armed agency members up here plus René, Henri, Lilly, and the DuBoises. We're practically standing room only around here. How many do you need?"

"As many as I can get—enough to fend off a swat team of kung-fu-trained warriors or whatever, if it comes to that. Enough to get me out of trouble if the pulley jams. I'll be back in no time. I figure that the object I'm looking for would have landed nearby. Straight down the hole, in other words. I should be able to locate it in minutes."

With that I climbed up onto the edge of the oubliette and settled into the sling. It was almost comfy.

I gazed out at the gathering dusk, heard an owl hoot somewhere, a nightingale sing, a bug buzzing past. Above my head, the first stars were pricking the sky and I imagined that the moon wouldn't be far behind.

Rule number one: never descend into the darkness without filling your heart with light. If Confucius didn't say that, he should have.

"Okay, lower me down," I called.

Whenever I am faced with a distasteful task, I focus on the intent to get it done without allowing my thoughts to stray either right or left. It's a similar technique to balancing on one foot while fixing on a spot on the horizon. Keep an eye on the ball, in other words.

As the pulley lowered, manned by Peaches and René, I thought only of reaching the bottom and scanning the space using my phone app. With a flashlight thing around my neck and my phone open in one hand, both arms encircling the ropes on either side, it seemed an easy enough task to manage. I was not going to think about the bones I fully expected to see down there or the possibility of rats, which I assumed must be everywhere. I was looking for rectangles or cylinders, period. Geometric shapes in a sea of rounded organic objects should be easily detected.

And it helped that my friends above kept up a steady stream of shouts, comments, and questions firing down, especially when the first 10 yards or so seemed to be nothing but a rock-hewn well with its claustrophobic lack of surrounding space. They expected me to describe everything and I happily obliged. "I can't see anything but slimy stone around me but the ground is getting noticeably closer."

"I estimated it to be 30 feet down. You're like one-quarter of the way there," Peaches called.

And then the walls fell away and I was suspended in a cavernous darkness. Panning my phone in all directions, at first it was difficult to discern one object from another. Everything seemed a jumble of gloom, kind of sepia-toned with black pockets everywhere. The air smelled so foul I barely wanted to breathe. I didn't want to imagine whatever nasty molecules I might be inhaling. But try holding your breath while yelling.

"What do you see?" Nicolina called.

"Nothing yet," I cried back. "Keep lowering me."

The rope jerked and stilled for a moment before continuing.

"Sorry!" That was Peaches.

I swore. "Do that again and I'll start seeing my life pass before my eyes," I said with a laugh I didn't feel. Suddenly I was too aware of being suspended over a death pit. I began imagining what it must have been like to be somebody who had angered the castle owners enough to be dropped down this place to die frightened, in pain, and alone. For a fleeting second it was as if I could feel the press of souls against me, hungry for warmth, light, life, compassion.

"I'm sorry," I whispered.

"What do you see now?" This time it was Rupert and the sound of his voice yanked me back into line. "Still nothing," I said, "but I'm almost at the bottom. Ease up a bit!"

My descent slowed and at last my feet hit the bottom. Maybe hit wasn't the right word—thunked, I supposed. No, *squelched*. It was strangely mucky down there, not bone-dry the way I had expected. I had a horrible thought that maybe all this organic matter had just settled into a kind of stew. My stomach lurched. I shook myself out of that and scanned the chamber with my phone.

"It's covered in silt," I called. I took a brief glance at the hole above. The light shone down on me like a beleaguered moon as my friends' heads peered down in silhouette. A flashlight raked my eyes.

"Sorry!" Peaches again.

I turned away and cautiously got to my feet. Walking was tricky in the oversized waders but I was grateful for the layer of rubber between me and whatever. Holding the phone with care, I clicked the ground-contouring app and panned it around the chamber. Nothing geometric in sight, just a bumpy surface. "I need to walk a little farther," I yelled up.

"Don't leave our sight."

"It'll only take a minute," I replied as I took my first step away from the safety of my sling with its shining path to safety above.

What if the object tossed down the hole didn't arrive alone? What if a person was clutching it when he fell or was pushed into the oubliette? I hadn't considered that until now but it made perfect sense. These were desperate times and somebody was escaping somebody else while clutching political dynamite and possibly the first somebody wanted to ensure that what he grasped would never be seen. Maybe if it was witnessed by a ruling power, another person—maybe a friend—would be harmed. Such secrets needed to be protected, even buried. Such secrets might have to be plunged deep into the darkness of the forgotten room and take their carrier with them.

In which case, the object I was seeking may have been moved, maybe dragged, by a wounded man.

What would I do if I was sentenced to die alone with this object that had cost me my life? Wouldn't it seem like my only companion, perhaps a spark of humanity in this horrible place? Maybe it told the story of bravery and sacrifice, maybe dreaming of it would be the only thing to bring me comfort as I struggled for my last breath. Fix on the light, always fix on the light.

Fixer sur la lumière.

Several steps later and I realized that I was treading on crunchy things below the slimy muck. I must be walking on bones. I stifled a sob.

Somebody was calling for me to return but there could be no return for me. I had given that up long ago when I took the oath to defend all that was holy and true and vowed to protect this beautiful tapestry that told the true story of our maiden's betrayal. Would its beauty never see the light of day? Would I? No matter, what was my sacrifice next to hers?

I tripped and my phone went flying, jolting me out of my trance. I landed facedown in the muck, my chin hitting something hard. With the light around my neck stuck in the mud and my phone gleaming weakly to my right, I was blinded, yet somehow I could see.

Lifting my head, I gazed straight into the hollow eye sockets of a human skull. Scrambling to my knees, I crouched, trembling. It was as if I knew him. I *did* know him.

"Where is it, *pére*?" I whispered. The blank gaze was fixed to my left. I turned toward its gaze. *"Merci."*

Seconds later, I had plucked my phone from the silt, wiped it and my neck lantern off on my waders, and fixed the geocontour app straight ahead. Right on cue, the outlines of the upper part of a cylinder appeared on the screen like a ghostly sketch against the darkness. It seemed to be poking out of the ground against the end wall, close to where I knew the first chamber narrowed into the second intestine-like drop. *Shit.*

I dragged my feet deeper into the darkness while speaking in French to my imaginary (perhaps not so imaginary) companion. Voices and shouts sounded from somewhere behind me but they all seemed so far away, so irrelevant. I remained fixed on the object ahead. It was sticking out at an angle, definitely a cylinder embedded at least one-quarter of the way deep. I hope it wasn't wedged in something. I would have to yank it out with both hands and somehow drag it back to the sling.

But now I seemed to be gasping for air. Suddenly I couldn't breathe. Reaching the cylinder, I blinked down at it, dizzy. Lead casing. Slimy coating. I pocketed my phone, grabbed the object, and tugged. It slipped from my hands and flung me backward.

Luckily, I blacked out before I could feel myself sliding deeper into the forgotten room.

13

I lay on my back shivering. Somebody was wiping my face with a damp cloth. I blinked up at the stars overhead and all I could do was push gulps of fresh air and heaps of gratitude deep into my lungs.

"What happened?" I gasped.

"You passed out," Nicolina told me, her hand warm on my forehead.

"Not enough oxygen. Should have remained near opening as I said." That was Seraphina's voice.

I jolted upright and gazed straight into Peaches's glaring face. "Yeah, we got it back up safely, too." She pointed to the muck-covered lead cylinder lying on the ground behind me over which stood Rupert, Eduard, and René. I moved to get to it but Nicolina held me back. "We will open it once you are recovered."

"I'm recovered now," I said, struggling to my feet.

Peaches held me down. "You're recovered when we say you're recovered. Lilly and Natalie have gone to get a hot bath ready and fetch you some clean clothes. Then you'll have something to drink—"

"Tea," Rupert instructed as he crouched beside me. "Tea is always the best restorer, Phoebe. I've brought my own selection, along with a particular soothing favorite."

"I'm fine," I argued.

"You are not fine," growled Peaches. "You passed out. Seraphina and I had to go down and drag your sorry butt back through the muck and bones before returning to get the canister. I can't believe you bloody insisted on doing this alone, woman! We had to go down there, anyway, so why not bring us in the first place?"

Nicolina tried to silence her with a look but Peaches refused to meet her eye.

"Can't explain right now, Peach. Just know that I needed to be alone in that pit to find out what I needed to know."

"Holy shit, you better not be speaking about spooks down there because I'm not having it. I—"

This time Nicolina chopped the air with one hand, a gesture as close to witnessing a royal command as we'd ever receive. Peaches fell silent, though her expression was still filled with admonishment.

"We will help Phoebe into the château now," Nicolina ordered while adding directions for René and Seraphina to bring the canister into the library after wiping it down. Peaches then lifted me into her arms and marched toward the château.

"Let me walk," I protested.

"Forget it," came the reply.

I kept looking around. "Where's Henri?" I asked.

"In the loo," Peaches responded. "He almost peed himself for fear for you."

"I've got to tell him something important," I said.

"Will have to wait, won't it?"

I resigned myself to helplessness for the rest of the way. I couldn't even pull my phone out of my pocket to message Evan. I just had to wait. I hated waiting and I was desperate to get at that canister.

But first came the shower—no bath, takes too long—then I climbed into one of Lilly's red silk Chinese robes that was just roomy enough to work over my second pair of leggings while my clothes were being washed. Then came the tea, which I was grateful to sip while munching croissant sandwiches Natalie had put together. The last two activities were at least performed while I shot a quick text to Evan.

Me: *Survived the ordeal.*

Evan: *I know. I held you safe in my virtual embrace.*

Me: *The story is beginning to weave together at last.*

Evan: *As I knew it would. Go bury your face in a flower. Bright beautiful things are necessary after penetrating something so dark.*

There was a posy of roses and baby's breath in my room. I buried my nose deep inside the peachy-colored petals and breathed deeply, a smile on my face.

Seconds later, I was heading downstairs, tea in hand, accompanied by Peaches, who had remained on guard outside my bedroom door as if she expected an armed attack.

"What's the status of the Tengfeng-Mimi dot?" I asked.

"It stopped briefly at a little church on the other side of the river but is on the move again," Peaches told me. "The camper has been abandoned and there's been no sign of activity anywhere around the château. Seraphina set up a perimeter scan around the property but there's been no disturbances there, either."

"They are off on another track," I remarked.

"That's what I think, too."

"Or maybe they want us to think they are."

Everybody was in the library gathered around the now-wiped-clean cylinder, which lay on a towel on one of the library tables. All eyes were on me as I entered.

"I've been running the X-ray app over the canister, Phoebe. Though the exterior is lead, it contains nothing metallic, as you've probably gleaned, and the receptacle is not long enough to hold a precious tapestry," Rupert informed me.

"No, it's not," I agreed, "but what it does contain is important enough for a man to lose his life over." I sought out Henri sitting by the fire nursing a glass of wine. "Henri," I began. "I found your ancestor Pére Louis Saint Chappelles."

He jolted up from his seat. "What do you mean?"

"I mean that Louis Saint Chappelles was either thrown down into the oubliette to protect the secrets contained in that canister or he jumped, taking it with him. I think he jumped."

"But how do you know this?" he demanded.

"I wish I could explain that convincingly but trust me, I do. He knew where the tapestry was hidden, too, but this was a piece of evidence he needed to secure against the enemy. I think the clue to its location is hidden in the canister. When all this is over, you may want to retrieve his bones and give him a proper burial. I'm not sure why his spirit didn't escape the oubliette but it could be because he believed he needed to guard the canister. I'm honored that he let me take it."

Peaches swore while I blithely continued. "Either that or he committed suicide, which, as a Catholic, may have convinced him that he deserved purgatory. Anyway, I think he'd like somewhere in the orchard overlooking the Loire or near the chapel. For now, let's see what he gave his life to protect."

All eyes turned to the receptacle, which appeared to be bound with four deteriorated leather straps with brass fittings. "Who will do the honors?"

"Henri, perhaps it should be you, old chap. Here, Eduard has brought us a set of wire cutters." Rupert stepped forward flexing the cutters, which he handed to Henri. The DuBoises and the rest of us gathered around.

"I wish I knew this ancestor of mine who plays such a role in French history," Henri whispered as he cut the remains of the strapping and snapped the brass closures open. He then lifted the top and gently tipped the receptacle backward to look inside. "Hello? Whatever is there, it appears to be wrapped in some kind of cloth. Canvas, perhaps?"

"A painting?" Nicolina asked, likely remembering our Botticelli mission.

"Or something else. Tip it out, Henri, please," said I.

Of course, in a perfect world, a delicate operation such as this would be performed in a lab under stringent conditions but here we only wanted a clue that might save an even greater treasure. Onto the table fell a roll of what looked to be thick rust-colored fabric.

Seraphina leaned forward. "Waxed textile."

"Something is rolled between the layers," I said.

Rupert donned a pair of surgical gloves and gently unrolled the piece, or pieces, which turned out to be four large squares of paper, placed one on top of the other and rolled in waxed wool. The top piece appeared to be approximately one and a half feet by one and a half feet and had absorbed so much of the dye from the fabric that it was almost indiscernible.

"I can see faint lines and color," Lilly exclaimed. "It's a drawing or a painting."

I almost forgot to breathe. "It's a cartoon quadrant!"

"Isn't a cartoon a joke?" Natalie asked.

"Originally a cartoon referred to a drawing that is hung behind the loom while a tapestry is being woven. It's the guide the weaver follows and is never drawn by the weavers themselves but by an artist commissioned for the purpose," I said. "This one's very old. Hardly any have survived down the ages. The best collection is at the Asmolean in Oxford. How many are there?"

Rupert counted the layers while carefully separating the sheets. "Four."

"Then it's a complete set. Spread the quadrants out on the floor now," I instructed, so excited I nearly squealed.

Rupert and Seraphina obliged, weighing down each of the corners with the DuBoises' collection of glass paperweights, until we stood facing a large red-tinted picture measuring nearly five feet long and slightly less wide. It was challenging to tell which quadrant went where. We shifted a couple of them around once or twice. The images were mostly indecipherable, rendered on a deep red background with a crackled surface as if the fabric's dye plus some of the wax had been absorbed by the parchment. Obviously, it had been damp down there so possibly the wax had even preserved the paper to some extent.

Whatever lay below the dye and wax was impossible to decipher. One section must have encountered a more highly waxed section of wool in a deeper, dryer position because the dye transfer there was much lighter. At least the outline of a figure emerged: a gowned lady, a look of pain registered in her features, staring sorrowfully off to the left. I leaned closer to the image, running my phone magnifier close to the surface, my heart banging against my chest. "I think there may be a unicorn under there. I can't tell without scraping and manipulating the paper, which is bound to destroy it further, but I can just make out a hoof."

Sitting back on my heels, I sent a quick message off to Ella at the Cluny Museum describing our find with pictures included. When I looked up moments later, Nicolina and Rupert were trying some of the X-ray apps, trying to capture the drawing's outlines.

"Drat!" muttered Rupert. "Had the drawing been with a lead pencil we might be able to detect more of the outline but, as it is, I believe this was drawn in ink and then washed in watercolor, which has mostly run."

"Once a conservationist investigates this, we may learn more but right now we can't risk damaging it further." I stood up. "Still, I'm guessing we just found the cartoon for the final Lady and the Unicorn tapestry."

"But what does it tell us other than the drawing must have somehow been explosive in some way?" Lilly asked.

"I don't know," I said. "Like the rest of the tapestries, it would be layered in symbolism and allegory but this one somehow completes the story of the Lady and the Unicorn in such a way that it tells a much more dangerous tale. Once we can see the whole design, we'll understand why Father Louis had to hide it."

"What do I see there? Look," Henri demanded, leaning over the cartoon segments. "Up there in the upper right-hand corner. Perhaps it is just my eyes but I see a sword. A line, perhaps, with what could be the cross of a hilt below it."

Rupert studied the segment from Henri's perspective, nearly toppling over the other man as he leaned in. "I dare say, I believe he's correct: a sword flanked between two wings, perhaps, or are those smudges? Blasted difficult to tell."

"It may only be a mark made when the paper cracks, *no?*" inquired Nicolina.

A discussion followed as each individual weighed in on whether it was a flaw or an actual drawing emerging from the ancient sheet. Meanwhile, I stood back, calibrating, calibrating... If it really was an image and not a splotch, why a sword and why in the upper right-hand corner?

All the other completed tapestries filled the background with millefleurs but the fact that those details may not appear on the cartoon itself didn't mean that they didn't feature in the actual tapestry. Millefleurs was perfected by the Netherlandish weavers and added by them during the weaving process so did not require the help of a drawing. There were also birds, rabbits, dogs, and plenty of other wildlife in the tapestry fields, but a sword? More likely the unicorn would hold the sword or possibly the lion but to have one hovering in the upper right-hand side? Too strange. How I wished I could see the entire drawing.

We decided to leave the cartoon where it lay, anchored flat in the library overnight with René and an electronic sensor keeping watch while we had supper and then headed for bed. René was ordered to bed, too, but insisted on camping out beside the cartoon. In the end, we decided he was too big to push around so we let his decision stand.

The major point of discussion over dinner was where to go next. The Tengfeng-Mimi contingent was on the move and, according to Seraphina's tracking map, appeared to be following a trail of small churches and chapels across the countryside.

"Any similarities among the churches?" I asked Seraphina over a dish of beef bourguignon served with new potatoes and cottage vegetables.

"No. I watch always," she replied. "All churches or chapels but nothing to link them. I made list. I send."

"Thanks." I gazed at the central table bouquet without focusing. They were after churches, just as we had investigated the chapel on the property. They also suspected that there had to be a religious connection and perhaps even that Father Louis was behind the conspiracy, too.

Then, as if catching my thoughts, Rupert said: "If they are investigating religious sites, I daresay it must be because they believe the tapestry is hidden in one."

"And they didn't check the chapel on this property because they already knew it wasn't there," I remarked.

Seraphina pulled out her phone to check the screen again. "They are heading for Paris."

"Perhaps they'll try the older churches, those that were active during the Middle Ages. Maybe they'll even go to the basilicas of Sacré-Coeur and Sainte-Chapelle," I continued. "I would if I didn't have a clue."

"Do we have a clue?" Peaches asked.

"We do," I replied, "but we just don't know what it means yet." I was referring to the cartoon, a major find that so far told us nothing.

"They believe they are ahead of us," Nicolina said as she set down her knife and fork. Nicolina never spoke and ate at the same time. She gave herself fully to either one task or the other but never both simultaneously. Maybe it was a countess thing. "They believe they know the tapestry is hidden in a church."

"But not in which church," Lilly said.

"But they pay no attention to us now," said Henri. "Suddenly they take off. No more break-ins."

"No doubt they are aware that we found out about their surveillance devices," Rupert began. "In fact, I guarantee they know that much since one of Lilly's went dark suddenly. They must believe themselves ahead of us in the search and have temporarily dropped us from their radar."

"Nothing will ever drop me completely from Mimi's radar. She'll find the tapestry and then make sure to lord it over me," Lilly said.

"She won't find the tapestry without my help," I said, turning to her, "but you can believe that they know exactly where we are at all times. We may have caught all the surveillance devices but not every tracker."

"Don't underestimate them, Phoebe." Lilly again. "Maybe they are listening in on us right now. They could be two, three even, steps ahead of us. They'll try to trick us just as we tried to trick them but they'll be better at it because they've had more practice. Promise me that if anything weird happens, you'll do the opposite of what they may expect."

I pondered that for a moment. "Okay," I said slowly. "I can be really impulsive sometimes so you may need to remind me to act strategically if the time comes."

"Deal." Lilly nodded. "So, like I'm nervous about leaving the château because that makes us vulnerable."

"It is true that military tactics always prefer to draw the enemy out of the castle." Rupert nodded. "However, what choice do we have since we are convinced that the tapestry does not reside here?"

"We have to find it, obviously." I gazed off into space. "We just don't know where to look but we have to begin somewhere. Churches really are a logical next step."

"Are we going somewhere?" Peaches asked.

"To Paris," I said finally. "That makes the most sense."

Across the table, Nicolina smiled. "To the old churches in Paris as if we are on the same path as they."

I nodded.

"Sainte-Chapelle houses King Louis IX of France's Passion relics and was where the kings of France traditionally worshipped. It would be a perfect place to look for a piece of hidden art," said Eduard, looking up from serving another round of wine.

"At least on the surface. The revolutionaries did massive damage to that lovely structure, though indeed it has been rebuilt. Definitely worth a bit of investigation. What say you, Phoebe?" Rupert had caught my eye over the rose bouquet and silently toasted me with his wine.

"I think that since we believe this tapestry tells a story that may be uncomplimentary to a certain French king, and the church itself, for that matter, hiding it in a place of royal worship wouldn't make sense but maybe they don't know that so we should make on like we're checking it out, too," I said. "At least until we can work out its true location."

"Plus there are others," Nicolina added.

"Many others," I agreed.

"There are not that many churches and basilicas in Paris of the correct age that have not been destroyed or damaged by either war or the revolutionaries," Rupert reminded us. "I have narrowed it down to two: the Sainte-Chapelle, Kingdom of Light, and the Saint-Denis basilica. Notre-Dame would have been the ideal place to start but we know that's out of the question. We might even have a go at Saint-Germain, the oldest church in Paris."

"But we don't know what church the tapestry may be hidden in so that makes us even with Tengfeng and Mimi," Peaches said.

"Not quite. We still have the cartoon in our possession and a theory," I said.

"Neither of which assist our endeavors for the moment but I trust this will change," Rupert added. "Meanwhile, we need to go to Sainte-Chapelle and Saint-Denis to make it appear as though we believe that is where it is hidden."

Lilly lifted her head from her plate and smiled. "'Make a sound in the east, then strike in the west.'"

I grinned back. "Something like that."

"Only we don't have a clue as to where in the west to strike," Peaches pointed out.

"Not yet," I acknowledged, "but hopefully while they are expending their energy scrambling over those churches and we pretend to be doing the same, we'll figure out where the tapestry is really hidden and send them on the wrong path. After all, we have the cartoon, they don't."

"But we can't decipher it or even see it properly," Peaches repeated.

"Not yet." I picked up my fork and stabbed a carrot.

The rest of the meal passed in more of the same. Seraphina excused herself early to go upstairs to comb the rooms for bugs again. All agency members knew what she got up to every night when she supposedly went to bed early. We also knew that she'd probably plant a few devices of her own in the DuBoises' room, just in case. Seraphina's policy was to trust no one and, at this point, we weren't going to disagree.

As the evening ended and we were heading up the stairs for bed, I broke the news about the Lucky Ho Export Company to Lilly.

"Seriously? Why am I not surprised?" She paused. "Mimi and Uncle Tengfeng are united about making money any way they can and those of us in the West are merely the opponents in the game, me especially."

"I don't think this is all personal," I remarked.

"Not totally," she agreed, "but most of it feels personal to Uncle Henri and me."

Once alone in my room, I read the latest message from Evan, a few lines from a poem by Victor Hugo provided in French and English: *Life is a flower, love is its honey. It is the dove united with the eagle in the sky.*

Nothing else, just the poem, and for a moment I imagined his spirit, the spirit of the dove mingled with the fierceness of the eagle, both predator and lover all at once. A thrill hit me. The man I loved was chasing a dangerous foe, making him as much the eagle as the dove, but he was doing so in part for me. Was he saying that because he loved me, that he was determined to vanquish my foe?

Wiping away tears, I sent him a heart, which symbolically best caught the multiple emotions surging through me just then. Words escaped me. Somewhat parochially, I added a photo of the cartoon quadrant with the barely distinguishable figures in the upper field.

Then I read the message from Ella that told me she would be traveling down to retrieve the cartoon as soon as she could make the necessary arrangements. Max also messaged me to say that he had just purchased an amazing seventeenth-century carpet, and Zann, our newest member now in charge of our US office, texted me to say that she thought she had a lead on a hoard of Roman gold.

My head spun. Not surprising, my sleep was filled with dreams. I was trapped in an airless chamber while a bodiless monk floated around my head asking about the weather above ground.

"Why do you want to know about the weather?" I asked him.

"Because here it is always dark always unless the angels visit," he replied in French.

There was more but I couldn't remember much of it when I awoke about four hours later. By then it was three-ish and the time I often wake for no good reason. Do I have an internal alarm clock or something and, if so, how do I turn the thing off? When at home, I'd fix myself tea and knit for a bit before returning to sleep, and since I'd barely touched my needles since leaving Paris, I decided that tea and knitting would be my soother of choice.

I plugged in the room kettle, placed one of Peaches's herbal tea remedies into a cup, and settled down in the room's only chair to dig around in my tapestry bag for my sack of French confection-colored silk yarns. Meanwhile, I'd cast about in my subconscious for strands of what still elluded me and, with a little luck, catch something.

Nearly thirty minutes later, I yawned and crawled back to bed none the wiser.

* * *

THE NEXT MORNING, we divided into two groups: Peaches, Lilly, Rupert and I would travel together in Rupert's spiffy rented car, while Henri, Nicolina, and Seraphina traveled in Henri's Peugeot. René would remain with the DuBoises on cartoon guard duty.

We found tracking devices under both cars, as expected, which suited our plans perfectly. The idea was to confound the enemy. While Nicolina's group investigated the Sacré-Coeur basilica, my team would take on Sainte-Chapelle and Saint-Denis, all the while pretending to be searching the floor tombs or hidden underground recesses. I suspected that Tengfeng probably knew by now that we used handheld devices with X-ray capabilities but I figured he didn't know that those devices could not yet detect a textile through stone. Let them track us.

We said goodbye to the DuBoises and promised to let them know what we were up to as soon as it was safe to do so. Meanwhile, we left a few surveillance devices around to catch any interlopers should they be lurking. We gave René a short session on how the things worked and left him with a program to check on his own phone. By the time we were under way, the sun was rising in the east and the air promised a warm late-spring day.

About a half hour after we were on the road, Seraphina texted to say that the Tengfeng-Mimi tracker had arrived at the Île de la Cité and stopped, which meant they'd parked. Two main cathedrals lay in that area, Notre-Dame and Sainte-Chapelle.

"Damn. They beat us to it," Peaches muttered.

"Maybe not," Rupert remarked. "Sainte-Chapelle does not open its doors for another ten minutes and Notre-Dame is of course closed until further notice."

"We should spot them in line when we enter," Peaches said.

"If they intend to tail us, they'll need to divide up eventually, too," I muttered. "Somebody will have to follow each of our groups, which will be useful when we discover the tapestry's true location."

Or that was the idea.

"And you expect to figure out where the tapestry is really hidden while we pretend to be searching for it?" Lilly asked me in amazement.

"Something like that."

"But what if you don't figure out where it is?" Lilly asked.

"We will." I truly believed that but had absolutely no way of explaining it convincingly. "It may take a few more days but it will come to me."

"Should be interesting. It always is watching Phoebe work," Rupert murmured as he navigated the lanes heading for A10. "By the way, I have requested that Seraphina report regularly as to their location."

We sat lost in our thoughts for a while. "Lilly," I asked as the signs for Paris began to appear, "was Père Louis Saint Chappelles a monk, by any chance?"

"I have no idea," she admitted, today back in incognito gear in a wide-brimmed hat and sunglasses. "I don't think very much was ever written about him or that he wrote much about himself. Then again, maybe everything that had existed along with any correspondence was all destroyed except that one letter."

"Speaking of that letter, I understand that you called the Cluny Museum asking about it's veracity," I said.

"I did no such thing," Lilly assured me. "That had to have been Mimi."

A few minutes later, a sign for the Île de la Cité appeared to our right. Meanwhile, the enemy's tracker hadn't moved.

"I'll give you directions to the nearest parking lot," Peaches, who was up front with Rupert, said as she peered at her phone. "Take the first left off the ramp."

"Why do you ask about Père Saint Chappelles?" Lilly turned to me and flipped up her glasses.

"Just a dream I had. I imagined myself talking to a bodiless monk."

"Sounds scary."

"It wasn't. Just odd."

She smiled. "Maybe that was Père Louis. Maybe you're on to something."

Rupert called from the front seat. "Speaking of Louis, did you know that King Louis IX, the king who ordered the Sainte-Chapelle cathedral constructed around 1242, could have easily born the descriptor 'aggrandizer' attached to his name? He built this cathedral with the intention of making Paris the new Jerusalem. The cost of the holy relics he accumulated far outstripped the cost of building the cathedral itself."

"I think entitlement is clearly the kingly way," I remarked. "He probably hoped to pave his road to heaven. Wasn't he sainted in the end?"

"He was," Rupert acknowledged.

"And wasn't some of the structure destroyed during the French Revolution?" Peaches inquired. "They did have that anti-royalty thing going on."

"Also correct," said Rupert. "However, it has since been reconstructed. Fortuitously, most of the stunning stained glass has survived, despite the marauding populace razing down the epitome of wealth and excess while crying 'Viva la France!' as if France isn't as much about its history as it is about its future. Poor deluded sods. Nevertheless, they helped pave the way for democracy. Let us visit the upper chapel first."

Along the way it was necessary to pass Notre-Dame, that day a mass of webbing and scaffolding that all but obliterated the magnificent structure beneath. The ravages of time had fangs of fire in this case. Our hearts fell looking at it as we hurried along.

"Prepare to be astounded," Rupert said as he ushered us toward our destination.

Being astounded while simultaneously pretending to be seeking something of value and looking out for our enemies at the same time was more challenging than I expected. Once we had joined the line (Peaches had purchased our tickets in advance) and climbed the narrow stairs to the upper level while attempting some modicum of social distancing, we entered the magnificent upper chapel only to be struck dumb. Or at least I was.

"Holy crap! Pure Gothic magic! Look at that vaulted ceiling!" enthused Peaches, gazing upward at the huge rosette window inset into the front nave.

Never had so much color and light beamed over me all at once. With 15 glass walls over 49 feet high, it was as if we had stepped inside a magnificent multifaceted prism, as if a thousand Tiffany lamps were washing brilliant illumination down upon our heads all at once. Bathing in color and light was so overwhelming I temporarily forgot what we had come to do. When next I looked around, Rupert had his phone in hand and was running it over the mosaic floor.

"I'll watch your collective backs," Peaches whispered. "There may be lots of space in here but that leaves plenty of places to hide, too. If your guess is correct, they'll be watching us. Luckily, the first group is still relatively small. I only counted forty people to enter with us."

Lilly was keeping an eye out for any individual who could be either her sister or uncle in disguise. "Don't expect them to be all dressed in black, either. They're smarter than that. They'll probably look like tourists and tag along with an Asian tour group. Most people don't bother to distinguish between Chinese and Japanese, anyway. Still, I don't see any tour groups, for that matter."

I checked my phone. No message from Seraphina, though Nicolina had texted to say they had just arrived at the Sacré-Coeur and that there was no sign of any likely suspects there, either. Okay then, time to pretend to get to work.

As I held up my phone as if to run an X-ray app, a guard strode up to me with a pleasant but definite *non.* No pictures allowed. Now what? Somehow I had to pretend to use my app on the sly. To that end, I veered toward the side of the chapel that was richly gilded and elaborately decorated, though the stained glass clearly stole the show.

Still, since the whole place had been restored long after the Hundred Years' War, I knew there was likely no place there to hide a tapestry. The logical thing would be to head down to the crypt, anyplace, in fact, where the revolutionaries might not have ravaged. And then it hit me: *there was no place that the revolutionaries hadn't ravaged.* According to the guide I overheard speaking to my right, they'd even melted down the reliquaries and stolen the jewels. What tapestry could survive that? And I bet Tengfeng and Lilly knew that, too.

I was crossing the mosaic floor toward Rupert just as he was approaching me.

"Nicolina texted to say that the enemy's tracker has not yet moved but that she sent Seraphina to do a reconnaissance and that Seraphina believes she has spotted two who may be our enemy checking out Notre-Dame!"

"Through the barricades and scaffolding?"

"Just so."

"That's crazy! That place was badly damaged." I knew the tapestry wasn't in Notre-Dame, though the dates fit and a court priest would have had access to that facility. There were crypts, of course, but Louis wouldn't have hidden anything that close to his king. "Let's head for Saint-Denis. Maybe they'll start following us."

Peaches arrived with Lilly. "What are you talking about?"

We filled her in.

"Well, they're not here, that's for sure. We were the first ones in when the doors opened for the day."

"We're heading for Saint-Denis now," Rupert said.

"Where the kings of France were buried?" Lilly asked.

"Exactly."

And so we left for our car, me reading a text from Nicolina as we strode along. "No sign of Tengfeng and Mimi in the basilica, either. What does that mean?"

"That they believe the tapestry may be hidden in the remains of Notre-Dame?" Rupert inquired.

"But it can't be," I claimed. "They are off on the wrong track."

"So are we," Peaches mused, "since we don't know where the right track is."

Unfortunately true.

"That's a good thing that they're on the wrong track, isn't it?" Lilly was striding along right beside me.

"Yes, it's a good thing. It means we don't have to lead them along on a wild-goose chase because they're off on one of their own but it's not the way I'd hoped this would happen. Let's continue to Saint-Denis and see if they track us there."

But it was unsettling. What if Louis had hidden it in Notre-Dame? But no, I reminded myself, he couldn't have. Don't ask me how I knew that but I just did.

The basilica was in a northern suburb of sprawling Paris and required maneuvering traffic, taking several wrong turns, and probably frittering away our time to get there.

"Where would you hide a tapestry if you were a monk?" I inquired to no one in particular.

"In a monastery," Peaches replied. "Don't mean to be so literal but, really, why not?"

We had reached the car park by then and Rupert was pressing the horn button on his key fob to find our rental. "Well, indeed, why not? There's the blasted thing. The basilica of Saint-Denis was, in fact, a former medieval abbey church and contains the remains of every French king dating from the tenth century. It sounds like an ideal place to hide a tapestry on one hand, except it would be extraordinarily well-guarded on the other, and why would this Louis chap make things so difficult for himself?"

Peaches ran her scanner around the car in case something worse than a tracker had been attached. She paused somewhere near the fender. "The bastards." And she swore under her breath.

"What?" Lilly asked.

We watched in silence as she slid her hand under the car, emerging minutes later holding a wafer-like object about the size of a stick of chewing gum. In moments, she had ground it under her heel and tossed the remains down a drain. "They were here and fastened that thing under our car. I have no idea what it was but let me check the interior before we go anywhere." Five minutes later she emerged with another one, glaring at it in disbelief before taking its photo and performing the same crunch-and-discard ritual.

"Surely it isn't an explosive device?" Rupert asked.

Lilly blanched.

"Couldn't be or we'd be nothing but bits and pieces by now," Peaches told him. "Just never seen anything like it. I sent the pic to Ev but the scanner indicated a listening device merged with a tracker—ultra-high-tech, like man-on-the-moon high-tech, which, now that I think about it, is so last year."

"Technically so last century," I remarked. "Let's get going."

We piled into the car and took off, and while we cut across Parisian traffic, all I could think of was how it was folly to underestimate one's enemy. They should be following us by now but apparently weren't; they appeared to be investigating Notre-Dame instead but probably weren't. Did they have a lead that we didn't? It was baffling, unsettling, and left me at loose ends.

And now we were hoping to trick them into thinking that we, too, believed the tapestry was hidden in a church, specifically a tomb. Hence, Saint-Denis. The sight had a fascinating history. Any structure that begins its tale with a saint who was supposedly decapitated by the Romans and carried his own head to the spot where he wanted to be buried is worth hearing. However, while en route, Rupert also informed us that most of the monastery sections were destroyed in 1792 and that the revolutionaries had melted down the artifacts and reliquaries there, too. Even the lead roof had been dismantled to make bullets. It was boggling how much destruction this basilica, in fact Paris herself, had endured through the ages. Still, she rose proud and inspirational over the collective imaginations of Europe and beyond.

By the time we had arrived and parked our car, still no one followed us. Our tracker remained resolutely in the same spot. Meanwhile, back at Sacré-

Coeur, Nicolina and team likewise found that their activities were garnering no interest on the surface or, at least, not enough.

"It's a game and they're winning," Lilly remarked as we strode toward the imposing exterior of the basilica. The visitor line was depressingly long and Peaches had been too preoccupied to nab tickets. "While we think we are leading them on a false trail, they intend to do the same to us. How do we know that their car hasn't moved?"

"Seraphina found it in the same car park as us, but," I said, my mind racing, "suppose they left that vehicle and transferred to another one? They must know that we're tracking them, too."

"Of course they know," she said.

"I shall just pop into the ticket desk and see if I can throw Interpol's weight around to get us a special pass," Rupert announced before scuttling off.

Lilly stared at me. "We need to deploy another strategy."

"Any ideas?" I asked.

"How about we find the real tapestry first?" Peaches always preferred the most direct approach.

Then somebody recognized Lilly and swooped in for an autograph while Peaches and I stood aside to watch.

"Peach, I agree that we need to find that tapestry but I just don't know where to go next. Maybe I need to return to the oubliette and confer with Louis?"

"I'll just pretend you didn't say that. Still, it looks like we're being played while we think we're doing the playing. At least we didn't go dashing into Notre-Dame to follow them, did we? Maybe they thought they'd jump us or something while we were scrambling around the scaffolding," she pointed out.

"Maybe, and maybe they never went to Notre-Dame in the first place. Maybe they went elsewhere and only wanted us to think they went to Notre-Dame." I shot a message off to René, who replied within seconds: no signs of interlopers at the château. Still, I remained uneasy until Rupert returned and beckoned the three of us to follow him. He had used his Interpol pedigree to get us a special pass to the most sacrosanct parts of the basilica, which left him as plump-feathered as the king of the barnyard.

"Indeed, it was surprisingly easy. All I need do was show my credentials, wait while they made a brief phone call, and voilà!—we're guests. Truly, I do love it when things work as they should with the least amount of effort expended on my part, and am sorely tempted to use a similar technique for getting us a prime table in one of the top Parisian restaurants—Le Cinq, L'Oiseau Blanc, the Carette—"

I slipped up beside him. "If only we had time for fine dining."

He adjusted his ascot and sighed. "Just so."

Moments later, we were descending into the underbelly of the basilica toward the crypts, a long dimly lit area with various interconnecting stone chambers that spanned the centuries from Charlemagne on to the seventeenth century.

It was a perfect place to hide a tapestry if someone needed the location and privacy to manage such a thing. A court priest would certainly have access to those vaults and be allowed to pray in solitude for the souls of the dead while he secreted something of immense value in one of the tombs. But why would he? If he thought his secret damaging to the crown, wouldn't he want to hide it someplace as far away as possible and not in the midst of them? Also, tombs were hardly dry and tidy. One didn't need to be a textile conservator to figure that one out.

"Henri believes he recognized a sword in the cartoon," I mused aloud. "In keeping with the Joan of Arc theory, Joan was a warrior so that sword could represent her triumph. I thought at first that maybe the tapestry might be hidden near Joan's remains but there were no remains. She was burned in Rouen and her ashes tossed into the Seine."

We stood gathered around one of the oldest sections, gazing at the crumbled and worn sarcophagi that had been arranged—and looted—centuries ago. We had been left alone.

"However," Rupert began, clearing his throat, "a recent scientific discovery investigated an apothecary jar that supposedly contained Joan's ashes and found a piece of linen hailing from the fifteenth century."

"Along with the femur of a cat, right? It was typical during the execution of a supposed witch to throw a black cat onto the flames to ward away evil spirits," I added.

"Hell, if I were an evil spirit, that wouldn't work on me," Peaches whispered. "I'd want the kitty to keep me company wherever I was going."

"You'd probably be burned as a witch, too, then," I said. "Me, too, actually."

Peaches nodded. "Bright, kick-ass, rebel women were easily branded as witches back then. Both of us are 'sistas' in time."

"Anyway, speaking of time, this is wasting it in bucketloads. We've got to stop pretending and start finding," said I. "Our enemy are on to us."

"I'm all for that," Peaches said.

I turned to Rupert. "Name some of the major sites in France that factored during the Hundred Years' War."

"Crécy, Orléans, Agincourt—" Rupert began.

"I don't mean battles, just locations."

"Phoebe, all of France was involved in the war that continued for well over a hundred years. It would be most difficult to determine a location that wasn't affected."

We began walking back the way we'd come. "What about significant castles, châteaus, or fortifications that factored in the war?" I tried again.

"The Château de Castelnaud," Lilly offered. "It was captured by the English during the war."

"Not a likely place, then," I said. "Our priest and his confederates would want to hide this secret someplace they believed the English would never conquer."

"Surely there was no such place?" Rupert said.

"What about the royal Château de Tours?" Lilly again. "That's where King Charles VII married Marie d'Anjou and it was the site where they hosted Jeanne d'Arc's victory at the Battle of Orléans."

"Too close to the seat of the mighty again," was my response.

"I thought you believed that it must be hidden in a church?" Peaches pointed out. "Why are we thinking castles all of a sudden?"

"Just brainstorming," I said.

"Hold on a minute. I have to find a toilet," Lilly said. "I think I saw a sign near the entrance. I'll meet you back here."

"Wait, I'll go with you," Peaches said. "We need to keep eyes on you at all times."

Lilly flashed her a smile. "I've been doing this on my own for a long time, Peaches. You guys can wait nearby if you insist but I'm entering the toilet alone. Do you see the *toilette* signs?"

We followed Lilly to the entrance where we all reapplied our face masks in the interest of germ avoidance because by now the place was swarming with visitors. While Rupert waded through the throng to thank the guard for letting us in, something caught my eye.

I nudged Peaches and Lilly. "Look at that," I whispered as a tour group squeezed by us chattering away. "Are those saints?"

Peaches stared at the painting that was probably done in the late seventeenth century, situated beside the information booth, and portrayed four radiant figures descending through the clouds. "I have no idea, being a Baptist from birth, but do saints have wings? That top guy is brandishing a sword."

Lilly just stared before announcing, "Right, off to the loo. See you in a minute."

We watched her stride away as Rupert arrived beside us. "Those are four of the top archangels. Really, you two, don't you know Gabriel, Uriel, Raphael, and Michael?"

"Not personally," Peaches remarked, "but that explains the wings."

"The topmost image is archangel Michael, the most powerful angel in the celestial realm and also the angel of protection. He's often portrayed as a warrior, which is why he holds aloft a sword and—" Rupert's words trailed off as he stared transfixed at the image.

"A sword with wings," I whispered.

"Which angels did Joan of Arc see again?" Peaches asked.

"The archangel Michael…" Rupert said.

I licked my lips. "I think we just found our next clue."

"Wait!" yelped Peaches, swinging toward the entrance. "Where the hell is Lilly going and who is she with?"

14

We burst outside in time to see Lilly wedged between two men running toward a white van parked at the curb about 50 feet ahead of us. Short, powerfully built, only one of the men appeared to be Asian, though it was hard to tell since both were wearing hoodies. I took a photo of the license plate while Peaches and Rupert dashed toward the van, which pealed from the curb seconds before they reached it.

"Shit, shit, shit!" Peaches was crying. "They bloody kidnapped her! We've got to follow them!"

That was my first instinct, too, but our car was parked several blocks away. Peaches began hailing a cab while Rupert spoke into his phone.

"Alerting Interpol!" he said over his shoulder. "This is now a kidnapping case."

"I just sent you a picture of the license plate and the van," I said, running up beside them. Turning to Peaches, I added: "Forget the cab."

"What do you mean 'forget the cab'?" she blurted. "We've got to chase after them!"

"No, we don't. That's what they expect us to do, what they *want* us to do. Leave that to the police. Lilly won't be harmed. This is her uncle and her twin sister we're talking about, remember? They want us to chase her to divert our attentions away from what they are really up to. We fell into the first trap, let's not stumble into another."

I called Nicolina to fill her in.

"They must have another vehicle that we do not track," she said. "We must locate them quickly. I will put Seraphina on it at once and use our network. Do we need a helicopter?"

"Maybe," I said. "At least we will once I know where we're going."

As soon as we hung up, I opened a map of France on my phone.

"Brain-think, everybody!" I said to the others. "We now know that the tapestry cartoon may contain an image of the archangel Michael. In fact, I'm sure it does. That must lead us somewhere. I feel like the answer is hovering between my eyeballs but I just can't catch it."

"The cartoon may also reveal the images of Saint Catherine and Saint Claire, both of whom, along with Saint Michael, Joan of Arc claimed emboldened her to save France," Rupert pointed out. "How can we consider one without the others?"

"But surely an archangel trumps a saint in the holy hierarchy?" I said.

I turned away and sent a quick message to Evan, who had been raised Catholic and knew all about saints and sinners. Hopefully he would respond right away:

Me: *Evan, if the archangel Michael is a clue to a location of a church or fortification in France and you were a priest and a dissenting member of Charles VII's court following the Joan of Arc crisis, where would you hide a priceless object?*

"Are you seriously going to just let Lilly go?" Peaches had arrived at my elbow.

I looked up. "I assured her that I'd think strategically and wouldn't fall into another trap. This is a trap, Peach. They want to lure us off-track. They must know where that tapestry is hidden and are heading right there now, if they haven't already arrived. All this—" I waved my hand around "—is a smokescreen."

"The police are on their way. I shall remain here and submit our report but you had best leave now or you'll be tied up in questioning for at least another hour or more," Rupert announced. "Here's the keys to the car." He dropped them into my hand. "Let me know when you determine a location."

"Thanks, Rupert. Come on, Peach," I called as I dashed away.

"Where are we going?" she cried as she ran next to me.

"I have no idea."

"Seriously?"

We reached the car park just as the peal of sirens ripped the air.

"Seriously. You drive."

After performing a quick scan around the car where we discovered and destroyed three more trackers all inserted in different locations from those found last time, we climbed into the front.

Peaches banged the steering wheel with her palms. "There's too many buttons on this damn thing! Give me a switch any day. Where are we going exactly?"

"I don't know exactly," I said. "Just take us as far away from Paris as fast we can go."

Then the phone rang. Evan. I put him on FaceTime while I watched that beautiful face on the screen.

"Hi," I said. "So glad you called right away. Peaches and I are leaving Paris to parts unknown. I need you to be a good Catholic boy and think like a priest for a moment—okay, maybe think like a monk. I believe Father Louis became a monk. You've seen the pictures of the cartoon I sent? We think one of those smudges could be the symbol of the archangel Michael."

"I've reached the same conclusion, but first of all, good morning, Phoebe and Peaches. Nicolina's filled me in on the status. As for the next piece of business, I haven't done many monkish things lately for which I have you to thank. I have you on my tracker map, by the way. Is Peaches driving?"

"Yes, Ev, I'm bloody well behind the wheel of this souped-up car Rupe insisted upon renting."

He smiled. Such a fabulous smile that warmed every cell in my body. Totally irrelevant, I know, but still. "Take the sign for the A14 toward Évreux."

"Evhoo?"

"Évreux," he repeated, spelling it out. "You should see it on the dashboard map as a destination to lead you out of Paris."

"Okay, so like do you know where we're going?" she asked as she merged into traffic. "Oh, shit, don't tell me we're heading for the Arc de Triomphe. Traffic there is like a zookeeper's nightmare."

"Stay calm, Peach," I said in my most soothing tone.

"Yes, I have an idea," said Evan, "and if you take the next left, I'll navigate you away from the congestion. Your location is open on my map here."

"Where are we going?" yelped Peaches.

"Phoebe, it should strike you momentarily. Look at the map."

I pinched out the map on the dashboard screen, locating Évreux. My eyes traveled along the route to a spot so obvious it shocked me to the core. "Oh, my God!" I cried. "I should have thought of that! We're going to Mont-Saint-Michel! Evan, you're brilliant! I just adore you!"

"And I feel the same way about you." He grinned. "I just wish I were close enough to show you in person."

"Get a room, you two! Ev, where next after I take that left? There's a garbage collection truck ahead the size of one of our ambulances back home plonk in the middle of this lane. Looks like they're chewing up boxes one at a time. We'll be here all day." And then she caught sight of something in the rearview mirror. "Shit! I think we're being followed."

I turned to see a black Rover rapidly approaching from behind, a guy hanging out the window aiming something at our tires.

"Over the curb!" Evan ordered.

"But—"

"Now!"

Peaches veered to the right of the truck, swiping stacks of wooden boxes and crunching something under our tires, leaving the sanitation workers swearing at us with waving arms.

I fell back into my seat. "They're following us. Not the sanitation guys but the bad guys."

"Yes, they are," Evan said calmly, "so we must outmaneuver them and get you outside of Paris to rendezvous with the helicopter we're trying to organize. I'm guessing that they don't want to kill you, just capture you."

"Me, why?" Peaches asked.

"Not you, Peaches. Phoebe," he said gently. "They believe she'll lead them straight to the tapestry."

"Of course it's Phoebe they're after. Sorry—distracted." She leaned over and patted my knee.

"So they must believe that the tapestry is hidden in Mont-Saint-Michel," I said. "Peach, eyes on the road, s'il vous plaît. Leave my knee alone."

"No doubt they know that much but not exactly where. They'll need you for that. Take the next right and then a hard left. I have a fix on your pursuers and they're not far behind. Keep going straight until I say otherwise."

"But I don't know exactly where it's hidden," I protested, holding on to the door as the car swerved to the right.

"Not yet," Evan said in that calm measured way of his, "but I have full confidence that you will. Tengfeng and Mimi Yu Ho are professionals, Phoebe. You can believe they've done their homework and know that you have a sixth sense for finding lost art. You've been monitored from day one. We just don't know how."

"You believe that we were under surveillance even after we ran the scanners and found Lilly's yin yang pendant?" Peaches asked.

"We must have been. I've always suspected it but didn't know how," he said.

I stared straight ahead, shocked by the realization that Tengfeng and Mimi must know everything, including the Joan of Arc connection, which I thought had given us a powerful advantage. "They must have known about the cartoon after we found it, too, maybe even figured out the archangel reference before we did. Damn! If it's not a device sending them information, then it has to be a mole."

"A mole!" Peaches exclaimed. "You mean somebody in our trusted circle has been reporting back to Mimi and Tengfeng?"

"A mole is my conclusion, too," Evan said. "I just spoke to Rupert and Nicolina and we concur. Peaches, at the next stop sign you'll merge onto a road that will eventually become the A13. Stay the course and follow the signs. How well do you know Lilly?"

I gazed into Evan's eyes. "Not particularly well but it can't be Lilly. She was the one who hired us to find the tapestry in the first place."

Peaches whacked her horn with her palm. "Get your smelly old Renault butt out of my way! That thing is so old it shouldn't be on the road. Yes, but Lilly believed that all we needed to do was find the tapestry to make Uncle Henri richer. What if once she discovered it would be confiscated by the government, she decided to throw her hand in with Uncle Tengfeng and Mimi? Let them steal it and sell it on the underground market like for a percentage. They're family, after all."

"Did you do that with your criminal brother?" I asked. "Did I?"

"Course not but everybody's different. We're very different."

"I just can't believe that it was Lilly. Her competition against her sister is real, plus she has a career she needs to protect, plus she warned me about how to play this game. Lilly's legit. The mole can't be her."

"But we can't rule her out, either," Peaches insisted. "After all, as soon as you pointed out Saint Michael's symbol, she conveniently ran off with a couple of dudes."

"Kidnapped," I pointed out. There are other potential moles to consider—the DuBoises, for instance. What about René?"

Peaches glanced at me. "René's a sweet guy but not the brightest bulb in the box. Maybe Henri."

"But he detests Tengfeng and would want the tapestry to stay in France."

"Focus on the road for now," Evan warned. "We still have to get you safely out of Paris. It should take roughly four hours to get to the mount, barring any mishaps."

We glued our eyes back on the road where dark clouds were gathering in the western part of the city. "Where are our tailgaters now?"

"They've fallen far behind but they may have glommed on to the direction you're heading." Evan spoke in such a calm manner that it could only mean trouble.

"And?" I prompted.

"And if I were them, I'd wait until you were in the countryside heading for the coast before making my next move."

"Which would be?" Peaches inquired.

"I'd find a way to stop you long enough to kidnap Phoebe. I wouldn't waste my time and energy chasing you all over Paris once I figured out where you were heading. The other option would be to wait until you arrived at the mount and ambush you there."

"Thanks." Peaches swore. "Here we come, a pair of *canard assis.*"

"You're hardly sitting ducks," Evan said. "You have the strength of our network behind you, plus the two of you are dynamos."

So why didn't I feel like a dynamo? Suddenly, I felt more like a fool. Why didn't I sense a mole sooner? "Do we have agents on the ground in the abbey yet?" I asked.

"No, but they're on the way and so am I. I'm sitting on a plane as we speak." Relief washed over me.

I sat gazing into his eyes, letting them give me strength because I had no idea what lay ahead and I needed all the support I could get. Unconsciously, I fingered the key beneath my shirt. "The tapestry would have to be hidden in the medieval part of the abbey. I gather that the site is very old. I haven't had a chance to do my research yet."

Evan was like a walking history book—with benefits. "In the eighth century, the cult of the archangel Michael inspired Father Aubert, the bishop of Avranches, to build a sanctuary on Mont-Tombe, now Mont-Saint-Michel. The story goes that the bishop was slow to comply so the archangel poked a finger into his skull to bring the point home. The bishop's skull, complete with indentation, is among the abbey's relics."

"A holey skull, in other words. Never argue with an angel," Peaches muttered as she followed the signs to the Normandy coast. "They'll always have the upper hand."

"And the abbey part?" I asked.

"The site became of strategic importance in 966 when the Duke of Normandy established a community of Benedictine monks, which continued there for over eight hundred years," Evan told us.

"Which included the Hundred Years' War," I remarked.

"Absolutely." Evan quirked his mouth in a half smile, trying to keep me calm and possibly distract me from a sense of impending doom. "Mont-Saint-Michel never succumbed to the English no matter how hard they battered its defenses. As you know, it's perched on a pinnacle of inhospitable rock in a tidal estuary that is now linked by a causeway."

"A perfect defensive position," I remarked.

"The best. Though it withstood the English, its formidable location made it a perfect place for a prison, which it became in the seventeenth century when it was named the 'bastille on the sea.' It's designed in the hierarchal style: first comes the abbey with a golden archangel perched on top representing God—a later addition, by the way—next comes the monastery, then the great halls and the dormitories, after which follows the town beyond the walls on the very rock foundations with the sea crashing below."

I looked up at those dark clouds scudding in from the English Channel. "Crashing? What's the weather report?"

"Gloomy with a side of disaster," Peaches muttered.

I smiled. "Oh, just stop."

"I have to talk to French Interpol for a while. We're having trouble locating a helicopter on short notice. Stay the course, Peaches, and I'll be back as soon as I can."

As the buildings began to recede and the French countryside opened up around us, I pulled up my phone and dug into my research.

"So Charles VI, Charles VII's father, strengthened Mont-Saint-Michel's ramparts and added courtyards," I said. "Sometime during his son's reign and following the Joan of Arc debacle, Père Louis Saint Chappelles may have requested the king's permission to join the monastery for a time, which could have given him the opportunity needed to hide the tapestry."

"Going to monasteries was a medieval priest's idea of a vacation, I take it?" Peaches asked.

"Yes, either that or on a pilgrimage and the mount was also a pilgrimage site for a time."

"What I don't understand is why he and Le Viste felt compelled to have that tapestry made in the first place if it was such a treasonous act? Couldn't they have been burned at the stake, too, if they were ever discovered?"

I sat back in my seat and stared out at the gathering clouds. The first drops of rain splattered the windshield. "Possibly. I think Saint Chappelles and Le Viste needed to express their outrage at Joan of Arc's treatment by church and state. Art has always given subversives a voice and these were subversives. Maybe they believed that the archangel demanded that they do this."

"Maybe."

"To true believers. Joan of Arc was a simple peasant girl who went to war after she was supposedly commanded to do so by archangel Michael and two saints."

"And Louis was a priest, too, and to him Joan of Arc must have seemed like a miracle."

"And a beacon of faith to everyone, an agent of Saint Michael himself. Like all great women, she delivered what she promised, and in what must have seemed to be in a miraculous manner."

"Yeah, Joan was a badass."

"A true medieval superhero, a real one. Anyway, the first tapestries in the series were just leading up to this grand finale panel, which I'm convinced was not designed at the same time as the others."

"So they'd really risk their lives for a tapestry?"

"For art, yes, and they wouldn't be the first."

After that we fell silent, focusing on our thoughts while preparing for whatever lay ahead. As if we could. Rupert informed us that the police had found the kidnapping van abandoned on the outskirts of Paris. It had been stolen, apparently, but there was no sign of Lilly.

"Hopefully they won't harm her," Peaches replied.

"I doubt that they will but I'm betting they'll piss her off."

"Do you think the Yu Hos will go into the abbey disguised as tourists?" The first glimpse of the coast came into view way off to our right.

"Maybe. They'll probably hide out somewhere. If they don't try to kidnap us first, they'll let me find the tapestry, then nab it. The site shuts its doors at seven p.m., as in an hour's time."

Those banks of dark cloud gathering over the English Channel aligned with my mood.

"Does anybody stay overnight at the mount?"

"There are about sixty inhabitants, which probably include shopkeepers, bed-and-breakfasters, plus a handful of monks and sisters."

"The monastery is still active?"

"So I understand."

Peaches stared at the gathering gloom. "Damn. Why does nature have to be such a set stager? Is that a storm I see blowing in?"

"Yeah, really. We could do without a squall hitting tonight."

"And I don't have a gun on me. That just leaves my knife and our super-phones for protection. Will that work against a bunch of kung-fu bat-shit überwarriors?"

"Peach, stop panicking. Leave that to me, will you?"

She laughed and fell silent again. That left miles and miles of beautiful cloud-scudded farmland, small towns whizzing by, and plenty of traffic that gradually intensified as we neared suppertime and, after dusk, dissipated once again. The rain, too, would intensify and then reduce to a splatter here and there before resuming with more vigor.

Still no one attempted to stop us, ambush us, or do a single disruptive thing. We had a moment when we were forced to slow for roadwork but the slowdown ended up being exactly as advertised, allowing us to continue on minutes later without mishap.

"I think there's a seagull following us," Peaches commented. "I've seen the same black speck hovering overhead for the past ten miles."

"Must be a drone. Since none of our peeps announced anyone tagging us, it must be theirs."

"First sign to Mont-Saint-Michel ahead," Peaches announced. "Where's Evan with our helicopter?"

I glanced down at my phone. "He just messaged me to say that they can't locate one on such short notice but he's still trying. It won't be much help in this weather, anyway."

The rain began whipping the car as the dark descended dense and ominous.

"Drone still overhead. I think," Peaches muttered.

"It's times like these I just want to be at home knitting."

"Right. That's my first thought, too: bad guys, art thieves, a spy drone, and sneaky bastards who want to kidnap me equal 'where's my knitting?'"

"I'll turn you into a convert yet."

We were cruising along a road called Route du Mont-Saint-Michel lined with restaurants and B and Bs interspersed with farmland. Most of the traffic was heading in the opposite direction. We could just see Mont-Saint-Michel puncturing the sky in the rain-whipped horizon ahead.

"So what are we going to do, just drive up and demand to be let in?" Peaches asked.

"Pull over," I said quickly. "There's a restaurant/B-and-B combo on the left. See the sign? Turn there."

Peaches turned into the parking lot while I rang Evan. He didn't answer but had sent a text minutes earlier that I read aloud: *"Just landing. No helicopter. Rupert and I will get there as soon as possible. Nicolina and Seraphina en route now."*

"Now what?" Peaches demanded.

"We eat, of course. We have to assume that the Yu Hos and their crew are waiting for us somewhere in the monastery or in the village itself or maybe up ahead by the causeway. You can believe they'll have that causeway watched. We need to do the unexpected. When's high tide? Maybe we'll wait until dark and then commandeer a boat."

"Shit. I was afraid you were going to say something like that. Need I mention that it's wet as hell out here?"

"Let's order supper and think this through."

I ordered a croque monsieur with plenty of hot coffee on the side while Peaches slurped up a bowl of onion soup with crusty bread. Between bites, I was on my phone trying to locate boats for hire, which turned out to be futile. Only the tour boat variety were listed, which meant a slew of after-hour recorded messages telling me to book online without a single live human attached to a phone. But we wanted a boat now, as in that night, not the next day. I went through five phone numbers before exhausting the available options.

"This isn't going to work," I said after a moment.

"You're damn right it isn't." She had the Google map open on her phone and was switching back and forth reading background accounts. "It's crazy to tackle that estuary by boat at night unless you know the currents and even then. Nobody does it, not even the locals. There's marshland and an estuary leading up to the mount. Once the tide comes in, everything is pretty much obliterated with some of the strongest currents in Europe washing around that rock."

"Okay, but I'm pretty good with boats."

"Did you miss the crazy part? If you're nuts enough to try scrambling across the sand flats at night," she continued, "the chances are high that you'll hit quicksand and be sucked to your death. In other words, take the causeway. Maybe we can ward them off with our phones."

"Just the two of us against we don't know how many 'kung-fu bat-shit überwarriors' as you call them? Where are we at on the tide cycle?"

"The next low tide is at 9:45 p.m."

I stared straight ahead without speaking.

"I hate it when you do that."

"Means I'm thinking. So…we'll leave the car and proceed on foot to the causeway. Maybe we can escape notice if we blend into the shadows. At least that drone will be useless on a rainy dark night. Let's book into this B and B and hopefully convince anyone who may be watching that we've decided to head over in the morning."

"And then what?"

"And then we wait for reinforcements to arrive."

We nabbed one of the few available rooms, a twin-bedded motel room overlooking the mount with an image of the monastery etched into each headboard. An added bonus to our location was the green belt at the back of the motel that ran along the estuary that fed into the mount's bay. It appeared to head directly toward the causeway.

After booking in, we climbed into our black stealth gear, sneakers, and rain hoodies, made certain our phones were completely charged, and waited for word from the team. Nicolina informed us that they'd been held up with the roadwork, which now appeared to be completely blocking access to all routes heading in our direction. I checked the time. "Road work at 8:15?"

She texted moments later: *Ambush!*

"Damn it. The enemy is swooping in!" I said. "We have to get to the mount one way or the other."

"Yeah, let's get out of here. I hate being a *canard assis* even if it means we may be walking into a trap."

We scrambled along the wet grass. To the left, a fringe of tall grasses and stubby trees lined the estuary while, somewhere ahead, the lights of the mount twinkled in the dark like some beacon in the jaws of hell. I had no idea how we were going to get across unseen and kept hoping to borrow a boat in a pinch. But there were no boats of any kind anywhere, which told me plenty in itself. My hopes to cruise up to the mount was abandoned.

"Low tide is when?" I hissed.

"In 32 minutes. We can't walk across that bay. Don't even think about it."

It had stopped raining but the blustering continued with the kind of howling wind that made it nearly impossible to walk at times. The marsh grasses on one side offered a bit of shelter, but by the time we could see the causeway off to our right, the air had suddenly become surreally calm.

"I don't like it when the weather plays games like this," Peaches whispered.

We stood together staring out at the rock with its pinnacles and monumental foundations uplit with spotlights. Mont-Saint-Michel seemed to hang suspended in a dark, slick sweep of receding waters that twisted in channels and pools like a shadowy luminous snake.

"Doesn't look real hospitable or holy, for that matter," Peaches remarked.

"No, it doesn't, and it's totally surrounded by those fortressy walls. The only way to get in is through the main entrance, unless we feel like scaling the defenses."

"Nope. Let's sneak closer to the causeway."

When we arrived at the entrance to the road and crouched down in the grass, I brought up my Google map to a flyover image of the causeway with its roads, walkways, and side parking lots. "It's long," I remarked.

Peaches gazed down over my shoulder. "There's a bank of grass running beside the road. Let's creep along there. We probably won't be seen with our black hoodies."

Which is what we did, trying to keep our heads down as we clambered across the scrubby grass banking the causeway. Ahead, the medieval rock fortress hovered over slick sand, the lights glinting off the occasional rivulet as the water receded.

Everything smelled briny, a scent I usually found comforting after growing up in Nova Scotia, though here it hit me as ominous. I knew we had to be under scrutiny by somebody somehow but couldn't see them, couldn't detect them. I had the horrible sense that the enemy tracked us every step of the way. And my friends had been ambushed! Where were they now? I texted Evan but had yet to receive a response.

Eventually we ran out of grass as the causeway became a bridge.

"Shit." Peaches added a few more pithy expletives. "Let's just take the road."

Only we saw two black-clothed figures looking down at us from overhead at the same time that a mechanical whirring approached us from behind.

I turned. "Run!"

15

"What the hell is that?" Peaches cried.

We were slopping out over the wet sand heading for the mount with something like a mini-tractor chugging up behind us, its headlights raking the way ahead.

"Some kind of ATV! Keep moving! If you stop, you'll sink!"

"How many people driving?" Peaches called.

"Don't know. Maybe two."

Though the vehicle wasn't exactly racing toward us, at the pace we were making it may as well have been.

"We'll never outrun them!" Peaches called.

Every second step, the sand sucked us down, making our progress slow and laborious. Both of us were covered in grit from the knees down.

"Then let's outthink them!" I cried. The wind had picked up again. Maybe she couldn't hear me when I shouted: "Fall!"

I had my phone in one hand when I landed flat on my stomach. Quicksand wasn't nearly as effective for sucking you down when spread across a larger surface and I figured my body qualified.

I kept my gaze fixed on the approaching vehicle while out of my peripheral vision I saw Peaches drop on her stomach, too. The guys driving the ATV were speaking Chinese as they pulled up beside us and cut the engine. Bastards thought they had us. Poor little girls caught in the quagmire.

The moment the first guy crouched down, I rolled over onto my back and phone-tasered him right in the chest while Peaches beamed her laser into the other guy's eyes. One screamed, the other fell unconscious into the sand. I tried to jump up to grab the side of the ATV as one leg began sinking.

"Peach!"

She was scrambling on her hands and knees toward the tractor thing and managed to haul herself up into the driver's seat before reaching down to pull me free and up into the seat behind her. The five causeway guys were yelling and scrambling toward us by now but the engine turned over and the vehicle lurched across the sand.

It wasn't fast but it made steady progress toward the mount on its tank-like traction system.

"So, when we hit a wet patch does it float or something?" Peaches called over her shoulder.

It had begun to rain again, which made it hard to see. "Don't think so. How could it with those track plates under there? Is there a button that indicates a propeller or something?"

"Nope," Peaches called back.

"Then it can't float."

And it couldn't speed, either. What it could do was keep steadily on while the men on foot plodded along behind us, occasionally getting stuck along the way. Two were trying to help their wounded comrades back to shore while the others talked into their phones.

It had begun to rain and blow, wet lashings whipping across the expanse. I checked over my shoulder to discover that our pursuers had stopped pursuing. "They won't try chasing us. They'll change tack and ambush us up ahead instead. The main gates are the only way in."

"Unless you have a vehicle that can zoom you around the outer walls looking for another route."

"Zoom" wasn't quite the right word, but why quibble? It made a lot of sense to try entering the fortress another way. After all, the mount was no longer under attack except by swarms of tourists, which should mean that the battlements were no longer battle-worthy.

"Besides," I said aloud. "They might not have eyes on us on the other side, whereas they definitely will at the entrance."

And so we made our slow progress around to the channel side of the mount, our vehicle bumping and lurching along over the uneven ground, occasionally splashing through tide pools and over sandbars. We kept the headlights off until out of view of the causeway, proceeding along deeper into the shadows of the high defensive walls. Here the lights were less frequent and mostly hidden by the thick rock overhead.

Though just as forbidding and impenetrable-looking, the walls in this section had fewer cosmetic features, like window boxes in the arrow slits. Also, it appeared as if plenty of flotsam and debris had washed up against the foundations over the months, including pieces of wood, plastic jugs, part of an upturned dory and a tangled fishing net. As we puttered around the circumference looking for an access point, our ATV crunched over shale while I flashed my phone light over the walls.

We both saw it at the same time.

"Is that a door?" Peaches asked, pulling the vehicle up to the wall.

I climbed off and strode up to investigate. A thick metal door about four feet high sat in a deep indentation in the wall. "I'm guessing it's an access door so workers can get in and out of the fortress to make repairs. It's certainly modern."

"Any way in?" Peaches asked.

"Not from the outside unless we laser-cut the hinges off."

Peaches studied the foundations. "This level has to be a seawall. See those arrow slits there? They are so low down that this whole level must get flooded during high tide. If we cut our way in, it won't damage it structurally. Let's get to it."

Using the ATV's headlights for illumination, Peaches set her phone's laser feature on high and began to cut into the metal door.

"You'll probably exhaust your battery," I said.

"No choice."

Finally, one last spark-filled sweep around the door and the thing groaned. We stepped back as it toppled off its hinges before we slipped inside a dark, foul-smelling space, me flicking my light along the slippery, seaweed-slick floor while Peaches cast one longing look over her shoulder at the ATV.

She ran back and turned it off, pocketing the keys. "If we can get this over with before high tide, maybe we can drive that thing back to safety."

But right then, all I could think about was getting out through the walls to the other side. We found the outside door almost directly adjacent to the seawall door and this one had a simple lock we could easily disengage. Minutes later, we were gazing out at scrub brush and rock overhead. From this vantage, we couldn't see any lights.

"Must be on the other side. If we climb up that way, we should reach the village," I said.

Which we did but only after scaling boulders and scudding down the other side until we arrived at the roofline of medieval houses stepping upward toward the abbey.

"The Grande Rue," I whispered. Directly below us, wedged between a building and the stone, lay a tiny garden the size of a table. "Should we scramble up the roofs or take the street?"

"Looks like the streets are deserted thanks to the weather. Let's go that way."

We squeezed through the alley between two buildings until we reached the street. Luckily, the restaurants and souvenir shops were all closed, the medieval buildings huddled together over the street in a manner that would have been charming any other time. Keeping close to the walls, we began the long trek upward, the cobbled streets slick in the rain. Peaches kept turning to scan for stalkers while I did the same thing ahead. Nothing.

"They're waiting for us here somewhere," I whispered while checking my phone, "waiting for us to lead them right to the tapestry. Evan and Rupert are still en route from Paris while Nicolina, Seraphina, and Henri remain incommunicado."

"Think they've been captured?"

"Hope not."

The farther we climbed, the more intense the wind blew, lashing the rain across the cobbles with bone-chilling intensity. We were high enough now to see the lights of the village and other towns way across the bay while ahead the road stretched on.

We were about halfway there.

"Has Louis told you where to look yet?"

She was only half joking. "It doesn't work that way," I said. "I have no idea where's it's hidden."

"It would be great to find out soon. Can you send an ESP text or something? Look." Peaches pointed to an almost indistinguishable stone building with a bell tower.

I checked my phone map. "That's the Église Saint-Pierre, the parish church for the community. Let's cut around behind it. There's a shortcut up to the abbey."

"How old is it?" Peaches now walked half-turned, trying to keep watch both ahead and behind. "I keep thinking I see movement on the street back there."

"Fifteenth century." I plodded along, exhausted by now. I longed for someplace warm and dry to rest but nothing on my agenda fit that description. "But its foundations date back to the eleventh century." I paused to turn back long enough to study the little church with its side door while wiping the rain from my eyes. "Is that a statue of Saint Joan I see?"

She was tucked into an alcove at the entrance to the church, so deep in the shadows that we nearly missed her. We ran up to investigate.

"It is!" Peaches exclaimed.

"She must be the patron saint of the parish." I studied the statue for a moment, at the way Joan gazed off into the distance, one hand on her sword, always fixed on her goal. The statue was late seventeenth century, was my guess. I took it as a sign that we were on the right track, whatever that was.

I stepped back, turned, and strode on. "Come, the abbey's just overhead." I meant that literally. A million tons of rock and turreted stone now rose above our heads, lights twinkling in the rain but looking about as welcoming as a dungeon.

Peaches clutched my arm and pointed behind us. I froze, catching a flash of movement at the end of the lane leading to the Grande Rue. One, no, two figures followed, all dressed in long black slickers, or maybe those were robes? One paused to look around in all directions, missing us completely as we stood still as rock dressed in our own shadow gear, our phones shoved into our pockets.

"Shit!' Peaches hissed as they passed. "That has to be them, unless the monks are on patrol."

"The real monks are probably safe in their beds by now. Let's keep going."

Something tugged away at my spine, one minute feeling like a pulse of electricity, the next a tingling sensation. "We're looking for a statue," I whispered as we trudged along.

"A statue?"

"Something raised from the ground, something that could enclose a canister or a roll of something, maybe five or six feet long."

She turned back to stare at me, eyes wide. "Are you having one of those bolts of enlightenment or something? Did Saint Joan or Father Louis talk to you?"

"Neither. It doesn't work that way, either."

"What do you mean 'it doesn't work that way'? Creepy skulls talk to you in death pits, don't they?"

"That was a dream. Oh, look. More stairs."

"Oh, goody."

And we climbed and climbed until we reached a junction between two sets, one leading up, the other down.

"This way," I said, heading down the dimly lit stairway. The kung fu monks would be coming up the main street. They'd expect us to head directly for the abbey, which we couldn't afford to do. Nothing so obvious.

Seconds later, we were slipping against the wall leading to what I guessed were the lodgings and main halls, and soon enough, a door appeared—tall, imposing, and very locked. We had the electronic mechanism disengaged within minutes, slipping into a long stone hall lit with lowlights fixed on the stone.

Coats hanging on pegs and a filled umbrella stand with a puddle drying at its base indicated that the area was probably used for offices and lodgings. We had no idea which way to head next but our best guess was to head up, always up.

Another set of medieval stairs offered us a narrow curving climb, the stair-well so steeped in darkness that we half expected to see a living shadow blocking our path at any moment. When we finally reached the top, we stood there on legs trembling with fatigue, waiting for our hearts to stop banging. Another thick arched door lay ahead. Peaches opened it slowly so we could peer out into a broad stone hall with arches and pillars lining its long expanse.

"They had to build these huge vaulted ceilings to support the weight above," Peaches whispered. "All clear." Indicating for me to follow her, she crept out, our footsteps nearly soundless against the ancient stone.

The hall was devoid of decorations of any kind, just arches and broad-branching medieval stone. Stairs off to the side probably led down to the crypts and dungeons, but at that point, I still believed that any statues that existed would probably lay up, not down, so we continued on our way looking for another stairway. It was cold in there, cold with the kind of damp freeze that chilled you to the bone.

The next stairwell up led us to the abbey. We paused inside the magnifi-cent structure, awed by the enormity of it all: by the looming arched windows pushing bleary light into the expanse, by the sound of rain whipping against the glass, and the sense of vast emptiness pervading all.

"I'm sure when the candles are lit, it's beautiful, but right now—" Peaches began.

"Shh!"

I took her by the arm and tugged her inside an arched alcove where we huddled in the dark listening. Something like a scuffling sound was coming from the far end of the abbey. The rustling was followed by a sharp cry and then total silence. We waited breathlessly. Somebody began raking a light down the length of the abbey floor, sweeping it back and forth as if looking for something—us, I guessed.

We remained still until the light retracted and we heard a door click shut.

Peaches expelled her breath while I pulled out my phone and began searching for a map of the abbey's interior, scrolling by frame after frame until I hit one especially designed to guide the handful of lucky people who occasionally lodged there overnight. Pinching the screen open, I stared at the labels of every room, chapel, and hall. When I found it, my gasp was audible.

Peaches nudged me. Taking the phone from my hand, she pinched the screen open further. "Notre-Dame-Sous-Terre?" she whispered. "Our Lady of the Underworld? Why doesn't that fill my heart with joy?"

"It's the earliest part of the abbey," I whispered back, "Nothing left but one wall of the original chapel and that statue of Black Madonna."

"Black Madonna? There are black Madonnas?"

"Lots in France, yes. The most famous one is in Chartres. They represent the realm of the dead and actually hail back to pre-Christian times. When this site was called Mount-Tombe, it was a Gallic burial site and the black goddess reigned over the underworld. Our earliest ancestors worshipped the sacred feminine as protector and the provider of life after death. The power of the feminine is manifest in the Virgin Mary and Madonna figures today. Humans weren't always so patriarchal."

"I can't stand it when you go on and on like that. The short story is that black goddesses have ruled from the dawn of time! What did I tell you?"

"Let's go. The chapel's directly below and the entrance at the other end."

We stood up on our stiffened legs to silently cross toward the far side where we'd heard the noise earlier. By now, my heart was racing again, jolted to the quick by my conviction that I'd found the hiding place for the seventh tapestry, that I'd tugged at that thread until the unicorn of truth fell out into my proverbial hands.

But racing hearts and a fixed focus can make one careless.

The *Sortie* sign beamed red at the far end. I fixed on it as if that beacon of modernity was some kind of pilot light leading me on. Peaches was directly behind me.

"Look out!" I heard her cry just seconds before I tripped over the body and fell hard on the floor face-first.

16

The breath was knocked out of me. I lay dazed, staring out at my phone, which had skidded across the floor. Peaches was beside me in an instant, rolling me over. "You okay?"

"Okay."

"Don't know if that poor guy is."

I forced the air back into my lungs as she shone her phone light over the body I'd tripped over.

"He's alive." She crouched beside him and felt his pulse. "Just knocked out. Blow to the head, by the looks of things."

I crawled toward the man—middle-aged, bald, dressed in nothing but his white boxers and undershirt. "I think he may be a monk. Bastards stripped him and took his robe. That must have been the sound we heard."

Peaches sent a quick message to the team saying that the enemy was inside the abbey knocking out monks and stealing their habits. "Why isn't anybody answering us? I've sent messages to everyone and no one responds. Think he'll be okay here until help comes?"

"I hope so." I retrieved my phone and beckoned her to follow.

We had to leave him, as much as I hated to. Using the map, we took an exit in the far corner and began descending another twisted ancient stairway. Unlit, the way was steep, slippery, and appeared to be penetrating deep into the heart of the rock itself. Periodic new brick and mortar patches indicated recent repairs but most of what surrounded us was ancient to the core.

The deeper we descended, the danker and darker it became. My only comfort was in the conviction that our monk-garbed enemies were off somewhere way overhead goose-chasing on another track, leaving us to the underworld.

At the bottom of the stairway, we followed the hall into the arched doorway of a little chapel where we stopped and ran our lights across the stone. The statue was tucked into an alcove. "This part dates from the first millennium."

"Okay," Peaches whispered, staring at the wooden statue of the Black Madonna. "I feel like I should genuflect, curtsey or something. It's about time I found a Madonna that looks like me."

The Madonna's and baby Jesus's gowns were painted in gold, the figures tucked into an arch with a faded blue star-flecked sky above. The statue was lovely if a bit strange in her rough-hewn sanctuary.

"Too recent," I said, my disappointment so heavy I thought it would drag me down to the cold floor.

"Recent how?" Peaches whispered.

"Looks to be nineteenth century. We need something much older." I flicked to the map on my phone again and continued reading the article accompanying the map. "It says that one Black Madonna was destroyed by the revolutionaries but before then there was another, much older Madonna, which now resides in the crypt of the Twenty-three Candles, wherever that is. We've got to find that."

"Which way?"

I checked the map again. "Toward the dungeons."

"Fabulous."

But the route to the dungeons looked like the rest of this warren of ancient rock-carved crypts. In the end, we stumbled upon it by accident. Our lights flashed across another very old vaulted ceiling with more areas of old brick mingled by cement.

"There." I shone my light over the stone altar before landing on the plaster statue of a crowned Madonna perched on a shelf on one side.

"But she's white," Peaches protested.

"Sorry, but she's also ancient. Show some respect. Typical of the time, she's dressed like a queen." I came as close to the statue as I could considering that a spiked fence separated the viewer from the figure, and ran my phone scanner over the faded paint of her once-red gown. "Definitely thirteenth century or older. It would have been here in Father Louis's day and she's hollow, too." Leaning forward, I studied the Madonna's missing hand, the baby Jesus with his absent head. "Can you get me up there?"

"Up where?"

"Up to that shelf so I can get to her."

"What are you seeing?" Peaches asked as she looked around to rig up a stand somehow.

"See Jesus's neck? It has a hole right down the center where the head would have been attached to a rod of some kind. These medieval plasters were sometimes cast in hollow molds with the hands and heads fixed by metal rods. See the faint horizontal line below the plaster on the Madonna's neck? I'm thinking that if we take her head off, we'll find a hollow core with something hidden inside."

"Damn you're good! Sometimes." Peaches darted behind a stone altar, emerging seconds later carrying a wooden step. "This might not be perfect but it will help us to climb over the grille and hoist you up to the statue."

Which we did.

"Now you climb onto my shoulders so I can lift you," she suggested.

That worked. In moments, I was riding Peaches, eye-to-eye with the Madonna. "Hold still. I'm going to try to screw her head off."

"And you say that *I* should show some respect. What if she breaks?"

"She's made of sterner stuff than that."

But the neck barely moved. I tried again, pouring every inch of strength into my arms as I gently but firmly twisted to the right. The head finally scraped an inch or two, leaving the plaster eyes gazing calmly off to the side. Taking a deep breath, I turned steadily until the head lifted in my hands. "Ah, she's heavy. Quickly. Put her down."

Once the Madonna's head rested on the ground, I returned to my Peaches perch and stared. "Do you see what I see?" I whispered.

"Something sticking out?"

"Leather, I think." Leaning over, I lifted the object straight up, a stiff, mold-scummed narrow brown carrier that Peaches helped me to raise out of the hollow core and lower to the ground.

"We found it!" I exclaimed. I could hardly believe it while, at the same time, my heart filled with admiration for Father Louis. Of course, he could never have imagined that even the sacred statue of the Madonna might have fallen prey to the marauding revolutionaries. He must have thought such statues sacrosanct. But then, he would have believed that the angels, saints, and Joan herself would have protected the treasure. And maybe he would have been right, based on his beliefs.

"Snap to, Phoebe! Let's put the lady's head back and get the hell out of here."

The moment we had made the Madonna whole again and were staring down at the moldy canister on the floor, voices sounded far overhead.

"Is it my imagination or are they getting closer?"

"Shit. They're like bloodhounds," Peaches whispered. "They're coming."

"We need to find a way to carry this thing." It was long, heavy, and awkward. "Maybe if I sling it over my shoulders? I think these disintegrating strips were once straps." I lifted it up carefully but it was surprisingly heavy.

Peaches had gone to the door to listen but was back in a minute nudging me aside. "I've got this."

In seconds she had the carrier over one shoulder, fixed in place partly by her belt and partly by one of the rotting straps, the top end of the long canister sticking out of her coat up into her rain hood. Our phone lights made a monstrous silhouette of her profile but she could move and the treasure was protected from the elements—all that mattered. That and avoiding the Tengfeng gang.

"Put your light on night-vision mode," Peaches whispered.

"There's a night-vision mode?"

She plucked my phone out of my hand with an irritated sigh and tapped the screen. "You need to study Evan's updates for once," she hissed, passing it back.

"I've been too busy studying Evan." And I craved like anything to have his tall protective presence by our side right then, not that he could do anything differently. Escape was our only plan. How was another matter.

The strange blue night-vision light turned the ancient corridors into something even more underworld-like as we slipped farther away from the sound of voices. They had to be on this level now and, with luck, had not yet detected our presence, let alone our success. Meanwhile, we had no idea where we were heading except for as far away from those voices as we could get.

I kept a rough image of the map imprinted on my brain and knew that many stairways led from the crypts and dungeons onto various levels. All we needed to do was find one and escape the monastery, descend to the village, find the outer wall that we had entered, and retrieve the ATV to make our way across the possibly tide-flooded bay. In other words, we needed a new plan and fast.

I could only pray that the rest of the team were somewhere on the mount by now because the scope of what lay ahead seemed as monumental as the rock itself. A few Interpol agents would be helpful, too. We'd had no time to check our messages in the past half hour. Where was everybody?

We found a stairway maybe ten minutes later.

"Praise the Black Madonna!" Peaches whispered as we crammed into the narrow passage and up the steep stairs. "And the saints and angels, too! Is there anybody else we should add?"

"Is that the Baptist in you talking?" I whispered.

"Yeah, she arouses at times like this. I could almost pray right now."

Now there was shouting behind us, the sound echoing against the stone. Meanwhile, the stairway we pushed through became so narrow Peaches had to stoop in order to climb without scraping the top of the canister against the scummy ceiling.

What the condition of the tapestry might be after centuries rolled inside that thing was another matter. I only knew that under the care of the right conservator—Ella, for instance—the final unicorn tapestry could be brought back to life and take its place in the history of France at last.

But the way was long and steep for humanity, clambering around in the dark as we so often do, weary, half-blind as we often are, sometimes with nothing leading us forward but the light of our faith, if we were lucky enough to believe in something.

"Where the hell does this thing go—up to the steeple?"

"Keep moving," I panted.

We arrived at a door crammed into a landing so small it was impossible to stand upright.

"Look." I shone the light on an ancient bolt system where the rusty arm had been thrown back. "This has just been opened recently, maybe for the first time in a long time."

"And?"

Someone called out way down in the darkness behind us.

"And let's go!"

As I shoved the door open, a gust of wind wrenched it from my hand to send it banging against the stone wall, reverberating right down to the bowels of the mount. Damn!

"They must have heard that! Run!"

The howling wind swallowed Peaches's cry as we pushed out onto what seemed to be vortex of rain and wind. Around us, nothing but swirling rain-whipped mist with zero visibility. Then for an instant, the tempest abated long enough to see lights far away to the left while, above, an uplit golden archangel Michael flew through the storm.

Peaches saw him, too. "Sometimes I believe in angels."

"Angels are real, they just don't all look like him! We're on the upper terrace," I gasped. "This way!"

Only that way meant plunging headlong and head down into the wind, which also meant that we had no idea what or who we were running into.

It was like ramming into a moving wall when it happened. My first thought was that I had hit a mass of solidified darkness.

* * *

EVERYTHING FLEW BY QUICKLY yet seemed to be happening in slow motion. Faces flashing in my phone light, me trying to tap open the taser app while somebody tackled me from behind, the phone slipping from my wet fingers, something black covering my face. Then Peaches's cry was cut off in mid-curse.

I was bundled up in something like a black tarpaulin, bound at the ankles and hands before being half dragged with my feet scraping against the pavers. All I could think of was *Did they hurt Peaches? They have the tapestry!*

Minutes felt like hours as my feet bumped and bumped up over steps, the bastard dragging me by the shoulders not caring how hard or where or he clutched my flesh. The rain splattered on my plastic wrapping and my panting used up all available oxygen inside my casing. Panic hit. Maybe they'd toss our bodies over the wall to be smashed against the rocks below! Such an easy way to dispose of two women on a hellish night like this and what a stupid end to what I had hoped to be a long and interesting life.

Then suddenly the rain and wind stopped as if somebody had flipped a switch. The splattering on the plastic ended abruptly. Now the ground beneath my feet felt smooth enough for me to realize I was being dragged indoors. I was gasping for breath by then. Dizzy, too. The men around me were speaking Chinese, maybe accompanied by one French speaker. Four men, maybe five.

Moments later, I was dropped onto the floor, falling hard on my back. A knife slit the covering over my face to let in a crack of bright electric light and air, blessed air. Gasping, I blinked up into the faces of two masked men.

Somebody behind me gave orders in Chinese. I was dragged over, still in my cocoon, and propped up against a wall. Now I could see Peaches lying soaked and still as death on the tiles where she'd been dropped, her back toward me.

"Peaches!" I cried. "What have you done to her?" And then my gaze landed on the three gagged and bound men seated at the table in front of me, stripped but for their undies—the real monks. Only one was conscious. The others sat with heads lolling. The single alert monk's eyes found mine as if to give me strength. I tried to smile but couldn't pull it off.

"Do not fear, Mademoiselle McCabe," said a voice to my right. "Your friend lives still but she will die unless you do as I say."

I looked over at the man standing in a monk's robe, the fabric bunched around his waist and secured by a rope sash. His round pleasant face was smiling benignly at me as he stood with his hands tucked into his sleeves. A second non-monk stood over Peaches holding a knife and there were ten others standing around in black, ill-fitting robes. We were in a long table-filled room, a refectory, I realized.

"You must be Tengfeng Yu Ho," I managed.

He bowed. "And you are Phoebe McCabe. I am most honored. You are most well-known as locator of lost treasure."

"Why don't I feel honored after being hijacked and encased like a sausage? What are you going to do with us and—" I scanned the room, my gaze landing on the canister on a nearby table "—and with the tapestry? If you open it now in this damp, it may disintegrate on the spot." I doubted that would happen quite like that but it would certainly be damaged.

"The tapestry, yes," said Tengfeng, taking a step forward. "At all costs, I protect tapestry. Buyer in China waits with great anticipation as do team of experts when back in Beijing. But you real treasure."

Shit. What did that mean?

Peaches moaned on the floor. The man with the knife gave her a viscous kick.

"Stop that, you monster!" I tried to get at him but only thrashed inside my casing helplessly. "What are you going to do with us, I said. Where is Lilly, the other agents you hijacked, your favorite niece, Mimi? Surely you don't expect to get away with kidnapping a bunch of monks and stealing a French trea-sure? Interpol are on their way, if they're not on the mount already, and you'll never make it out of the country."

For that, I received a full-beam smile. "Dear honored one, look around. No Interpol here. None on island. Island blocked off. Causeway open to shuttles in daytime only. Monks imprisoned in rooms, phones confiscated, your friends all captive, and we have escape plan. You make error fighting battle without army. Very poor planning. This disappoints me but in other ways you very fine adversary."

Oh, my God, did that mean he had Evan, too—everybody? Damn, but he was a brilliant strategist. He'd had the details all worked out in advance. "You knew the tapestry was hidden on the mount all along, didn't you?"

He bowed. "When you find cartoon, we know. Not before. I send men here immediately and we infiltrate. As for weather, this luck. Luck follows Lucky Ho Export Company." And the bastard laughed.

"Who betrayed us or did you have us under surveillance the whole time?"

"No time for questions now. All answered later."

"When's later?" I cried. "You can't stay here but how do you plan to escape since Mont-Saint-Michel is closed off?"

"Ah," Tengfeng began, still smiling. "Most easy. Causeway open for emergency only. Wounded monks emergency. Ambulance waits below."

I had to keep him talking. "So I led you right to it, is that it?"

Another bow. "You are very good finder. You make good moves—stealing ATV very good move. You almost succeed but we have many bodies, you too few. Now you help with rest of plan."

"I will not help you!" Pure rage warred in me now. "Never! And I'm not getting in that ambulance!"

The monk sent me a pleading look. Maybe he'd seen enough of brutality in the past two days to try warning me but I wasn't in the listening mood. I was in the ranting mood.

"You dollar-driven murderous bat-scum creepos! I'm not going to help you steal a French treasure or let you get away with this travesty! I'm going to watch you rot in jail, that's what I'm going to do! Do you hear me?"

Tengfeng nodded and the man with the knife and three of his comrades stepped forward.

"If you do not do as I say, your friends die," Tengfeng said. "If you do not believe, I toss this one over walls first. You watch."

I froze as the men lifted Peaches up by the arms. Still out cold, her limbs flopped about. Don't ask me how I knew but he meant it.

"Okay, okay! Stop! I'll do what you want. Just don't hurt her, just don't hurt anybody else," I sobbed. "But what more do you want of me since you already have the tapestry?"

"You help me leave country," Tengfeng said. "And you will come with me to China."

My mouth opened ready to protest but before I could say a word Tengfeng shoved his phone in my face. It was open on a live feed of Rupert, Nicolina, and Seraphina seated, gagged, and blindfolded.

17

a deviously simple plan. Peaches and I would be removed from the mount on stretchers carried by the supposed monks. Because they remained hidden under hoods, no one would notice anything strange about them or think twice that the patients they shielded from the driving rain were bound. Furthermore, unless an onlooker chose to brave the elements long enough to investigate more closely, the fact that one wounded monk had curly red hair and her mouth sealed shut with duct tape would go unnoted. Ditto the long cylinder that had been strapped to her side like a splint.

The way down was hellish. My carriers made no effort to ease up on the bumping and jostling as they clambered down stairway after stairway. At least the bastards were sure-footed enough not to trip, but inside my plastic wrapping I seethed and shivered. At least my face was exposed to the air.

The sight of Rupert, Seraphina, and Nicolina bound and gagged with a masked man standing over them had shocked me to the core. Our team were not easily conquered and were a match for any force. The wall behind them could be anywhere but I had the sneaking suspicion they were photographed in a basement. Or a dungeon. I needed to speak to Evan, who as far as I knew remained free. But he had been traveling with Rupert so how did that happen? At least no one had mentioned him and it was my hope the Tengfeng gang didn't even know of his existence.

Our phones lay on the terrace in the rain and, without them, we were unarmed and helpless. Where had we gone wrong? Did we fail to recognize the enormity of our enemy in time? Did the mount itself conspire against us through sheer geography? And who the hell was the mole?

At last we arrived at the bottom where red flashing lights indicated the ambulance. Not until I was being lifted into one did I notice that there were actually two. Tengfeng and three other non-monks climbed into one vehicle with me while four others guarded Peaches in the other. I thought I glimpsed police officers around the vehicles but I couldn't be sure. I certainly heard French voices before the doors slammed shut and we pealed away, sirens blaring.

Obviously they had commandeered real ambulances but were the genuine first responders lying in a ditch somewhere? And did the escape plan include a hospital? The ambulances had to go somewhere.

But I had other concerns just then. I was allergic to many things including the duct tape over my mouth. The adhesive taping my lips together was causing my skin to swell. Visions of anaphylaxis shock danced in my head. I tried to catch someone's attention but my stony-faced companions sat staring straight ahead looking like soldiers out of Emperor Qin Shi Huang's terracotta army. My moaning was overridden by that damn siren and no one was paying attention to me, anyway. Death by duct tape was not how I wanted it to end.

Then, without warning, Tengfeng leaned over and whipped the tape from my lips while snapping instructions at his men. It hurt like hell but I was too busy gasping to care. I could see alarm in his face, hear blame in his tone. He snapped a question at his men. I guessed the meaning: *Who used such tape? Idiots!*

Soon, an icepack was pressed over my mouth—not much help since I was gasping for breath by then. Tengfeng had my casings cut and my hands released, helping me to sit up so I could breathe better. Hunching over, I heaved air into my lungs while pressing the pack to my puffy lips. I was dizzy, sick, and unable to focus.

"Most sorry. Please forgive," he said. I was too muddled to speak but still relieved to know that he had a vested interest in keeping me alive, at least for the short term. I could only hope that the same applied to the others.

Wherever we were heading took hours to get there. I dozed off and on, and listened to Tengfeng talking on his phone from what seemed like some faraway place. There definitely was somebody French driving the ambulance. He spoke to Tengfeng from the front seat but I couldn't catch the words.

When the doors finally flew open and a waft of fresh air entered the van, I was shocked to find it already dawn. The rain had stopped and a pale silver light was breaking through the clouds.

They removed me from the vehicle and carried the tapestry as carefully as though it was a wounded queen. I, on the other hand, was steered along on my own two feet, though my hands were now bound and my arms pinioned. A tall white structure loomed, very old, vaguely familiar. The blue turrets gave it away first. We were at the back of the Château Saint Chappelles. I expected maybe an airport or a shipping pier, not this. What was going on?

Ahead, Peaches was being carried on the stretcher, still unconscious.

"Peaches!" I urged my keepers forward so I could catch up but they held me back and I could barely stand up straight, anyway. "What have you done to her?" I demanded. "Head injuries are serious. She needs a doctor!"

Behind me Tengfeng laughed. "Proceed. We talk later." He added something in Chinese.

Finally, one of my keepers grew so annoyed by my stumbling that he threw me over his shoulder like a sack of potatoes. I was carried up to some part of the château I didn't recognize, at least not while hanging upside down, and tossed onto a bed in a dark room. By then, I was so dizzy that all I could do was lie bound until I blacked out.

I had no idea how long I remained in that state but I was vaguely aware of people entering and exiting the room, of being propped up to drink water, of being forced to swallow pills.

Hours later, I awoke inside a little room and sat on the edge of the bed trying to muster my brain cells. My hands were free and a night-light glowed in what had to be a bathroom ahead. Soon I was staring shocked at my image in a mirror. The ravages of my duct tape attack still burned an inflamed streak across my mouth and cheeks. Though the swelling had subsided, the whole event had left me weak.

Back in the bedroom, I drew back the curtains of a small window and gazed down at a cluster of roofs. I was way up in some part of the château I'd never been, captive in what may have once been a servant's quarters. It was still night. No, wait—it was night again. Somehow, I had slept away a full day. Shit.

My heart was racing. Where was everybody? What about Peaches, Rupert, and the others? Panic gripped me as I ran for the door. I was shocked to find that it opened easily in my hand but an armed guard stood waiting outside.

The man restrained me with one arm while speaking into his phone. After a moment, he nodded and smiled—smiled! Soon, he was ushering me down the stairs as carefully and graciously as if I was his old auntie. He'd caution me in Chinese any time we maneuvered some obstruction, did not allow me to descend steep stairways without his hand on my arm. I couldn't understand a word he said and yet I did. He was one of the good guys.

"What's your name?" I asked him.

"Hai," he said.

"I'm Phoebe."

He nodded and smiled.

"Why are you working for this murderous creep?"

His grasp of English didn't extend that far, and before I could launch a conversion campaign with hand signals, we had arrived in the main part of the château. I was passed over to one of the stony-faced minions and steered across the great hall by a much rougher hand.

Tengfeng stepped across the expanse to greet me, today dressed in a traditional Chinese Mandarin red silk jacket that looked to me to be very old and simply gorgeous. It belonged in a museum, in other words.

"Mademoiselle, I most happy to see you well. Very concerned."

"Seriously?" I could have said so much worse but my inner voice was screaming at me to keep quiet. I needed to assess what was going on here, formulate a plan. And eat.

"So, this is the famous Phoebe McCabe," said someone behind him.

A small figure dressed in another silk Mandarin-style jacket, this one sunflower yellow and richly embroidered in dragons and clouds, stepped toward me. In my weakened state, it was like being approached by a flock of butterflies, the rich fabric glowing in the subdued lamplight.

Mimi was nothing like her sister, it was true, but she was no less attractive. Round face, pale porcelain skin beneath a thick fringe of glossy black hair, and a sweet almost child-like expression that belied the hard glint in her eyes.

"So you're the miraculous locator of treasure regardless of the century or origin or even the cultural identity of the piece pursued." She spoke in French, stepping past her uncle to better study me.

"And you're the evil twin," I remarked.

That made her laugh. "And you are a speaker in stereotypes."

"If the shoe fits..."

"I think I may like you. We will make a good team. Why are your lips swollen with that red mark across your cheeks?"

We will make a good team? "Your uncle's henchmen were a little too slap-happy with the duct tape and I'm allergic."

"Careless. When you join us, I promise much better treatment." She nodded, her expression suddenly serious. I had no doubt that despite her pleasant countenance, the woman meant business.

I opened my mouth to protest but thought better of it.

"Mimi," her uncle interrupted. "Ship leaves in morning. Must hurry."

They planned to escape by ship?

She nodded to the man gripping my arm and once again I was propelled forward, Mimi and Tengfeng leading the way.

"Where's Lilly?" I asked, "And your other uncle? And my friends—what have you done with them?"

Mimi shot one hand up to silence me.

Into the dining room we went. I was shoved into a chair before a plate of crackers and cheese. Natalie was there placing a jug on the table but kept her head averted.

"Natalie, are you all right? What have they done to you?" I asked, reaching for the water and drinking deeply. Then it occurred to me that she might be the mole so I added: "Or should I say: 'What have you done to us?'"

That seemed to startle her into shooting me a quick, pained look. Dark circles under her eyes, no makeup, hair barely combed. If possible, she looked worse than I did.

"Natalie?" I asked, shocked.

"Leave," Tengfeng ordered, waving her away. "And make noodles for dinner tonight."

"We don't have noodles," she whispered.

"Then make rice."

Natalie darted from the room after which I turned to Tengfeng. "Have you made her your domestic slave, is that it?"

That annoyed him. "Eat," he commanded. "More later." The bonhomie had evaporated leaving in its place the little general with his eye on the prize. "Now I speak, you listen."

Mimi sat back with her hands folded on the table, a little smile on her lips. "And listen carefully," she advised.

Picking up a cracker, I popped it into my mouth and chewed. I needed desperately to fuel my body for whatever lay ahead.

"Tomorrow morning, we leave Paris for China. You and tapestry will accompany. I have arranged details—visa, everything. You work with Lucky Ho Export Company in Beijing to help find certain treasures. You most honored employee. Very well rewarded."

I gaped. Gone went any attempt to control my tongue. "You're joking? How do you expect me to do that—under perpetual gunpoint?"

"You do willingly," Tengfeng said with a nod, frowning at his plate. "Or I kill friends. I keep hostage."

I dropped the other half of my cracker. "You plan on holding my friends hostage indefinitely, trained agents who have already been reported missing by Interpol? How will you manage that?"

He pulled out his phone and scrolled to a photo of a huge container ship. "This way. Friends go to ship. Many containers made into many rooms."

"Converted cargo containers," Mimi clarified. "We've had them made into modified holding tanks with toilets and beds where we can keep people for a long crossing—feed them, keep them isolated, hold them prisoner. We've used them before for transporting sensitive goods to China. It works beautifully. You'd be surprised how little scrutiny a human being gets inside one of those things. Customs look for contraband, not people. China and Europe exchange stuff all the time. Your friends will be drugged and boarded in crates bound for China—this time a load of French clothing headed for the high-end shops in Shanghai. Very smooth sailing." She laughed at her little joke.

I was dumbstruck. "You've done something similar before? What, like human trafficking?"

"Not exactly," Mimi told me while Tengfeng gnawed at a biscuit. One of his men had just delivered him a plate of sliced meat. "No one is waiting for them on the other end. If you board that plane tomorrow morning willingly— you'll be disguised and provided with a false passport—your friends will be guaranteed the best treatment on the ship. Good food, wine even. Maybe books. As long as you work willingly, they live in relative comfort. The moment you get out of line, the treatment worsens. We will provide a live feed for you to watch. Oh, and if you refuse, you will be the one transported by container ship, only your friends will be dead."

Hell, they were monsters. My mind raced ahead to the only possible endgame: there's no way any of us would ever get out of this alive. How could we? They'd have to dispose of us eventually.

"I don't believe you," I whispered.

Mimi grimaced. She spoke into her phone before laying it facedown on the table and staring at me hard. Not a crack of a smile, not a hint of the earlier merriment. Cold and ruthless, this one.

Seconds later, the door flew open and in came Lilly. I jumped to my feet before being shoved back down again.

"Sit, sister." Mimi pointed to the seat beside her across from mine.

Lilly sat. She looked nothing like the glamorous, confident woman I had first met in Paris but somebody much smaller, cowed, almost colorless.

"Lilly?" I whispered.

She straightened her shoulders, her reddened eyes meeting mine. "Do as they say."

"Be their slave? Be blackmailed into submission?"

"Better to live than to die."

I stared at her in horror. "Lilly, are you the mole? But why? Is giving up your career worth the price of the tapestry?"

"Not the tapestry," Tengfeng said, looking up. "You. You biggest prize. Tapestry bonus."

"All this was just to trap me?" I asked, stunned.

"First, I test. You pass test." He cast me a charming smile. "Now you make us much money."

Struggling to get my mind around this, I couldn't speak at first. Lilly kept staring. I couldn't have been as bad a gauge of character as that. I knew she had been telling the truth back at the beginning of this nightmare. Yes, she was obviously being coerced now but there was more afoot here than sibling rivalry. She was trying to tell me something.

"Lilly?" I asked again.

"Tell her, sister," Mimi ordered.

"I have been shown the importance of one's family and cultural identity," she said, her voice devoid of emotion. "I have been misled by the glitz and glamor of Western life, corrupted by your values. Do as they say."

Like hell.

"Show her what will happen if she does not, sister dearest," Mimi said. "Take her upstairs and to see the others."

Lilly stood. I stood, too, following her out the door while being helpfully shoved along by one of the minions.

"Where's Henri?" I asked her once we were crossing the grand hall.

Lilly remained silent. Either she refused to speak or she wasn't permitted. Either way, I felt as though she was playing a role, the amazing actress that she was, and if Mimi and Tengfeng thought they had her reined in, they didn't know her.

We climbed the main staircase toward the bedrooms and with every step I grew more terrified of what I was about to see. We arrived first at what had been Peaches's room and I stood there inside the door blinking into the gloom. One man turned on the bed lamp so I could see the woman lying there, eyes closed, caked blood on her temple.

"Peaches!" I tried to run to the bed but the other guy restrained me. "Lilly, tell them to let me see her," I cried.

Lilly, who waited just outside the door, stepped in and addressed the men in Chinese.

"They say that was not their instructions but I told them that you must be permitted to see how bad she is because that's what my uncle wants."

One of the guards jerked his head at me and I was allowed to slowly approach the bed. Peaches was lying on her back, her hands and feet bound, breathing through her mouth. At a glance, I also took in the way the empty water glass lined up with the bud vase on the side table, fallen rose petals neatly piled in the center in the triangular arrangement. A jolt of pure joy shot through me. I knew my friend's signature when I saw it: she was much better than she appeared.

"You bastards are going to just let her die?" I cried.

Lilly translated and then I was pushed from the room. Before the door shut, I looked back and saw Peaches lift a finger of her bound hands. Best damn sight I'd had in hours.

We proceeded along the balcony to the end room where another guard stood. Lilly turned to me. "He tried to escape. They warned him but he wouldn't listen. See for yourself."

I forced my feet to move, and found myself standing in the bedroom, a spacious master suite with a huge canopy bed. A man lay on the bed.

"Eduard?" Stepping up, I reached for his wrist, relieved to find a faint pulse. "He's barely breathing! What did they do to him?"

"Uncle Tengfeng had him beaten. I doubt he will last the night unless he gets a doctor, which they won't do."

"What about Rupert, Nicolina, and Seraphina?" I demanded.

"In the dungeons. Uncle Tengfeng keeps them alive because they are useful to him against you. Peaches will end up there, too, if she survives."

"My, God, Lilly. They're animals! How many are there?"

She placed a finger to her lips before whispering: "I counted twenty-five."

And that probably didn't include the ones at the mount. "What about the man with Rupert?"

"I know nothing of that. Rupert was found in the grass outside, I understand."

"We have to escape!"

She was only talking to me now because the guards remained outside out of earshot. "Unless you want everyone to be killed, you'll do as they say."

"Where's René?"

"He was gone by the time they brought me here."

"And your uncle Henri?"

157

But one of the minions poked his head in and barked something in Chinese. We were corralled back down the stairs to the far end of the main hall toward the older part of the château. I sensed where we were heading, to the dungeons. True enough, after several more flights of steep stone stairs partially lit by a few modern spotlights, we arrived at a door guarded by two men.

"The DuBoises planned to open the dungeons to the public eventually," Lilly said.

"Silence!" one man commanded. Smart. The prisoners were guarded by men who could speak their language. Their every word would be monitored. And these guards were big-muscled, mean-looking, and carried rifles. *Shit.* "You must not approach prisoners," the man ordered. "You remain in doorway."

We were escorted through the door, me bracing myself for the worst. I could never have prepared myself enough. Rupert slumped unmoving against a wall, eyes swollen closed, his hands and feet bound; Nicolina, a bruise blackening one cheek, sat as if frozen with her hands bound in her lap while Seraphina lay sprawled facedown on the floor.

"Nicolina!" I couldn't suppress my wail of pain and outrage. "What have they done to you?"

Of course she didn't speak—she was gagged—but the eyes that met mine were filled with the kind of pained, resolute endurance I knew so well. Warrior first, countess second. She would not be defeated, only waylaid. As for Seraphina, I could only imagine that she had attempted something of the equal parts brave and foolish nature only to pay the price. Clearly she had been knocked out.

"I understand that they are granted one bathroom break a day and two small meals," Lilly whispered. "The guard goes in with the women and watches. That's when Seraphina flipped out."

I bit down on my lip to keep from screaming.

The guard's phone rang. He answered, listened for a minute, and passed the phone to me.

"Phoebe?" It was Mimi. "If you agree to our terms, we will immediately remove your friends from the dungeons and put them upstairs in more comfortable conditions with better food and en suite bathrooms. We will tend to the old guy, who seems to have a very weak constitution, and bandage the head of the short snippy one. Medical care will be provided before they board the cruise to China tomorrow morning. If medications are required, they will receive a good supply."

I didn't ask what would happen if I didn't cooperate and she didn't remind me. By then it was perfectly clear. "I'll do what you want," I told her.

"Of course you will," she said.

I shoved the phone back to the guard. Again, he listened for a moment before turning to me and bowing.

"You will be permitted time to visit them later in their new quarters, Mademoiselle Phoebe. Now you are asked to return upstairs to meet special guest."

Special guest? I turned to Lilly, who clearly had no idea, either.

"I'll see you later, then, Nicolina, Rupert." My gaze lingered on Rupert, who still hadn't lifted his head or acknowledged my presence. I thought my heart would crack right down the middle.

We had just regained the main floor level when a doorbell jingled through the hall. The guard brought us to a halt. We waited as Tengfeng and Mimi scurried up to join us.

A man in a suit and tie flanked by two minions and carrying a briefcase attached to his wrist was striding through the front doors toward us. When he was within a few feet, Tengfeng and Mimi greeted him with much bowing and handshaking. Finally, Tengfeng turned to me.

"Mademoiselle McCabe, this most famous textile scholar in all China, Mr. Tao. Mr. Tao, I introduce other expert, Phoebe McCabe. She joins team also. We dine, then see priceless tapestry."

It was all I could do to squeeze out a smile.

18

The congenial Mr. Tao was first allowed to wash up after his long flight and it was strongly suggested that I do likewise. In my case, my luggage was still in the motel room so Lilly was pressed to find something that might work, which resulted in me donning her kimono again. Natalie fetched the robe from the laundry room.

I could only imagine her state of mind with her husband near death and now forced to be slave to the Tengfeng army. We were not allowed to speak when she passed over the kimono. She still refused to meet my eyes. I figured out that she blamed me for every hellish thing that had befallen her since our arrival and I didn't blame her.

I showered and dressed in my old room—an upgrade, no doubt; a reward for my apparent compliancy—and, using the château's amenities, emerged at last, fluffed and fragrant to rejoin the supper party. Wearing my muddied leggings and sneakers beneath the silk probably spoiled the effect but who cared? I had hoped to visit my comrades in their new chambers but that was strictly forbidden. Dinner first, visitation rights second.

The gong reverberated through the château as I crossed the hall. All I could think of was that there were so many men it may as well be an army, and here we were occupying a fortified château. My colleagues would have a hell of a time rescuing us unless we helped them from the inside. Where was Evan? How did he become separated from Rupert? Nothing made sense.

Mr. Tao was already seated in the dining room talking pleasantly to the

Tengfeng contingent when I entered. Lilly was also present wearing her game face. The two men rose when I stepped in as though I was joining a lovely dinner gathering for new colleagues. It was all I could do not to throw my food at someone but the stakes were too high.

I sat down smiling. I picked up my fork smiling. I smiled while I ate the stir-fry Natalie had prepared with the help of one of Tengfeng's men and continued to smile all through the meal. Most of the conversation was in Chinese but occasionally either Mimi or Lilly translated on my behalf. I gathered that the esteemed guest did not speak English.

"Mr. Tao says that he is most delighted to meet you and looks forward to a long and fruitful partnership," Mimi said.

I looked up from stabbing a piece of broccoli and smiled. I wondered if the esteemed expert thought it odd that I had a perfectly rectangular red strip across my mouth and cheeks and that both Lilly and I looked haggard. "Likewise. Perhaps Mr. Tao can tell me a bit about his experience with fourteenth-century French textiles, tapestries in particular?"

Mimi's smile tightened but she managed to respond without missing a beat. "Mr. Tao has much experience with venerable textiles and has worked extensively with the Warring States textiles dating from the Qin and Han dynasties." There was no point asking anything more pointed because I knew it wouldn't survive translation.

Still the Warring States bit was impressive considering that those dynasties spanned 475 to 221 BC. "Amazing," I said truthfully. "Does Mr. Tao believe the conditions here at the château to be ideal for investigating a tapestry, which I presume he has come to do?"

Mimi turned to Mr. Tao and spoke Chinese to which the expert replied in kind.

"Mr. Tao says that the conditions are very poor here but that he would like to inspect the fibers with your assistance using tools he has brought for the purpose. He says that unrolling is unadvisable but he wishes to ensure that the tapestry is part of the Lady and the Unicorn collection as believed. We have brought him here for that purpose," Mimi added. "Our guest will inspect the tapestry on behalf of our client to ensure authenticity before transport."

Lilly said something in Chinese. Tengfeng replied with an abrupt tone, causing Mr. Tao to pause startled and glance at the uncle and niece combo. Then it hit me that the venerable expert had no idea what he had fallen into. Whatever Lilly had said had clued him in to the fact that all may not be as it seemed. I briefly caught Mr. Tao's eye before both of us lowered our gazes and returned to our meals.

The remainder of dinner passed in conversation that I didn't understand, though Lilly occasionally added a translation for my benefit. Mimi and Tengfeng no longer maintained that courtesy, although a few times some bit of pleasantry was added in English to make it appear as though I was there voluntarily.

Meanwhile, I counted the minutes, fearing for all the wounded souls in the château that night and trying to figure out a way to save them. I wasn't alone, I knew that, but how could my allies help us when we were holed up in this fortification? If there was one chink in Yu Ho's armor it was that he was on foreign soil and that sometime before the dawn he planned to leave the château to make a run for the coast. And maybe the airport, if I understood correctly. His most vulnerable moments, then, would be in the early hours when most of his house would be sleeping.

Until I had an opportunity to strike, I vowed to play my part. Mr. Tao and I were ushered into the library after supper where the canister now sat on a table. Relieved, I saw that the cartoon remained in its position on the floor.

Admittedly, I was preoccupied. I couldn't believe that René and Henri had just left. No one had said what happened to Henri after the hijacking of Nicolina, Rupert, and Seraphina. Either he had escaped or he was working for the enemy. As for the absent René, that was just boggling. It was hard to concentrate on anything else.

"What do you think, Mr. Tao?" Mimi was asking as the textile expert studied the canister.

Tao spoke, Mimi translated. "I think this is of a great age and of much importance to be hidden as it was for so many centuries." He entered a code into his briefcase and flipped back the lid to remove a long clear tube that looked a bit like an electronic turkey baster and a pair of gloves. "With this device, I test the fibers for age without damaging textile."

"Really, you can do that?" I said.

Lilly translated that part. She had been allowed to join us while Tengfeng removed himself from the proceedings long enough to stand at the back of the room and argue with somebody on his phone. I could only hope that his plans were going awry.

"China has made many new developments in the preservation of rare textiles," Tao responded through my translator. "I am most pleased to be working in the study of our rich textile heritage. I wish our nations were on better terms to exchange such knowledge."

"Me, too. Maybe we will be when the world finally begins to think like a global entity instead of a bunch of warring tribes," I said.

He smiled when Lilly translated. "Let us hope so one day. Chinese heritage is world heritage just as this precious tapestry belongs to human history."

"I agree," I said, smiling at him with genuine warmth. A kindred spirit is always a joy to meet. "But this one still belongs to France first."

Mimi interjected with something that sounded a great deal less pleasant.

"My honorable sister says not to waste time," Lilly told me. "She urges Mr. Tao to get back to work."

Which the man did at once; opening the lid of the canister, gummed together as it was, he gently inserted the turkey baster deep into the core of the folds. When he removed the device moments later, he sat one end on top of a metal platform hooked up to a laptop and waited for the data to calculate.

"Ah," he said through Lilly. "Estimated creation 1435."

"1435? Can that meter really date with that much precision?" I marveled.

"It tests the wool to the estimated life of the sheep based on a complicated carbon dating process that can assess accuracy within a five-year span," Lilly translated. "He says that with more time, the textile can be studied as to location of weaving and source of wool and dyes."

"But that's amazing!" I exclaimed. But it also meant that this tapestry was older than the others in the series, which I knew, predating the previous panels by almost three decades. It would have been completed just years after the death of Joan of Arc. It was the *first* in the series not the last. I was stunned by what that could mean and longed to see the piece unfolded, which could never safely happen under these conditions.

Mr. Tao began to carefully replace the canister's top. "He'll use another device to remove all air and moisture from container. When left in place, it will protect the textile until it goes to a lab," Lilly said for my benefit.

Tengfeng marched up to the table and spoke rapidly in Chinese. I knew that wasn't good. The little general was annoyed about something.

Lilly caught my eye. "He says to unroll it."

"No!" I gasped.

Mr. Tao immediately protested, his alarm evident in his tone and features. Tengfeng, with reddened face, pointed and repeated his order. The textile expert cast me a worried glance and offered me a pair of gloves. He then raised the canister.

"Tengfeng, this is nuts! Do you want to destroy the very item you worked so hard to steal?" I demanded.

"You I try hard to steal," he countered. "This rug will get same price no matter what happens now. It can be ruined—no matter. Amount negotiated as is."

Bastard. I assisted Mr. Tao so that Tengfeng wouldn't intervene and wrench the delicate fabric from our hands. As it was, we had to gently tug it from the canister because the fibers had swollen. When we finally laid it out on the table and began to roll it open, tears burned my eyes and Mr. Tao appeared just as stricken.

The tapestry had faded to a mostly muddied red and blue with vibrant patches here and there where the wool had survived the onslaught of time, yet nothing could suppress its energy. Clearly Flemish in origin, the tale it told was buried in the moldering fibers. To anyone who didn't know better, it was a muddied mess.

"Very poor condition. Is it valuable?" Tengfeng demanded.

"Not in this condition," I replied.

Tengfeng scowled.

Lilly translated for Mr. Tao, who straightened and said: "Tapestry must not be removed from France. Mr. Tengfeng, you have been untruthful to me."

I cringed at what I feared would come next.

Tengfeng swung toward him speaking rapidly in Chinese, causing the poor man to flinch. Lilly tried to translate for me but Mimi silenced her. I captured enough of the gist when two guards arrived and made as if to drag the textile expert away. He threw up his hands and spoke rapidly, bowing and smiling while backing up against a bookshelf. The man was begging for his life. I was betting that he promised to behave from now on. I knew what that felt like.

After a moment of silence, Tengfeng nodded. The minions left and Mr. Tao straightened, though he appeared to need to sit briefly to regain his composure.

"We must secure the tapestry for travel," I said, stepping in as tapestry expert numéro deux. "I see from Mr. Tao's briefcase that he has brought absorbent archival muslin, which can be used to re-roll the tapestry into its original shape. Perhaps we can use a case for transporting rugs? I saw a few in the storerooms when I was investigating the château earlier. If we use one of those it will look as though we are transporting a carpet out of France and nothing more valuable." I nodded toward Tengfeng, resisting the urge to bow. That was too much even for me. *See what a good little minion I am?*

Tengfeng gave me a curt nod and added a few words to poor Mr. Tao, who jolted up out of his seat to stand by me. Together, we covered the tapestry with a layer of white muslin-like fabric and proceeded to roll it into its original shape. Mr. Tao inserted another long clear device into the folds, something I assumed was designed to absorb excess moisture from the fibers. In the meantime, I gathered that one of the minions had been sent to find a rug carrier.

When I looked up minutes later, Lilly was eye-to-eye with Mimi and Tengfeng was back on his phone.

"Do you call this freedom, Mimi?" Lilly was asking in English. "You are as much a servant to our uncle as the rest of his crew. You jump when he says jump, march when he says march. Is this what you call success? You're better than this. You don't have to be a crook to measure your success."

"Don't lecture to me, sister dear," Mimi replied, also in English. "You were always the weaker one, so willing to acquiesce to please everyone, always the favorite sister, the apple of everyone's eye. You aligned with poor foolish Uncle Henri, the family buffoon. And where is he when you need him? Went running off into the dark when our men attacked the agents. Lily-livered like you. 'Lilly-livered'! Oh, I like that! Sometimes I love English better than any language. Anyway, I've made my success my way."

"You've made your success his way—" Lilly indicated her uncle with a jerk of her thumb "—the easy way, the way he's schooled you for. He's given you everything so you don't need to make your own luck. Mother warned us about Uncle Tengfeng. She avoided spending time with him because she knew he was up to something criminal. Now look at Lucky Ho—an underground smuggling ring. And you're proud of that? Are you kidding me? Look at you!"

Their voices were rising.

"Look at me? Look at you! All you do is pretend to be something you're not. An actress for the American films? What kind of job is that? You strut and pose using your looks like you always have. What have you done? Nothing!" Mimi looked ready to strike, her fists clenched, her eyes narrowed.

"It takes talent and brains to bring a character alive on film, plus a level of sensitivity and care for humanity that you've always lacked. You can't even be true to yourself let alone to another. All you care about is bettering yourself at another's expense!"

Mimi screamed something in Chinese, causing Tengfeng to lurch from his spot and step between the two sisters. He yelled at them both, ordering them from the room with a point of his finger. *Bad girls.* Unbelievably, they seemed to accept this, at least they left the room in the care of a minion. Lilly caught my eye just before the door shut behind them. Damn she was good. She orchestrated that on purpose.

After the sisters exited, Mr. Tao and I snapped out of our suspended animation. We had been standing with our hands frozen on the tapestry. Tengfeng caught sight of us and barked an order. In seconds we were back to work. One of the minions delivered an old rug carrier and soon we had the tapestry packed for travel.

When I checked my watch, I was startled to find it 11:15. Tengfeng was on the other side of the library still talking into his phone, giving me a chance to wander over to the window, leaving Mr. Tao to fiddle with his briefcase. I pulled aside the curtains, startled to feel fresh air on my face. There was a window open? A chill hit my spine. There was a window open and something was on the move.

And then the Bao gong resonated through the château.

19

_T_engfeng flung open the library door and shouted for the guards. In seconds, Mr. Tao and I were being steered across the hall by one of his men.

Pandemonium everywhere. Guys running and shouting. A woman screaming from the balcony. We were being hurried up to our rooms, but once we hit the landing, I saw that the guards stationed outside Eduard and Peaches's room had left their posts. One was dragging a fallen comrade down the hall. A gunshot fired somewhere below and our guard was shouting questions at another.

"They've escaped!" Lilly was standing outside her room waving.

"All of them?" I asked.

"All but Rupert. He's still in there but the others have gone. Mimi's taken off but nobody's paying her any attention. I'm screaming periodically to throw everybody off. Seems to work."

The guard shouted at her in Chinese and Lilly shouted back, though she retreated into her room, shutting the door.

The gong sounded again and our guard shoved Mr. Tao and me into a room, the lock clicking shut behind us. I pressed my ear against the wood, guessing that nobody was on guard. I pulled back, caught Mr. Tao's eye, and pointed at the old-fashioned warded lock. He nodded and I began searching the room for something long and thin.

"Mademoiselle McCabe?" he said after a few moments.

167

I turned. Mr. Tao stood by his open briefcase holding a long pin-like device. I hadn't noticed that he'd even taken the case with him. Flashing him a grin, I took the object and wiggled it around in the mechanism until it sprung free. On the way out the door, I shrugged off my kimono, leaving me in full stealth couture.

Lilly was standing outside holding a key. "I was about to release you."

"No need. Tell me what's happening," I said while dashing down the hall to Rupert's room, Lilly and Mr. Tao scrambling after.

"Peaches jumped her guard, took his gun, and knocked out a couple more on her way into Nicolina and Seraphina's room. They're loose, too, and everybody's armed. I heard that one of the guards found a back door open on patrol seconds before all this started, which means that we may have other friends within the building."

"That's fantastic! Where's Natalie?"

"In her room with Eduard."

"Come on, we have to get mobilized. Can you fire a gun? Ask Mr. Tao if he can," I whispered.

"I've been trained to handle a firearm but Mr. Tao says he is pure scholar."

"Tell him to be pure warrior." I entered Rupert's room. He lay on his back on the bed as I approached, one hand covering his eyes.

"Rupert?"

"It's about time," he rasped, propping himself up on his elbows. "Dear Phoebe, how relieved I am to know that you are well but do be careful out there. There's quite a few of these chaps running around. Peaches knocked a couple on the head; Seraphina did damage to a few more."

I stepped up to him and gripped his hand, breaking down just a bit when he pulled me in for a hug. "Rupert!"

He patted me on the back with his one good hand. It appeared that they had broken the other. "I am in no condition to be much help since they gave me a rather nasty knocking about but I have learned a few things as I lay here. I studied a touch of Mandarin in my school days, you know—not much, just a trifle, really—but enough to understand a word here and there."

"Rupert, make it quick, please!"

"Yes, well, I chanced to overhear the guards whispering and it turns out that only a handful of Tengfeng's men are properly trained while the others are makeshift toy soldiers hired on the fly, hence the current disarray. However—" he took a deep breath and let me ease him back to the pillow "—those that are trained are masters in several of the Asian martial arts, black belt sort of thing, and deadly."

"Where's Evan?"

"Our plan was to use me as an infiltrator while he musters our forces to storm the Bastille, so to speak. Lad's around here somewhere."

"Stop talking," I told him as I headed for the door. Lilly and Mr. Tao stood watch in the corridor. "Stay here and rest until we can return with help. Do you have a gun?"

"Nicolina gave me one but perhaps you need it more than I."

"You're defenseless. Keep the gun." I was at the door.

"One more thing."

I paused.

"Eduard, the man who owns this house...he was working with them but then rather changed his mind...at an inopportune moment."

We could hear Tengfeng shouting down below, heard footsteps pounding on the stairs.

"They're coming!" Lilly whispered.

Two men hit the landing running. Lilly shoved Mr. Tao out of the way as she leapt into action in a maneuver that was all flying legs and arms. I was too busy tackling the second guy with my basic armed combat moves to pay much attention.

It shocked me how unprepared that guy was as I kicked him in the groin and pushed him backward. Amateur. Lilly crept up behind him and crashed a vase down on his head as a final effect. I whipped the pistol out of his hand and shoved it into my waistband. Tengfeng must have sent his weakest men to take on the ladies—idiot.

"Get the bastards!" Lilly cried in French.

"With pleasure," I said as we bounded down the stairs to the main hall. I could see Tengfeng waiting for us below flanked by two men—all black clothing, carrying rifles. These must be the elite and they probably intended to capture us, if we let them.

"Lilly, can you take on your uncle?"

"No way," she whispered back. "He's a kung fu master."

"At least they won't shoot us. Get ready to run."

"Head for the kitchens," she whispered. "I know this place better than he does. Mimi's another matter."

"Tell Mr. Tao to wait here. He'll be safe enough. It's us they want." We were still moving, though more slowly now, working out our strategy on the descent.

"I did. He refuses. He feels guilty falling for my uncle's spiel so now he's looking for retribution."

Pure exasperation hit. "Tell him to wait here! Retribution is better when alive!"

And then the lights went out. Sudden, complete darkness.

Our team had to be behind that. The timing was perfect in one respect and not another. I had already mapped out an escape path—jump over the banister on the last set of stairs and bolt for the back of the château—but now I couldn't see what lay below the six-foot jump and crashing into a set of armor wasn't in the plan. I knew there was one standing there, I just couldn't recall whether it was two feet to the right or farther to the left.

But I had to try. I leapt over the railing, Lilly following, leaving Mr. Tao to scramble down the stairs. We landed on the tiles without obstruction and dashed for the back of the château. Behind us, I heard thudding sounds and scuffling, which made me think that Mr. Tao was doing something with that briefcase of his.

Lilly was tugging me to the right. Now I was following her blindly down a corridor, through the kitchen, and down a set of steps. Behind us, our pursuers' flashlights raked the walls but had veered off to the left. I couldn't see a thing but Lilly seemed to know her way around in the dark well enough. She pulled me into a linen closet and shut the door.

We stood for a minute still as death, not daring to breathe. A linen closet, I realized, not that I could see anything, but the scent of starch and detergent gave it away. Lilly was wiggling a shelf.

"Secret passage?" I asked hopefully.

"Right. Only Mimi knows about this and Uncle Henri, of course," she whispered. "You'd have to have grown up here."

"Lilly, what's really going on? You know, don't you?"

"Not exactly but I know Uncle Henri. The lights going off has him all over it. The fuse box is way down in the basement. Nobody knows about it except the DuBoises and Uncle Henri but he used to turn off the lights when we were kids so we could play hide-and-seek."

"I felt a draft in the library. Do you think he's here somewhere?"

"Definitely! I argued with Mimi to distract everyone—I know where all her trigger points are—and she fell for it. But still, it shocked even me to see how brain-washed she's become."

"What happened when they kidnapped you?"

"Nothing. They just gagged and blindfolded me and I ended up here."

"Shh!"

The sound of voices came from somewhere beyond the doors, along with pounding footsteps. After they'd faded, I whispered: "Where does this lead?"

"To the old keep. It links several rooms along the way." She was fumbling around for something. "We always kept flashlights here for emergencies but they're gone."

"A light would certainly help." Without either my phone or a light, I felt naked and blind. How would we be able to tell friend from foe?

Something creaked.

"Got it. Help me push this open."

Applying shoulder to wood, I felt something budge before the whole shelf slowly swung forward, revealing a wall of dark beyond. Using my hands to steady myself, I followed Lilly down a set of stairs into a musty-smelling corridor, both of us fumbling along using our hands and feet as feelers.

"Be careful here. The floorboards are rotten. Keep to the edges," she warned.

The planks groaned beneath us and one cracked ominously underfoot as we passed. Dust irritated my nose, forcing me to suppress sneezes. My eyes were watering and my nose running by the time I heard Lilly pushing on something ahead. When I reached her side, a slice of air washed in pale moonlight leeched into the corridor.

"Where are we?" I asked.

"Inside one of the old halls. It's been closed for decades."

We gazed out into the space. A body lay facedown in the center of the floor, illuminated from the moonlight penetrating cracks in the boarded-up windows.

"Cover me," I whispered, passing her my gun. I crept out to the center of the floor, and knelt down to feel for the guy's pulse—one of Tengfeng's men and very dead. I stood up. "He's been shot," I said.

"By your people?" she asked.

"Who else? They must be here somewhere."

We froze at the sound of voices speaking rapid French—a man and a woman.

Lilly put a hand on my arm. "That's Mimi and Uncle Henri. Come on!"

She led me through another room, down winding corridors, and out through an exterior door. Now we were running across the grass. Seconds later we were climbing through the wall of the ruined keep and ground to a halt deep in the shadows. There, on either side of the still open oubliette, circling one another, were Mimi and Uncle Henri.

Mimi, dressed in her black martial arts gear, appeared small, fierce, and lethal but her adversary seemed equally dangerous wielding a long sword. It took a second to realize that Henri wore the tapestry strapped to his back like a long quiver. How did that happen?

"Do not make me hurt you, uncle," Mimi was saying. "Hand over the tapestry."

"You take me for a fool, me the man who helped raise you, and now you come to steal my family treasure?"

"Isn't it my family treasure, too, uncle? Only we know that's not true, don't we? A Chinese adoptee does not lay claim to her adopted family's French fortune. She only stands by like the outcast she is."

"You make yourself an outcast! Your father and mother would be so ashamed!"

They inched around each other step by step encircling the dark hole between them. Why wasn't the cover replaced on that thing?

"Not my mother and father," Mimi sneered. "Pass me the tapestry and I will permit you to leave unharmed. You are no match for my skills with your puny sword. Are you kidding me? Such a joke! Do not force me to make a greater fool of you than you already are."

Henri emitted a cry either of outrage or pain, I couldn't tell, but at that moment my attention was drawn to the shadows moving along the walls of the keep above, black-clad figures climbing into position, but to what purpose? Were they ours or theirs or both? Shit. I turned to Lilly but she was slipping around to the other side as if to line herself up with the combatants. I didn't know what she had planned but knew it couldn't end well.

I stepped out of the shadows, thinking to draw attention away from Henri and Mimi long enough for Lilly to activate her plan, but Henri took that moment to leap over the oubliette at his niece. Then Lilly sprang toward her sister just as a chorus of cries erupted overhead. I was distracted by the clamor, which is the only excuse I have for the fact that someone grabbed me from behind.

I kicked out only to be flipped onto my stomach in an instant. My assailant was knocked sideways and I turned in time to see Peaches slug him with the butt of a rifle.

I was on my feet in seconds. "Glad to see you!" But I couldn't wait to play catch-up because Lilly was tackling Mimi while Henri was using his sword to fend off a kung fu adversary. The two sisters were not evenly matched, either, but even so, Lilly was holding her own. I worried more about Henri just then. He was battling none other than Tengfeng himself.

Henri brandished his sword and lunged; Tengfeng kicked the weapon from his grasp and swiftly delivered a chop to Henri's throat. In seconds,

Henri went down flat on his back and stilled. Lilly cried out, losing her focus and leaving Mimi with an opening. In seconds, Lilly was on the ground with Mimi straddling her, hooting a cry of triumph.

I sprung toward them, thinking surely to hell she wouldn't harm her own sister, but I wasn't sure with this bunch.

"Don't hurt her!" I cried, but suddenly two things happened: I felt myself wrenched backward by my neck and someone shot Mimi. I saw the woman clutch her shoulder and scream, more in fury than in pain.

But I was a bit preoccupied. It took a few seconds to realize that I was being dragged up to the edge of the oubliette. My feet scrabbled to find the earth beneath them, finally ending up partly propping my weight on my toes. I struggled for breath, furious with myself for getting into that position.

"Stop!" Tengfeng commanded in my ear. "You move, she dies!" The cold metal of a gun pressed to my temple.

20

There was comfort in seeing friendly faces amid the carnage. Nicolina stood over one of the felled minions while a guy in uniform held another at gunpoint, and from what I could see out of my peripheral vision, some kind of black-clad op team was rappelling down the walls into the keep. It had to be ours.

Tengfeng released the safety catch in my ear. I remained strangely calm but I have no explanation why. It was not because I believed that he wouldn't kill me because I knew him quite capable of pulling that trigger. It's just that when the situation reaches the possibility of no return, I ready myself for the ultimate adventure. Only, and I was way too angry to just give up.

Peaches's gaze was fixed on my face. She held a gun pointed at Mimi, who now clutched her wounded arm with a snarl on her face. By the expression in Peaches's eye, anyone who didn't know her would believe that she could happily finish Mimi off. I wasn't so sure.

"Let Phoebe McCabe go. You are surrounded," a deep voice announced over a megaphone.

Oh, my God, I knew that voice! It didn't matter that I hovered over a gaping black hole with a gun to my head, my gut still did that butterfly thing. Evan! But for the record, I detested this helpless woman shit. I'd rather be the one doing the rescuing.

Tengfeng leaned forward until my legs dangled over the pit, leaving me kicking into empty space. No breath entering my lungs now. He was strangling me. Maybe I only imagined everyone holding their breath at the same time. I needed to remain alert but dizziness hit. Suddenly, he pulled me back and released his grip long enough for me to gasp a lungful of air before tightening it again. My attempts to kick out at him were expertly avoided.

"One false move, I shoot!" Tengfeng called.

"And if you hurt one hair on her head, I'll pull the trigger on your precious niece!" Peaches cried out in broken French.

"You would not kill in cold blood," Tengfeng said contemptuously. "You weak, all weak."

"You've got me all wrong, Teng. I'd shoot this little bitch in a microsecond. Just give me another reason to pull the trigger. Let Phoebe go and your niece lives."

"You are surrounded," Evan announced. Did I just imagine a tremor of emotion in his voice? "You'll never get out of here. Most of your men have been captured and we are in possession of the tapestry."

They were? I strained my eyes trying to see what had happened to Henri but couldn't see anything from my perspective.

"Your army is outnumbered so what do you have left to gain?" Evan asked?

"Her." He jostled me in case anyone doubted his intended victim. "You let me go safely to China and I take McCabe. No one killed. You make wrong move, she dies." But he sounded less confident now. "Sniper has gun on her. You try anything, he shoots."

The enormity of the force against him must be finally hitting home—no army, no might—but if he had nothing to lose, I was as good as dead. So, was there a sniper in those walls with a gun on me? Probably. My predicament was hitting me now, too, but first I needed to breathe.

There was a long pause.

"All right. We'll give you safe passage as long as you release her neck," Evan said.

Tengfeng loosed his grip long enough for me to shove in a lungful of air. Evan was going to play along, I realized, knowing that there would be multiple opportunities to ambush Tengfeng before we ever reached a car let alone an airport. Tengfeng had to know that, too. If I didn't do something, more people would get hurt, but my options were a bit thin at the moment. Peaches and Mimi stood in my direct line of vision. Peaches was trying to communicate something. I was trying to think.

Suddenly, I let myself go limp in Tengfeng's grip. Though he might know what I was up to, it still made things difficult. He couldn't hold my weight and the gun for much longer and he needed me to walk out of there on my own two feet.

He cried out and tried to shake me into standing. I felt his gun arm move. He swung toward Henri, who I now realized sat propped on the ground. He intended to shoot him! I kicked out at his knees just as a bullet whizzed by my ear, hitting Tengfeng. He dropped me like a bag of rocks.

While I was scrambling for a handhold at the edge of the oubliette, Tengfeng was yelling, "Stop!"

Everything went still except me. I had just hauled myself to safety and crouched about three feet away while Tengfeng stood with the gun pointed to his own temple. It looked as though he'd been shot in the shoulder, maybe by his own sniper.

He called out, "I die with honor!"

"Uncle, no!" Mimi cried.

And then he pulled the trigger.

* * *

WE ALL SAT in the grand hall, countless people moving back and forth throughout the château, ambulances parked outside along with police vehicles among others. We had been interviewed by French Interpol agents attempting to piece together the story while Evan periodically joined in long enough to weave in knowledge of his side of the operation. Mostly he remained occupied in organizing the multiple agencies that had descended upon the château. We hadn't yet had a moment to speak.

It turned out that he and Rupert had come up with the idea of dropping Rupert onto the château's doorstep in order to infiltrate the Tengfeng bastion. Rupert's knowledge of Mandarin along with a surveillance device inserted into his ear was designed to gather the necessary information to tackle the twenty-three-person-strong Yu Ho team. They thought wrongly that an older man would be unharmed. What they couldn't have anticipated was the beating Tengfeng ordered on Rupert almost immediately, taking his bile out on the man in pure spite. Though tougher than he looked, Rupert had been badly shaken by the ordeal but assured me he'd be fine.

René did not fare as well. He had been hiding out in the château once Tengfeng had arrived, awaiting his opportunity to stymie the gang, which he did in countless ways, more of the annoyance variety at first. He had located and destroyed all of Tengfeng's monitoring devices before managing to disarm Peaches's guard and helping her and the others escape. Then, deep in the older parts of the building, he had attacked one of Tengfeng's guards and snatched his gun. The two scuffled, the gun went off, and both the Tengfeng dude and René were shot. René's wound, though not fatal, was nasty. He remained unconscious during most of the action from thereon in.

Meanwhile, Henri had played a cowed, frightened man during the ambush when he, Nicolina, and Seraphina were on their way to Mont-Saint-Michel. He had a dramatic flair of his own and wielded it to play sniveling coward once they had bound him. He said that everyone was always a little too ready to believe him a coward when it took more guts than anyone anticipated just to survive daily life being himself.

While Nicolina and Seraphina fought the attackers, he waited for his opportunity to escape. He could not, he explained, overcome five armed men but he could sound the alarm, make his way back to the château to rescue Lilly and the rest of us, who he knew had been kidnapped. At his first opportunity, he let down the tires of the cars and slipped away to hitchhike his way back to the château, finally arriving later that night. There he had entered the complex through a secret entrance, cut the power, and stole back the tapestry, encountering Mimi on his way to rescuing the rest of us.

After Interpol finished their interviews, we remained seated in the baronial hall in various states of shock and exhaustion. Henri slumped inconsolably in one of the couches, Chouchou in his arms, after having his head attended to by a medic; Rupert, René, and Eduard had already been transported to the hospital while Mimi and eighteen Chinese nationals headed to jail. Tengfeng left for the morgue along with a few of his hapless supporters. A Chinese lawyer had arrived threatening retribution along with a French lawyer arguing against him while Ella and her team arrived to claim the tapestry on behalf of France. I had only time to smile and wave at her as she passed with her team.

"Eduard was the mole, seriously?" Peaches asked, gazing around our motley gathering, slurping back mugs of coffee and devouring croissants while she was at it.

Natalie sobbed. "I didn't know at first, I swear! He made a deal with Tengfeng, who promised him thousands of dollars if he passed along information. That's all he thought he must do but no, then Tengfeng demanded that he help capture Phoebe and that's when he refused. They beat him, they beat him so badly!"

Lilly sat beside her holding her hand. "Eduard will be fine," she whispered. "You can visit him at the hospital as soon as they give the word. Be warned, though, they may lay charges."

"Everything is gone, *non?*" moaned Henri. "The tapestry, the château, Mimi, everything. You will need to auction off the château now and it will never be in the Saint Chappelles family again. I have failed."

"You have not failed," we all said more or less at once. "You are a brave man and helped win the day," I added.

After all, he had launched a noble mission in the attempt to release us but, in the end, it seemed that taking advantage of the ensuing chaos to snatch the tapestry had brought him face-to-face with his niece. That had shaken him emotionally more than anything. "I could not convince her that I loved her," he sobbed. "She did not believe me and said such hateful things. I should have loved her better when she was young."

Lilly leaned toward him. "Uncle Henri, you are not responsible for Mimi's choices. She made them, not you. Besides, you'll always have me and we'll have one another because we're the only family left that matters."

That caused him to muster a sad smile.

"I'm ashamed of my sister and ashamed that she chose to represent the worst part of humanity instead of its best," Lilly continued. "China deserves better ambassadors than Mimi and Uncle Tengfeng."

"And I've met many, some here," I assured her.

"Anyway, I'm hoping that a few years in prison might temper Mimi's ways and give her a chance to think. I'll visit her often and try to win back the sister I love." She looked across at Henri. "We'll try to amend our family, won't we Uncle?"

"We will try, of course. One must never give up hope," he acknowledged, "but sometimes this is so difficult when so much has been lost."

Nicolina sat straight and elegant in her ripped leather couture. "I have an idea that may solve the issue of the auctioned château but perhaps we speak of this at another time?"

"Now, please," Lilly urged.

Nicolina folded her hands. "Very simple. I buy the château as part of a..." She sat struggling to find the correct English word.

"Conglomerate, cooperative, group purchase?" Peaches suggested.

"Perhaps one of those," she acknowledged, "but I am only the money person—"

"Financier," Peaches said triumphantly, snapping her fingers.

"Financier," Nicolina agreed with a nod. "I finance the hotel operation until the château pays me back. Natalie and Henri manage it together."

Lilly translated that in case Natalie missed it.

Natalie and Henri gazed at one another.

"That is if Eduard spends much time in jail," Henri said in French. "If not, he joins us and I will forgive him. Natalie, I would be most happy to work with you to bring the château to life again with this financial backing. We can make this work, yes?"

"Perhaps." Natalie gave a tentative nod.

Then Mr. Tao entered accompanied by the Chinese lawyer. "I say goodbye now," he said with a smile and a nod. He spoke to Lilly, who translated.

"Mr. Tao thanks you very much and wants you to know that he is most glad that the tapestry remains on French soil. He invites you, Phoebe, to come to China anytime where he will ensure you a very warm welcome."

I grinned. "I hope someday to take him up on that."

"Make sure he invites me, too," Peaches added.

Another bow and he was gone.

By the time the château cleared out later that afternoon, we were half-asleep in our chairs. We began heading for our rooms, me planning a detour to see Evan.

Peaches sidled up to me. "He's outside being manly and organizing the last of the forces. Look." Taking me by the arm, she led me to one of the windows and pointed below. "Total babe magnet."

Evan stood discussing something with a gendarme, hands flying in the air —tall, broad-shouldered, too handsome by far, all I could do was sigh. I didn't have enough energy left for much else.

"Right," I said after a moment. "I'll see him later."

Some things are worth waiting for.

21

A maiden sat weeping under an orange tree in a field of flowers with a dead unicorn in her lap. The beautiful creature's tongue hung out and a bloodied sword had been plunged into its side. Rearing overhead, a lion roared victorious, waving the Le Viste pennant while a second banner lay burning in the grass amid a patch of lilies. Above the scene, the archangel Michael flew in a swirl of fire with his sword glowing in the upper left-hand corner and the holy cross in his left.

The textile was still in the process of being restored but had garnered so much attention in the interim that the museum relented long enough to give VIPs a special glimpse. It remained enclosed behind glass in a clear temperature-and moisture-controlled environment, the fibers badly deteriorated in parts and most of the colors faded. It would not be fully revealed to France until it was able to hang in some semblance of its former glory.

"It tells the story of the betrayal of Joan of Arc," I whispered. "The maiden is France, the unicorn is Joan, the lion England, and the pennant burning in the lilies bears the arms of King Charles VII of France, which contained the fleur-de-lis as his emblem."

"And a Le Viste could be burned as a heretic for commissioning such an image," Rupert remarked.

"Definitely, as would his collaborators, the Saint Chappelles. Father Louis gave his life to protect another when he jumped into the oubliette with the cartoon," Evan said. "The tapestry says in summary: *the king of France and*

England killed the sainted Joan, a travesty against God and man. It's an accusation against the church and two of the most powerful earthly forces in the then known world. It's an act of defiance and an expression of treason coupled with the most extraordinary courage."

We had held a small private ceremony for Père Louis back at the château after having his bones removed and reburied on the property at a spot overlooking the Loire. Henri was commissioning a lovely headstone to commemorate his ancestor's bravery and the role he had played in preserving the seventh Lady and the Unicorn tapestry.

"And we celebrate all noble souls who go forth to battle injustice" , and for emphasis, Henri Saint Chappelles gave Peaches's shoulder a squeeze. He had yet to squeeze any part of me but I was all right with that.

"Indeed, your ancestor was a true hero." Rupert stood nursing his arm, which he'd encased in a lovely silk Hermès scarf that just happened to match his socks, should anyone choose to investigate that closely. He had assured me that, in Paris, people investigate that kind of detail very closely.

We were all standing together at the private unveiling of the seventh Lady and the Unicorn tapestry in the Cluny Museum, the public event having been slated for much later. Besides various French dignitaries, Peaches, Rupert, Henri, and I were in attendance along with Evan, who stood by my side. Lilly was on location filming her next movie so couldn't attend. Natalie did not receive an invitation but was busy readying the new Château Saint Chappelles with Nicolina for an onslaught of late-summer bookings. René had been hired on as the new hotel's security guard and refused to leave the premises in the meantime.

Ella stood at the front of the small gathering speaking to a handful of officials from the Ministère de la Culture. When she caught my eye, I left Evan's side to join her where I chatted with the esteemed company about my interpretation of the tapestries as a whole.

"And what do you believe may be the seventh sense in the allegorical sense?" Ella enquired.

I cleared my throat. "I've thought about that a great deal," I admitted, "and I'd like to suggest that the seventh tapestry refers to what is today known as one of the 'interception' senses, in particular the sense of balance."

Everyone turned to me.

"Balance?" one man queried.

"It could be physical balance," I continued, "as in the stricken unicorn clearly lost his when he fell into the lady's lap but the broader meaning also fits." I ignored the intense scrutiny fixed on me at that moment. "When the

English struggled to control France, all balance was lost and then there's the balance between good and evil, church and state, one nation over another. The English's influence over another sovereign kingdom disrupted the order of things and cast France into a hundred years of chaos. Joan attempted to restore this balance and eventually succeeded but only at the cost of her own life." I looked around at my companions. "Well, that's my take on it, anyway."

Whether the experts agreed with me or not hardly mattered because I was now convinced. A lively discussion followed and I left the group flushed with the stimulus of a good debate.

Minutes later, my friends and I left the Cluny and headed into a warm sunny Parisian summer day. Paris can do summer so magnificently and we were on our way to one of Rupert's favorite restaurants by way of a treat. It was a bit of a stroll but we were up for it and Paris appeared happy to oblige.

While Peaches walked arm in arm with Henri, and I held hands with Evan, I took Rupert by the arm so that I was flanked by two of my favorite men. "All right, gentlemen, it's time you disclosed what you've been hiding from me all along."

That provoked the usual expressions and protestations of bewildered innocence, all of which I allowed to peter out before I said anything further. I was temporarily distracted by the sight of lovers kissing by the Seine. I took a deep breath, thinking I could use more of that. Definitely later. "I realize that I've probably been handling this all wrong. Let me approach this another way by posing a direct question: Evan, you say that you were adopted by two lovely people whom you consider to be your true parents, but who is your biological father?"

I looked up to find him staring down at me, dumbstruck. Here was a man who didn't do dumbstruck often or well so I took pity on him and turned to Rupert.

"Rupert, is there any reason why you have spent the last five years hiding the fact that Evan is your son? I've seen how solicitous he is of you—when he's not dropping you off in the grass outside a château, that is, but every son's allowed a few transgressions. And I even wondered if you two were a couple —back then, I mean. This is before I knew Evan so well, er, in that way, and even if that had been true and you two were a couple, it still wouldn't have been anything to hide. This is 2022, right?"

"Phoebe—" Evan began.

"Don't deny it," I said.

"I'm not denying anything, I'm merely trying to explain."

"Oh, good. Please do."

Rupert and Evan exchanged glances.

To me the resemblance was unmistakable once I began to look for similarities—the same eye and hair color, only Evan's complexion leaned on the olive side whereas Rupert always remained pale.

"Well?" I prompted.

"Phoebe." It was Rupert who was about to tell the tale. "The fact that Evan is my son has remained a secret for a very good reason. Initially, it was because my dear late wife, Mabel, was not aware that I had sired a child before we met and, after we married, the conditions of my inheritance were determined by my having no progeny, thus I preferred to keep it that way. As it stands, my estate and title revert to Mabel's eldest nephew upon my passing but there is yet another complication in that Evan's biological mother, indeed my first love, also was at one time a wealthy woman and her estate belongs to…" He paused as if exposing the truth to the air might suddenly bring universal wrath upon his head. But then, he may have just needed to come up for air.

"Belongs to?" That was me again.

"Nicolina," he finished.

I allowed that to ripen among us until I could digest it fully. Then I was the one to gape. "Maria Contini is your mother?" I swung to Evan. "The Maria Contini who was Nicolina's friend and heir and whose murder we helped solve in Venice? You are the member of an old Venetian family?"

His expression, pained in a way I'd never seen before, seemed to be unable to release the word his lips were forming. "Yes," he said finally. "But Nicolina must not know. On no account do I want her to think that I will ever make a claim on the Contini assets. That's not who I am."

"Did you know two years ago when we were searching for Maria's killer?" I asked.

"I suspected." His eyes met Rupert's. "But it took several months before I discovered the truth."

"Oh." I could hardly speak and the emotion flowing between the two men was so thick with either reproach or love or both that I hardly knew which way to turn.

"What's going on?"

I looked up to find Peaches standing before us, leaving Henri up ahead gazing across the river.

"I've just heard confirmed what I knew all along," I told her.

"Which is?" she asked.

"If we tell you, you cannot disclose the truth to anyone," Evan told her sternly.

"Seriously?"

"This is very serious, Penelope," Rupert warned.

Nobody called her Penelope. She looked from Rupert to Evan before holding up one hand. "My lips are sealed—Black Goddess's honor. So, what's the big mystery?"

Rupert cleared his throat. "I suggest we wait until this evening to disclose the details over dinner along with a very fine glass of wine."

"Hell, yes," Peaches exclaimed. "By the look on your faces, let's make it the whole damn bottle."

THE END

JOIN PHOEBE and the Agency of the Ancient Lost & Found on their next adventure which plunges the reader deep into the secrets of ancient Rome. Unravel the tale of an emperor who is only as great as the woman who commands the world behind the throne ...and buries a secret against time itself. The Emperor's Shadow can be pre-ordered now.

AFTERWORD

Art has multiple interpretations which is one of the reasons it can be both enlightening and inscrutable. The Lady and the Unicorn tapestries have been the subject of much speculation among scholars but not until I began this book did I realize that there might really be a link between the Maid of Orleans and the Cluny tapestries. I really believed that I was making the whole thing up. Since the tapestries' execution dates are unclear as are so many other details surrounding the key players, why not? The truth, as often the case with history, remains a mystery but may be stranger than fiction in the end.

Meanwhile, Phoebe is just beginning to acknowledge her "Pythia Key" (see *The Artemis Key*, book 4) in the series. Though my character's intuitive pull is strengthening as the series progresses, I, too, am experiencing something similar. It's as if suddenly all the connective filaments linking my story's elements become clear in my head and even rings true, at least by in my world.

Both Phoebe and I invite you to follow her next quest deep into the heart of ancient Rome when *The Shadow of the Emperor* launches book 6 of *the Agency of the Ancient Lost & Found*.

ABOUT THE AUTHOR

JANE THORNLEY is an author of historical mystery thrillers with a humorous twist. She has been writing for as long as she can remember and when not traveling and writing, lives a very dull life—at least on the outside. Her inner world is something else again.

With over fourteen novels published and more on the way, she keeps up a lively dialogue with her characters and invites you to eavesdrop by reading all of her works.

To follow Jane and share her books' interesting background details, special offers, and more, please join her newsletter here:

NEWSLETTER SIGN-UP

ALSO BY JANE THORNLEY

SERIES: CRIME BY DESIGN

Crime by Design Boxed Set Books 1-3

Crime by Design Prequel: Rogue Wave e-book available free to newsletter subscribers.

Crime by Design Book 1: Warp in the Weave

Crime by Design Book 2: Beautiful Survivor

Crime by Design Book 3: The Greater of Two Evils

Crime by Design Book 4: The Plunge

Also featuring Phoebe McCabe:

SERIES: THE AGENCY OF THE ANCIENT LOST & FOUND

The Carpet Cipher Book 1

The Crown that Lost its Head Book 2

The Florentine's Secret Book 3

The Artemis Key Book 4

The Thread of the Unicorn (pre-order) Book 5

SERIES: NONE OF THE ABOVE MYSTERY

None of the Above Series Book 1: Downside Up

None of the Above Series Book 2: DownPlay